TIME WHEEL

by
Rosemary DeTrolio

Time Wheel

Book 1

Copyright © 2020

by Rosemary DeTrolio

Middle Grade fiction

ISBN 978-1-7339869-5-3

Grow Your Spirit Books

Any resemblance to a person
living or dead is purely coincidental.

Prayer wheel - a cylindrical wheel on a spindle made from metal, wood, stone, leather or coarse cotton. Traditionally, the mantra Om Mani Padme Hum is written in Newari language of Nepal, on the outside of the wheel. The inside holds a prayer on a scroll of paper. The more the barrel is turned, the more powerful the prayer becomes.

DEDICATION

To those that find a gem in the pile of rocks, sunshine behind the clouds, and adventure in their own backyard. One person's trash is another person's treasure.

Table of Contents

CHAPTER I

Hopeless in Hope

TOMMY DELO, age 11 ¾, a friendless, vertically challenged boy sat in Mom's car. Summer vacation slipped through his fingers like sand. Two weeks of freedom left before entering grade 6 in a new school in Hope. He held in an urge to barf and frowned. *I'm hopeless*. He laughed at his own sad joke.

"What's so funny?" Mom asked.

"Nothing. Nothing at all," Tommy said.

If someone would have told him, soon he'd find a can on a lollipop stick that could zap him through time, he would have laughed his head off. Good stuff like that only happens in the movies, not in real life. Even a ton of fairy dust couldn't bring Dad back from the *better place* everyone mentioned on funeral day. Tommy puffed a humid breath at the car window. He traced a sad face with his fingertip before it evaporated in the summer heat.

Tommy eyed his mother suspiciously. "Why are we stopping here, Mom? Are you lost?"

"I have a surprise to show you!" Mom drove up Main Street.

"Surprises aren't good," Tommy muttered.

She parked in front of a dilapidated three-story building. "Ta-dah! What do you think?" She pointed to the storefront in a row of small shops that faced the Main Street.

"You mean that homeless-looking building?" Tommy glanced up at the worn-out building, its faded blue paint peeling like potato skins from the exterior clapboards. "I think a bulldozer needs to knock it down."

A wide smile crossed her lips. "It's perfect! And… it's all ours."

"You mean you bought this old junky place and you didn't even ask me?" He fumed and his brows knit.

"I thought you'd be thrilled."

"I'm not. What would Dad say?" He didn't mean to shout it, but the words flew out like an angry hornet from his mouth. He regretted them as soon as they stung Mom. Tommy watched Mom's face crumble even though she tried to hide it from him. "I'm...I'm sorry Mom," he mumbled. The counselor told him his moods flew up and down. Dad's been gone for over a year, but it seemed like yesterday. This was one of those times.

"I miss him too, Punkin'. No need to apologize to me." Mom dove a hand into her huge orange bag, riffling around for the shop key. She pulled an old key on a leather fob and said, "Got it. Think of the possibilities!"

He lifted the corners of his mouth attempting a smile, but it was no use. Tommy flung the car door open, his worn sneakers touching down on gravel. His eyes drew up to the rusty squeaking sign overhead that read Bell's *Treasure Trove*. It hung suspended by two chains as it swung in the breeze with a squeak, squeak sound. He half-smiled pretending to be agreeable. He searched his brain for something nice or kind to say... just like the counselor had advised him ka-gillion times last year. "Maybe the possibilities are inside?" He pressed his nose against the dingy picture window and peered into the shop. "Well, they're not inside. Just a bunch of junk and an old rusty sign." He rubbed his nose on his sleeve.

"I thought you'd be excited about this."

Guilt twisted his gut when he noticed the crushed expression cross his mother's face. Tommy grimaced, realizing he'd hurt her feelings...*again*.

Mom tousled his hair with hand. "Some possibilities are invisible *until* they happen. You'll see." She wiggled the key into the lock. A dusty brass bell dinged over the entryway when she pushed the heavy glass door open with her hip. "Our new future awaits us." She flipped the lights on.

"I miss the old one," Tommy mumbled.

Spider webs decorated the door jam. His eyes trailed the ceiling as he stepped in behind her. "I hate spiders. Remember? I told you about the big hairy one that crawled on my cot at Boy Scout camp."

"Yes. I remember. We'll have these spiders swept away soon enough. Why the sad face? An open mind is like an umbrella, it's no use unless it's open."

Mom was famous for dumb sayings. Tommy viewed the jam-packed room. Dust-covered shelves were stacked high with goods. He sniffed the musty odor of old magazines, basement, and dirty socks. "There's a ton of stuff in there and it smells. Who owns all this junk?" Tommy curled his lips and gave her the side-eye.

"Don't you get it? We do! We can open the shop and sell these treasures... you and I— a team, like Batman and Robin!"

"Treasures? More like trash." Tommy shook his head. He wasn't buying her Batman and Robin sales pitch. He wished he could turn back time. All he wanted was Dad, his house, and his friends. Instead, all he saw were invisible possibilities, a butt-load of junk piled sky high. A fastball of sadness hit him in the gut.

Once inside the shop, he felt a tingly chill crawl up his spine, as if unseen eyes watched him. He whipped around toward the tall gray shelf. Was it a ghost? His eyes caught the tiniest spark of light and he heard a crackling sound. "I hear weird noises, like a sparkler on the fourth of July, coming from right over there." He pointed in the direction of the shelf.

"The old heating system hisses." She walked to where Tommy pointed to investigate. "I don't see or hear anything. Look around, you love adventures, don't you?"

"This doesn't look like an adventure— it looks like a mess." Suspicious of her motives, he asked, "How'd you get money to buy this place? You said we didn't even *have* money for shoelaces. I'm too old to wear Velcro, you know." Tommy looked down at his worn sneakers. He didn't want to ask about new ones especially if there wasn't money for shoelaces.

"Yes, certainly are. I said we're on a *shoe string* budget, but I managed to save a little here and there," she said. "Look around. There are tons of interesting saleable items."

Tommy's hand flew to his head. An insistent buzzing made him feel anxious and edgy and woozy. "What's the buzzing sound?"

"Old buildings are noisy places. Fluorescent lights buzz and hum, or maybe there's a bees nest somewhere." She walked to the middle of the store to set a bag of cleaning supplies and big orange purse down on the wooden counter. "Hmm. I don't hear it."

Tommy's feet melded to the floor. He cupped a hand to his ear when he heard a swishing sound, like a can rolling back and forth. Then the buzzing hum filled his head making the back of his neck prickle and his head ache.

Green shards of light flew up from the top tier with a crackle and a snap. Tommy dashed around the boxes near the tall shelf and ran to the shop's center. "Mom! Mom! I saw flashing lights on the high shelf. I need a ladder. Something weird is happening up there!"

"Oh my! If it is an electric wire, I don't want you anywhere near it. Besides, I haven't found a ladder in this mess," she said. She rifled in her big orange bag for a cell phone. "I should get it checked. I hope an electrician can get here on short notice." She looked up local electricians in the search bar and touched the numbers on the key pad. "Hello? I'm the new owner of Bell's Treasure Trove, on Main Street. My son saw sparks. I need it checked on right away. Oh...not till *next week*?" Her voice fell flat. "I need someone *immediately*. Oh...Sure, thank you. What's his number?" She dove a hand into her bag to rummage for a pen. "Ok, thanks." She jotted a phone number on a cardboard box top and ended the call.

"What'd he say?"

"He gave me the number of a local handyman." She tapped in the number on her phone and recited her dilemma. "Great! Thanks." The call ended. "He's going to stop by in a few minutes. He's working right down the street—lucky for us!"

A short time later, Tommy heard a bang on the front entry door. He ran to open it. "Mom, the fix-it guy is here." Tommy's eyes drew up to the tall man with huge muscles and a tattoo peeking out from his tee shirt. Right away, he smelled trouble. He looked like the movie star Mom said was so handsome.

Mom paced over and turned the key in the lock to reopen the heavy glass door.

The bell dinged. The man was so tall, his thick black hair smacked the bell above the door. His hand flew up. He laughed. "I didn't expect to ring any bells today." He swung his hand forward toward Mom. "Jackson Stanton. Nice to meet you. Mrs. Delo, I assume?" Mr. Stanton's perfect white shiny teeth gleamed.

"I'm Mary Delo, and this is my son, Tommy. Thank you for coming by on such short notice."

Tommy didn't like the grin on his mother's face— or the girly way her voice lifted as if he told her a joke. Only he didn't tell one.

"No problem, Mrs. Delo. Pleased I could help out. He paused and shot mom a lazy smile. "I was right down the road, so no prob." The tall man shifted on one leg, and stuck a thumb in his belt loop as if he had all the time in the world.

The man turned toward him and extended a hand to shake. Tommy squeezed his large calloused hand extra tight, just the way Dad showed him.

"You have a powerful grip, Son." His mouth corners lifted into a grin.

"My name is Tommy." Tommy didn't know if the guy was kidding him. The big bad wolf fooled Red Riding Hood with his big shiny chompers and friendly smile. Worse yet, Mr. Fix-it smelled of the aftershave men wear to attract women. Dad wore it on date night with Mom. Tommy noticed a wolf tattoo peek out under the tall man's rolled-up shirtsleeve confirming his suspicions.

Tommy decided to trail after him like a detective on a mission. He was the man of the house and had to protect Mom.

"My son saw sparks by the tall shelf. I'm sure it's nothing, but I wanted to be certain." Mom gestured to the three-tiered shelf crammed with boxes.

Tommy couldn't see past the second shelf.

"Do you have a ladder here?" Mr. Stanton asked. His head did a 180 turn.

Tommy folded his arms over his chest and announced, "We couldn't find one in all these possibilities."

"No worries, I'll get the one from my truck. I'll be back in a jiff," he said.

Tommy pulled Mom by the arm. "He smiles too much and he has a *tattoo*."

"I don't care if he has a pet gorilla if he can help us."

Tommy wasn't about to laugh to encourage her. He saw Mom's goofy smile and flushed face and didn't like it one bit.

The man returned, his arms circling the ladder in a hug. "You saw sparks?"

"Right up there. Green sparks and a rolling noise, like a soup can," Tommy said.

The man climbed up and investigated. "Hmmm. No wires or plugs here." He climbed down.

"Can I take a look in case you missed something?" Tommy a raised brow and met the man's inky black eyes with his own.

He eyed Tommy like he was reading clues. "Sure. Have at it, if it's ok with your mom."

She held the ladder as Tommy ascended. "Be careful, Tommy."

"Geez, I'm almost twelve." Tommy spat it out like a wad of used bubble gum. People always guessed he was younger than his age because he was so short. He wasn't a dumb kindergarten baby.

"You can't be too careful," Mom said.

Mr. Stanton laughed. "Sure you can. Sometimes life brings great surprises when you take a chance." Mr. Stanton shot Mom a big stupid grin. "My son is entering grade six this year. Name's Jake. Maybe you can meet up with him before school starts."

Tommy let his suggestion drop into a ditch. "I don't think so. I'm not ready for new friends. I have a ton of them back home." Tommy's face darkened and his brows knit.

"I'm sure you do," he said.

Tommy climbed up and felt around. He drew his hand back. His nose crinkled. "No surprises here, just a stupid globe and an old dusty magazine."

"Mrs. Delo, do you mind if I look around the shop? These old buildings are tricky." The man laughed.

"I had the place inspected already." Mom's face blossomed red.

"I'd like to check if the wiring is up to code. Never can be too careful." Then he laughed again.

"Sure. Call me Mary." Tommy watched Mom's face flush sunburn red. He wrinkled his nose in disgust at her bad behavior. *How could she forget about Dad?*

"Call me Jackson."

Mr. Stanton strode around on long legs and chunky work boots.

Tommy shadowed him in case Jackson was up to no good. Mom trailed behind the man with a notepad and pen.

The man tapped on the window frame with his knuckles. "You're going to need to replace these windows. See? Dry rot around the framing —not a good sign. With cold weather around the corner, you can't ignore this. I'll check the breaker box for you. See if anything's tripped."

Tommy laughed. "Like on a banana peel? Good one." No one laughed.

Mr. Stanton winked at Mom.

Tommy panicked. *Winking is flirting.* Tommy folded his arms over his chest. No way should Jackson be alone with Mom—ever. He needed to remind her of Dad— pronto. "Dad fixed stuff all the time *for free,*" Tommy blurted louder than he meant to, but it had the right effect.

The man hesitated, as if considering new information. He looked right at Tommy, folded his muscled arms over his chest and said, "Oh, of course you can check with your dad before I do any work here."

Mom held up a hand. "Tommy, let me handle this." She turned to Mr. Stanton. "I'm a widow. We're just scraping by. Let me think on it." Her fingers grazed her heart necklace. "Tommy and I had a hard time when Thomas... passed. But he's in a much better place."

"Oh, I'm sorry for your loss." The tall man nodded. "Seems like you had a hard run of it, Mary. Tell you what, I'd be happy to fix these windows at no charge. I renovate for a living, so I always left-over materials laying around." "It won't cost you a dime."

Tommy's plan backfired. He knew if for sure when he saw Mom's eyes fixed on the man's rippling muscles. She looked guilty, like she stole a cookie, then tried to hide her evil deed. The guy would probably try to kiss Mom if he wasn't around to supervise them. He'd have to keep his eye on him. He folded his scrawny arms over his chest and tried to appear taller. He challenged Jackson to a man-to-man show down. "No *dimes*, but how many *dollars*?"

An amused grin, as wide as a jack-o-lantern lit on the man's face. "No dollars. Pro bono...Free."

Mom's nervous giggle filled Tommy's ears like wind chimes. It had been a long time since Tommy heard Mom laugh like that. He didn't want a new dad...Ever.

She said, "How kind of you… but it's only fair I pay for your labor. No one works for free." The man's stark white teeth gleamed.

Tommy felt an ache bubble up like soda fizz. He was sick of everyone talking about The Better Place, like it was Disney Land for dead people. He glared at Mom, then stormed from the room and ran upstairs. He pinky swore with Dad he'd watch out for her. He'd keep his promise to Dad, but Mom was breaking all the rules.

That night, Tommy and his Mom drove back to their temporary apartment across town. "Why were you so rude to the nice man, Tommy? He was only trying to help us."

"He smiles too much… and you smiled back."

"Ahhh, I see. I was just being cordial." She pulled her car up to the apartment building.

"Does cordial mean *flirting*?"

"No. It means to be friendly and polite." She kissed the top of his head.

Tommy sat in his bed. Mom hugged him and said, "Everything will work out. You'll see."

Tommy punched his mattress with his fist. "Why does everything have to change? Change stinks worse than old socks and outhouses."

"Life will look brighter in the morning. We'll head back to the shop tomorrow. You can help me sort and toss. Get some sleep." She tucked him in and put his teddy bear near him.

"I'm too old for Teddy." But he took the stuffed toy under the covers with him all the same and closed his eyes. Mysterious lights, losing Dad, and a huge tangle of concerns jammed his head in a big tangled knot. Not even teddy bear could ease the mess in his brain.

When he couldn't fight sleep any longer, his head sunk into the starry pillow and he drifted into a dream. He imagined a glowing cylindrical object with a stick underneath it spinning around, humming a sweet song, and calling out his name. The melodious voice tickled his ears and made him smile. The copper object lifted and spun, dropping him through a portal of time. What was this object?

In the morning, only fleeting images of his dream remained, like wisps of clouds on a sunny day. For some reason, he felt just a tad brighter.

CHAPTER 2

Bell's Treasure Trove

Mom swept her arm out as if she was presenting a fine dinner to the king. "You do the honors this time, Punkin. Here are the keys to the castle."

Tommy turned the key in the lock. The overhead bell dinged.

"So, what do you think about the shop, now that you've slept on the idea?"

"No one knows what 'trove' means," Tommy mumbled in disgust. "We need a better name for the shop."

"Trove means *collection*. We have more fish to fry before we decide on a new sign," Mom said.

"What do fish have to do with a stupid sign?" Tommy wrinkled his nose and shrugged.

"Just an expression of speech. Why don't you think up a better name for our shop?"

His voice dropped to a low whisper and he pushed a cobweb out of his way. "How we gonna do it all, Mom? Dad isn't here to help us." *There I said it.* "And the place is haunted." His eyes shot down at his ratty sneakers. He kicked his toe into the wood flooring. Little curls of dust lifted in a puff around his feet.

His mother's face was determined. "We can do this. I'll be here each day. I won't have to go to an office anymore. This is a good summer project to keep our mind off—all of the changes."

Tommy knew 'all the changes' was a secret code for no dad, no friends, no house, and new *everything*, except for old boxes of junk Mom called *possibilities*. His stomach twisted like a knotted shoelace. "Are you sure about this, Mom?"

"Yes. Very sure." Mom scanned the room. "Why do you think it's haunted?"

"Buzzing noises." *And someone called my name*, he thought.

"Why don't you take a good look around today? You haven't even seen the best part...the super-secret Crow's Nest." She had a glint in her eyes.

He liked the way Mom's pretty face smiled at him and her eyes crinkled. His glum mood shifted ready to go for the bait. "There's a Crow's Nest? No way, really? Now, you have my attention." He slashed the air with an imaginary sword. "Arrrg, Matey." "You know I love pirates!"

"Right this way, Captain Hook." She motioned with her hand.

He pounded up the steps following at her heels.

She shoved her knee against the squeaky door that led to the second-floor apartment and grunted. The door swung open.

Tommy followed her in. As he wandered further through the second-floor room, Tommy scoffed, "More stuff up here."

"Four hands make light work," Mom promised.

"We need ten. That's three more people to help us." He kneeled down distracted by a pile of large black heavy bound books. "Hey, what kinda books are these?" He flipped them open. Rows of neat pencil marks, numbers, and fancy cursive names filled each page.

"They're old ledgers to keep track of money spent and earned by the business."

Tommy tipped his chin to her. "Couldn't they just use a computer?"

"Not invented yet."

"No way! How did they get anything done?"

"Pencil and paper— the original computer system." She tapped her temple and grinned.

"Were you kidding me about the Crow's Nest?"

"Scouts honor, it's here. Keep looking."

He walked around the room, randomly tossing objects aside. "No secret room yet, but good news, I found the other can!" He flushed the toilet and watched the water swirl in a circle. "The toilet flushes and there's a tub in here, too. I don't see any secret room."

She paused dramatically. "You'll find a secret entrance on this level. You're not giving up, are you?" She threw her hands to her hips in a superhero pose.

"No way." Tommy's eyes crinkled with delight.

Eagerly, he dashed around checking for clues. "No staircase or doors anywhere."

"I'll give you one little hint. Feel all of the walls."

Curious, Tommy traced his fingers over the perimeter of the room, leaping over stacks of junk. He pushed boxes out of his way to get to each wall. "Am I warm yet?" He stood near a large room to the far right.

"Ice cold."

He walked next to the smaller room on the right. "How about now?"

"Warmer."

He moved to the left of the doorway and noticed a panel of decorative wood trim which seemed out of place. He ran his fingers over it.

"Red hot!" She encouraged.

Tommy pressed his palm against the center panel and it shifted back with a squeak. "Mystery solved!" The creaky 3 by 5-foot panel eked open to reveal a narrow four-step stairwell just his size. "No freaking way!" He bounded up the staircase. He twirled around examining the small attic room with a circular window facing a creek. From it, he could see a row of historic wooden buildings Mom called the Old Long House. His eyes lifted to the arched ceiling then down to the cozy corner, just right for a desk, chair, and tall Lego tower. This was the perfect secret clubhouse hideaway if he only had some friends to fill it. This room was the only space in the building not filled with junk. He bounded down the stairs with a mile wide grin. "The Crow's Nest is a *perfect* bedroom. There's a creek out back! Can it be my bedroom?"

"We can't get a bed through the little doorway, but a sleeping bag will fit. "Are you sure you want to be up here alone? If you sleep walk, you might fall down the staircase."

"Aw, Mom. You worry too much. You know I don't sleep walk as much as I used to."

"We'll put your bed in the small room on the second level next to mine. Ready to help me clean?"

"Ready, Captain." He saluted her.

She headed down to the ground floor shop level.

He followed her. Mom gathered up cleaning supplies while he busied himself examining box contents. Then it happened. A loud buzzing sound filled his ears and he heard a voice call his name.

"Tommy, Tommy."

He froze in place and his eyes jutted around. Tommy sprinted to Mom. "Did you hear the buzzing sound?"

"No."

"Didn't you just call me?" His voice quavered.

"No, but now that's you're here, you can help me clean up." She handed him cleaning cloths.

No use telling her the voice might be a ghost. He tossed a worried glance over his shoulder.

CHAPTER 3

Trash or Treasure?

Cloth in hand, Tommy shook off a shiver, rattled by the disembodied voice. There was definitely something weird going on. But he promised Mom he'd help out. He pushed the fear away and investigated the crammed shelves stacked with boxes. His eyes roamed the room. Soon, he forgot all about the ghost.

His gaze landed at the middle shelf labeled, *Old Toys and Collectables 1950-1960's*. "That's what I'm talking about!" He tugged the dilapidated box from the shelf and set it on the wooden floor. His hand dove into it. "Wow! Old fashioned toys!" His mood lifted as high as a helium balloon and his face lit like sunshine. "Mom, If I find something really special, it's mine, right?"

"Sure is," Mom tousled his hair. "Remove everything before you clean each shelf."

He held up the 1960's spaceship toy. "Check this out, Mom." He zoomed the silver metal disk up and down imitating motor sounds. He thumped the disc with his hand. "This is made of good metal, not cheesy plastic that break in two seconds."

Mom scanned the room. "It's ours to sell."

"But not this toy." He held up the spaceship. "You said I could have it."

"Scouts honor." She held up a boy scout salute.

"It counts even though you're not a scout," Tommy said.

"I beg to differ. I was a girl scout back in the day. We have two weeks before school starts. Don't waste too much time playing around with the toys."

Tommy groaned and gagged. "Did you have to mention school?" He hung his head low and his mind drifted. "Maybe I can call Petey."

Mom's nose wrinkled. "Petey?"

Petey was a sore subject ever since Mom caught them browsing the Internet. She was steaming mad. *How was I supposed to know an innocent word would bring up naughty photos?*. "Petey tricked me. Oh, never mind," Tommy waved his hand. "He's probably busy with all his *new* friends, anyway."

"How about that nice boy, Harv? Why don't you call him instead?"

"He moved to California and we're in New Jersey. He might as well be living on the moon." He thought of his old house and the fun they had playing in the yard. "Is our house gone for good, Mom?"

"Hospital bills, Tommy. You know we had to sell it." Her voice drifted away so softly, he almost missed it.

He knew it was hopeless to pretend they'd move back in and Dad would be alive. It was just a dumb fantasy, but he still wished it were true. The counselor told him he was in the Nile...or was he in *denial*?

"Dad is cheering us on." She pushed a stray lock of hair from her eyes and sneezed a dusty puff out of her nose.

Tommy wasn't convinced by her everything-will-be-alright-smile. It didn't keep Dad alive. His mood dropped like a rock. He tried to imagine Dad, smiling from the better place everybody mentioned. *But where was this better place? Would it have baseball games, hot dogs, and dad's favorite books?* He twisted his lower lip and frowned. *Probably loaded with skeletons, creepy stuff, and old dusty boxes, like Davey Jones locker in the sky.* "He's gone."

"What did you say?"

"Never mind..." His voice drifted off. Every single blurt got him in trouble last year, especially in Mrs. Black's stupid reading class. She didn't treat him *special,* even though he went to her for special help. He only felt dumb. In a few months it would be Christmas and then Father's Day. *All the kids at school would have two parents and a happy life. His old life, before Dad got sick.*

"Will I have to see a counselor this year?"

"We'll see how you're doing... with all the changes." She hugged him. "Turn that frown upside down. I need your help, Tommy."

He looked up at her through teary eyes. "It's just you and me now, Mom." He'd watch out for her just like he promised Dad. He blamed himself for making Mom sad twice since yesterday. He'd have to do better. Dad told him to use his mile-wide smile to help her. He looked up to the ceiling and mouthed, "I'm sorry, Dad." Tommy pushed the corners of his mouth up and gave her an everything-will-be-alright smile. Dad used to say, fake it till you make it. So he faked it, swallowed his sadness and asked, "How'd you find this great place, Mom?"

"Mr. Bell's family sold the place to us for a song— and by song, I mean *cheaply*."

"I figured that out." He gave her a sly smile. If you sang for it, the store would've cost us double!" Peals of laughter erupted. "Get it Mom?" Tommy's humor reminded him of Petey. A fun friend who got him in trouble *all the time*. Jokes made Mom laugh— and when you laugh, you can't cry. His moods bounced like a ping-pong ball —one minute happy, pissed-off the next, even though that very phrase got him into detention last year. It was exactly how he felt. At times, he didn't have control of happy or sad, they just landed on him like bird crap.

"Sure do, Punkin."

Mom tossed her hands to her hips and studied the room. "We have lots to do, Co-manager."

"Sweet! Co-manager? I'll need business cards; after I help you fry all those fish."

"I'm on it." She laughed.

Tommy managed to bring a smile to Mom's face. He removed hefty boxes from the shelves when he heard a voice call his name. "What is it, Mom?"

"I didn't call you." She yelled back.

He went back to work sorting through the boxes when he heard his name again. Tommy cocked his head sideways and cupped his ear. This time, he ran over to her. "What is it Mom?"

"I didn't call you, but now that I have your attention, here's some extra cleaning solution and paper towels. Once the boxes are down, wipe the shelves." She handed him a pile of clean cloths, paper towels, and a spray bottle.

"This stuff smells like rotten eggs and old socks. Why can't we use Clean-Off?" he complained.

"Too many chemicals. Organic or nothing."

Above his head, he heard a shuffling sound, like a can rolling back and forth metal to metal. He headed back to the tall shelves, hurdling boxes as he sprinted. When the noise stopped, he dashed back to report to her. "I don't want to scare you, but we have a ghost."

"Ghosts don't like clean shops and hate elbow grease." She tossed a clean cloth to him.

"Do we even have elbow grease?"

"Sure do!" Mom chuckled.

"Good, then we don't need to buy any. Seriously, what can we do about the ghost?"

"Ghosts hate Zap-away." She smirked.

He realized she didn't believe him. "We need to hire a Ghost Buster, Mom."

"I have a Dust Buster, will that work?"

"Seriously. I heard something."

"Probably just noise from the air vents. Get crackin, Kiddo." She pointed to three boxes. "Trash, treasure, donate—then wipe the shelving 'till the dust bunnies hop away. When you think it's clean, wipe it again." She demonstrated and sneezed. She held up a soiled cloth. "See? More dirt."

Tommy pinched his nose and waved his hand in the air. "Are you sure ghosts don't like this nasty spray?"

"Positive."

"Then we'll need a ton of it."

"We'll move in upstairs once we have the rooms clean and tidy. Until then, we can pretend we're camping."

He sighed. "Move in? Maybe… but only if we can toast marshmallows. We already have more spiders than we need." And a ghost.

CHAPTER 4

What is a Prayer Wheel?

Tommy headed down the steps from the second-floor apartment. His feet stopped short when a glimmer of light from the top shelf caught his eye. He hammered down the rest of the staircase and dashed toward the shelf. He heard a chink of metal on metal. He looped the shop running around in desperate search for a ladder.

He explored the last corner of the shop and found a closet door partly covered by a tall stack of boxes. He strained to move the heavy boxes aside. He yanked the door open. A musty smell hit his nose, reminding him of his grandmother's basement of her old house.

"Finally!" He yelped. The tall wooden ladder was wedged behind a pile of junk and yellowing newspapers tied with string. "Yahoo!" He moved the newspapers out of his way. He tugged and pulled to release the ladder, but it was stuck tight under the door frame. Frustrated, he kicked his sneaker against the ladder, which only hurt his toes. He tugged and pulled, but he couldn't dislodge it. Mom would say she was busy, but he needed her help. He dashed to her. "I found a ladder in the closet. It won't budge and I really need it."

"I'll be a monkey's uncle. We own a ladder after all. Why do you need it? Can't this wait?"

"It can't wait. I have the gurgling stomach bubbles."

"Gas?" She seemed confused.

"No, the *other* bubbles the counselor told me about."

"Oh. You have a gut feeling."

"Yes. My guts are gassy and telling me I have to check something out on the top shelf."

"I see." She followed him to the closet.

She pulled and tugged, angling the ladder to release it from the door jam.

Once cleared, they pulled at the end of the ladder and it eased out.

"Now I can see what's been rolling around and glowing."

"Glowing? It's probably just...."

"Yeah, I know.... the reflection from the windows." Not. "At least it's not a live wire."

"Didn't you already check the same shelf when Mr. Stanton was here? What do you expect to find today that wasn't there yesterday?" She carried the ladder to the high four-tiered shelf.

"I'm not sure. My guts won't leave me alone until I check."

"Ok. I'll hold the ladder." She propped the ladder like a big A. She held the side rails. "Go for it. Be careful."

"Geez, Mom. I got this. It's not like I've never climbed before." *I've already climbed the roof at our house, Petey's garage, an apple tree by the mill, the baseball fence at the field....* Thoughts trailed away. He ascended and stood on tiptoes. He flung his arm toward the back of the shelf as far as his fingers could reach. He craned his arm back and felt a cold metal object teasing his fingertips. It rolled further back from his grasp.

"I knew it! There's something rolling around up there. Just another little stretch." He coaxed the object toward his fingertips which buzzed as he grazed it. Suddenly, the object rolled toward him. A spark tingled his fingertip as the cold metal cylinder rolled right into his hand as if he had a magnet in it. "Got it!" Excitement filled him like a red party balloon.

Something about the object spoke to his gut. A strange familiar memory tickled his brain. Did he dream about this metal object before? He couldn't bring the memory up.

"My gut was right, Mom." Tommy tucked it into his shirt pocket before descending the ladder. His feet touched down. He pulled it out of his shirt pocket mesmerized. He watched the strange writing whirl around as he rolled it in his palms.

"That's a valuable find!" Mom said.

"I told you so." He held the object by its handle and twirled the cylinder with his hand. "I haven't seen squiggly writing like this before ever. What is this thing?" The object warmed at his touch, then shocked him. "Ouch! It bit me!"

"It bit you?" Mom lifted a brow. "What do you mean?"

"It bit me... like the car handle does in the winter."

"Oh. You mean you got a static electricity shock. Dry air makes static electricity. We'll need to hook up a *humidifier* in the shop to get more moisture in the air."

She took the notepad from her pocket and jotted the word humidifier on her shopping list.

"I don't think it's the air." Tommy folded his arms over his check.

"Tommy, let me take a closer look at it."

"I hope it doesn't bite you." He handed it to her as if it were a snarling puppy.

"I'll be brave unless I see its teeth." She grinned and flipped the cylinder over, rotating it in her palms to examine the inscriptions on the barrel. "I'm not sure what kind of writing this is. It's not hieroglyphics. Once we have the Internet hooked in, we can find out more. It's quite beautiful!"

"Didn't it bite you?"

"No. I'm good with dogs." She smirked.

"I'm not even kidding. It bites." He picked it up with care. His palms heated as if he held a warm cup of soup in them. A low vibration hummed in his hands. He'd found something magical. "We can't sell this thing, Mom. It's really special and I want to keep it. Can I? What do you think this thing is?"

They walked over to the sales counter. "This seems to be a prayer wheel, Tommy, but I'm no expert. People in Asian countries would spin the can shaped part on the handle sending prayers to God. The metal looks like brass, copper, and silver. It must be worth a small fortune."

He saw her eyes light up dollar signs. "You won't sell this, right? Pinky swear promise me." Tommy held out a pinky.

She clasped it in hers. "I promise not to sell this, Punkin, *even though* it might be worth a small fortune. I've heard that the former owner was a world traveler. It's too bad he's losing his memory these days."

"Geez, I hope we have the Internet soon. I feel like we're in the dark ages without it," Tommy said.

She handed Tommy the artifact.

He heard a soft whirring noise in his head, like a song playing on a faraway radio. Suddenly, Tommy's brain got fuzzy. His hand flew to his head and his knees weakened.

"What's wrong? Are you ok?" Mom's concerned hand flew to his forehead in a mother- checking-for-fever kind of way.

"My brain got swirly and swishy." He didn't like the scared expression on Mom's face. She wore it every time she'd talk to Dad's doctors. He pressed the object into her hand. "Here, put this thig-a-ma-jig-whirly-gig on the counter ... but just for now."

"Sure." She took the object and set it on the old wood counter in the store's center."Sit down and rest."

In a few minutes he felt better. "I'm not sick, Mom, honest, don't worry." He did two jumping jacks to demonstrate then snaked through the piles of boxes. "See? All better now."

She took in a breath of relief. "Are you sure?"

"Yes. Hey, is this like an E-Store?"

"Before the internet was invented, people browsed for collectables at shops in person, just like this one." She paused to consider his words. "Come to think of it, posting an E-Store is a great idea!" Mom said.

"The Internet is a *necessary*," Tommy insisted.

Mom laughed. "A necessary is an old-fashioned word for a potty chair. The word you mean is *necessity*."

"Necessary is a dumb word for the can if you ask me. Do we have one here?" He twirled around looking for a bathroom.

"We do. In fact, there's an old potty chair near the back entrance of the shop by the other parking lot. But don't use it," She teased. "The real lavatory is around the corner behind that big stack of boxes and there's a second bathroom *and* a tub upstairs that goes with our apartment."

Let's get back to valuing the items. I'm sure some are worth a pretty penny."

Tommy held up an old doll from a dusty box and shook it at her. "I wouldn't buy it for an ugly dollar or a pretty penny. This doll is super creepy." He imitated the googly glass eyes with his own.

"I'll be right back." He leaped over boxes and dashed to the far end of the store. He found the potty chair. He flipped the lid open and saw an old tin pot in the center of the wooden chair and dashed back to report. "Now I know why it's called a potty. I saw the pot under the wood lid. I'm glad we don't have to plop into one of those." Tommy twisted his face and held his nose. "PU!"

"A toilet is a necessary necessity," Mom punned.

"Ahh, funny." Tommy giggled. "Who'd buy an old doody chair? It's so gross."

"You'd be surprised at the odd things people want to collect."

Tommy nodded in agreement. It was true. He owned every Lego set known to exist. He went through a collection phase at age eight. Harv collected toothpicks from restaurants and Dad used to collect old musty boring history books about places long ago. Tommy wrinkled his nose. Reading is hard. He'd rather collect Legos and toothpicks than books any day.

Tommy pushed the assorted knick-knacks aside on the shelf in favor of a well-worn tattered black leather catcher's mitt. He pounded a closed fist into it. "Hey Mom, this mitt looks just like Dad's old one!"

She nodded. "Sure does."

Tommy's eyes drifted away. "I miss playing catch with Dad." Tommy's happy mood dropped as fast as a missed fly ball. An ache blasted into his gut. Dad would've called it a major league pitch to the stomach.

"Why don't you keep that mitt?"

"You mean you're not going to sell it? Not even for an ugly dollar?"

"Not even for an ugly dollar."

"Now all I need is a pitcher," Tommy whispered and kicked an empty box with his sneaker.

He could have sworn he heard someone call his name. He whipped around. It didn't sound like Mom. He grabbed for the Zap Away, just in case.

CHAPTER 5

Sixth Grade Orientation

Four weeks later

September 1 Friday
Hope School Orientation

Late July, and August had passed. Tommy and his mom had tagged, sorted, and emptied most of the boxes in Bell's Treasure Trove. School hadn't started, but Tommy was signed in to attend a 2 ½ hour Orientation Day which was supposed to ease the students into the new school year. The night before, his eyes were wide open. Alone, exhausted and anxious, his stomach rumbled with bubbles of gas he tried to hold in, but poofs of air flew out. By morning, he was filled with gas. "Great. This is all I need," he muttered, moving away from the deadly deed.

Once inside the school, Orientation was a blur of new faces rushing around to greet friends. But since he had none, he did his best to be invisible, like a Ninja. A tall dark-haired boy *almost* waved and was about to walk over when the dismissal bell rang at 12:30, signaling the end of a tortuous two hour visit. A pin popped his balloon of hope. *Great. Another bad year coming my way. Hopeless starts here.* As soon as the bell rang, he hoisted his backpack and scooted out to find Mom. He stuffed the suggested reading list at the bottom of his backpack to hide it from her prying eyes.

Piles of kids rushed out of the building in a wave to board buses or cars in the semi-circle lot in front of the school. Tommy's face lit up when he saw Mom's red compact pull up to the circular driveway. He skyrocketed to the car, pitching his laden backpack on the floor before stepping in.

"Glad you're here, Mom. Soon, I'll go to the gallows." Tommy squawked like a chicken and pulled a pretend noose around his neck. "It's not too late to homeschool me." He batted his lashes and laced his fingers together in prayer.

Mom watched the cars and buses load and waited her turn to pull out. "Those puppy dog eyes won't convince me to homeschool you, Kiddo."

"Not even with a pretty please with sugar on top?" He knew she'd ask tons of questions about school work, friends, and the dreaded reading list.

"Not even…" She glanced at his face. "So, how'd it go?" She looked both ways and edged her car slowly from the circular school driveway.

He took a breath when her eyes were busy watching the cars. He released a tsunami of troubles. "First, we all sat in a big room while the principal yakked about rules, manners, and more blah, blah, blah. Last, we walked to the lunchroom and ate lunch —mac and cheese, but it wasn't *yummy* like yours. The skinny cooker-lady blah, blah, blahed — and we got menus. But I don't trust her, Mom. Dad always said, 'Never trust a skinny cook' except for you."

"Enough about lunch. Did you meet any of your assigned teachers? Did you learn *anything* today?"

"I learned I don't want to go to school. The real teachers weren't even in today. It'll be a big freakin' surprise tomorrow. I bet they don't even like kids…"

Or won't like me. Tommy gulped back his worried words.

"Some surprises are good, like birthday presents. This year will be your best one yet."

"Aww, Mom. You just don't get it. With school, surprises are *never* good," Tommy whined. "Like surprise quizzes, and surprise substitutes...get it? And who'd could I invite? Everyone's gone and lives far away."

She smirked. "You'll make new friends. Did you see your homeroom or meet your teachers?" She pulled out and turned left toward the town center.

"The real teachers weren't in today. Big whoop. I found the can in case I get gassy at school, which happened this morning. It's not polite to fart in public, but an air biscuit blew from my butt and I couldn't stop it."

"*Pass gas* in the *lavatory*... not the *can*, and you're right... it's not polite, but gas happens."

"A fart is a fart mom, no matter what fancy name you call it." Mom didn't like the word, but he didn't care. She's the one who made him go to a new school, sell their home, and live in a trash heap.

"What number is your homeroom?"

"Number 10. Big deal. I saw a bunch of new kids I don't know." He watched his mother's eyes tear up. "Are you ok, Mom?" Even though her eyes watched the road ahead, he recognized the sad eyes which mirrored his own... ever since Dad died. His emotions were flip flopping like a fish out of water.

"Just allergies." She donned her pretend cover-up happy face.

He *promised Dad I'd be brave*. So, he remembered his promise and donned his fake-happy face. He tried to think of something good to tell her so she wouldn't worry about him. "I saw a poster of Yoda." He imitated the character's voice to make her laugh. "I like Yoda, I do."

"See? A good surprise. Did you make any friends today?"

His fake-happy was short-lived and died like road kill. "Geez, Mom. I was only there a few stinking' hours. It takes time to make friends— maybe even years."

She rephrased her question. "Did you *talk* with anyone today? Did you meet the handyman's son?"

"No and I wasn't looking for him. The pretend teacher— who probably works at the gas station, interrupted me just when some kid was about to say hello. Then the dismissal bell rang and I left. That's my day in an acorn."

"You mean in a nutshell."

"Same difference." Tommy shrugged, not seeing the point of her correction.

"You have to make an effort, Tommy."

"I told you, I got interrupted or I would've." Tommy knew it was an excuse. He scrunched his face and felt his smooth chin. "I'm pretty sure all the kids shave except for me and the first graders."

"From the looks of your book bag, you have work to do."

"They might as well be bricks because they weigh a freakin' ton."

"Maybe you can call your buddy Harv tonight. See how California is treating him." The corners of her mouth lifted. "He's only a phone call away."

"It's not the same as seeing Harv every day. He's millions of miles from New Jersey." *Dad is millions of miles away too*, he thought. His stomach double-knotted, like shoelaces that don't untie even when you run fast.

"The same moon shines on all of us." She handed him a paper bag full of snacks.

"Harv might as well live on the moon." No way he could admit to Mom the awful things he'd said to Harv after he informed him of his California move. It was just one more person leaving him for good. Mom wouldn't understand. He dug his hand into the paper bag and pulled out a red apple and shined it on his pant leg.

"You'll acclimate to school soon enough."

"Acli-what?" He took a bite of the apple.

"Fit in— feel comfortable. I'll bet Harv feels the same way you do."

"I doubt it. He'll make tons of new friends. He won't even miss me." His voice drifted. "I'm friendless." Tommy's face contorted and he sniffled. He wanted to cry like a baby, but he held the tears in tight. Someone might see him through the car window.

She pulled over and hugged him. "Tell me something good about your day."

"It's like this, Mom. Fifth grade was super-hard for me. How can I acli-whatever in a new school with no stinkin' friends?"

"You'll make them. Besides, last year was... extra hard on us both. I couldn't help you with your schoolwork like I used to do... with Dad needing me. Now I can. It'll be different this year, you'll see."

Tommy knew she felt guilty about ignoring him last year. He saw it in the corner of her eyes, even though she kept them glued to the road. "I know." He dug down deep to make her smile since his jokes could make her laugh. "Get this...A huge ape asked me if I was a fourth grader 'cause I'm as short as a chimp. The kid has beard stubble and his King Kong knuckles scrape the floor. He probably smokes a pipe and lives in a tree."

She smiled with a twinkle of mirth in her eyes. "Maybe you can climb a tree and offer him a banana."

"Seriously?" He laughed in spite of himself, because it was funny. But even joking couldn't calm his jangled nerves. "Maybe I can get high-heeled shoes like Captain Hook wears. He must have been short guy like me, right?"

She eyed his small stature. "I think your sneakers will be just fine." She tousled his hair and pulled back onto the road. "You are a few months younger than your peers and a *tad* shorter. So what? You'll catch up soon enough."

"Not by Tuesday." Tommy shoved the apple in his mouth and wiped his face on his sleeve.

"Look on the bright side. We have each other. And soon, you'll have new friends."

He wasn't giving up so easily. "Maybe once the doors close, the teachers beat us with sticks. As soon as the buses leave, they lock us in the dungeon and make us recite our times tables until we puke." He bulged his eyes and poked his tongue out in dramatic grimace. "The real teachers were home today practicing to whip us into shape."

"Kids will enjoy your sense of humor. No need to worry."

"Easy for you to say. Bad things happen that aren't funny." Dark thoughts about funeral day clouded his heart. "Tommy stared out the window and traced a sad face with a puff of breath and a finger to the glass.

"You ok?" He saw her put a hand to her heart necklace Dad gave her.

"Last year, Mrs. Black said I wasn't funny." Tommy felt a dark cloud drift cover him. "She didn't get my jokes."

"That old battle axe? She wouldn't laugh at a monkey."

Tommy's face brightened despite his sour mood. "I agree."

"I heard that the teachers are patient in Hope School. Give them a chance… for my sake."

Tommy continued his rant. "I hate to tell you; teachers fool parents big time saying they're patient. All bets were off once they get us *captured*."

"*Captive*, kiddo."

"Whatever. Trust me; teachers *love* to give homework by the bucket load. They're really *impatient* if you leave it at home on *accident*." Tommy dug his hand in the paper bag to finish the last big handful of peanuts.

"This year, no excuses for forgetting homework… *by* accident or *on*-purpose," she scolded.

"Teachers stay up all night figuring how to make innocent kids barf up dumb facts."

"Really? How do you know?"

"Last year, Mrs. Black said she corrected papers *all night long*... Don't get me started about comprehension questions." He swooned and wiped his brow for dramatic effect.

"I see. So, you *do* have reading homework?" She stopped and pulled over into the dirt patch. "Spill the details, kiddo."

"Me and my big mouth." Tommy groaned and let out a deep sigh. "The pretend teacher *suggested* a reading book, so we don't really have to do it." Tommy dangled the lie like a little worm on a hook.

"Oh, a suggested reading list. Yes, you have to." Mom snapped his lie like a hungry fish.

He pretended to gag. "Newsflash, comprehension questions make kids hate reading even more."

"So, you've said. You'd might as well dig out the paper and let me take a look at it." She pulled the car over to a patch of dirt.

Reluctantly, Tommy shoved his hand into the backpack. "Here." He pushed a crumpled paper sticky with apple juice into her hand.

"Geez, Tommy. I bought you a nice new folder for important papers just like these." She unrumpled it carefully smoothing the edges.

"When I get some, I'll use the stinkin' folder," he grumbled.

She read the paper. "I see. The local library is just a town over. Let's head there. Hmmm, *Time Wheel*, a fantasy adventure genre by Rosemary DeTrolio. Interesting…the author was a teacher. I might borrow it when you're done reading it."

"A teacher? You're not making a good case for reading it. How 'bout you read it first and tell me all about it." Tommy winked.

"No way, kiddo." Mom handed him a wet wipe. "Here, use this."

"We'll head to the library before it closes." She plunged a hand into her orange purse for her cell phone. Her index finger tapped the screen. She pulled back out to the road and continued up to Main Street following the navigation from her phone.

"What's a *general*, anyway?"

"*Genre*, not generals." Mom sighed. "You don't remember anything from last year's reading test?"

Tommy wrinkled his nose, as if a bad smell was in the air, "My brain was filled to the top with comprehension questions. I had no room for *generals*."

"*Genre* is a type of story, you know, like fantasy, factual, historic and so on." She shook her head in dismay. "You'll have to study more this year."

"You know that I suck at tests." Tommy twisted his face into a scowl.

"Is that awful expression from Petey, too?" She lifted a disapproving eyebrow.

"No, sorry." *Yes definitely*. "I mean, I stink at tests. I heard a genius invented a flash drive for brains. It was on the Science Channel. I'm saving up to buy one."

"Till then, practice makes progress."

Tommy yipped, "I'd get an A if the test was about famous pirates!"

"Maybe this new book will 'hook you' in," she quipped.

Tommy formed his index finger like a hook. "Like Captain Hook, ha, ha. Not likely."

"Guess what? While you were at Orientation, I had the Internet hooked up."

"Sweet! I can see what the twirling can on a stick is for."

"First, we're off the town library to get a copy of your suggested reading. And by suggested, I mean you have to do it."

CHAPTER 6

Town Library

Hope Public Library the Same Day 1:40

Tommy checked the clock on the dashboard on Mom's car. He crossed his fingers and wished her navigation wouldn't find Hope Library. It was 1:40 pm when they arrived at the library. Mom parked the car in front of the large stone building. Tommy pushed to open the heavy glass doors. He heard the skinny librarian call out, "Patrons, a reminder that we will close at 2:00 today."

"Oh no. I thought they'd be open to 6:00 tonight. I forgot about Labor Day weekend." She groaned. "Bad mother moment strikes again."

"How can I find a book in *ten* lousy minutes?"

"Tommy, ask the librarian to help you. You have *eighteen* minutes."

He rolled his eyes and muttered, "Like eight minutes makes a difference."

On the large flat circulation desk, sat a gold sign emblazoned with the name, Miss Prim, Head Librarian. A tall countertop arced her territory like a queen's fortress. Arranged on the countertop were a tidy jar of pens and pencils, a flat screen computer, and a several large three-ring binders standing like soldiers on a shelf. Miss Prim turned and eyed him like he was a tiny minnow she wanted to snap up.

Tommy passed long semicircular counter and smiled at Miss Prim. Her red-pursed lips didn't look happy to see him. He dilly-dallied toward the shelves scanning the rows of books as if he was a traveler exploring a foreign land.

He tugged his mother's arm. "Can't you ask her for me... please?"

She tossed her hands to her hips. "Your homework. Not mine. Use your cute smile on her."

"I did and it didn't work." Mom was in her September-hurry-up-Tommy mode. She wouldn't give in even if he whined. But it didn't stop him from trying.

"Patrons, we're closing for Labor Day weekend and will reopen on Tuesday the 5th. We close in fifteen minutes." Miss. Prim readjusted red framed reading glasses on her sharp beak nose. "Make your selections quickly." She called out eyeing Tommy.

He looked around. No one except he and his mom were left in the library. The other patron headed out. Miss Prim's obvious warning was meant for him. "It figures," he mumbled.

Tommy strode over to Miss Prim. "How do I find this book, *Time Wheel?*" He lifted his brows and gave his best winning smile; one which got him out of trouble more times than he could count.

She pursed her lips in a little O like a fish and didn't return his smile. "Alphabetical— last name of the author. Letter D, for DeTrolio. Several of your classmates checked out copies *weeks* ago." Impatiently, she pecked on the computer keys. "There's only one copy left since you are here so *last minute*. Check the shelf." With a hasty wave, she pointed to the A through D aisle.

He winced at her clipped, unfriendly tone and red joker lips. Tommy saw a sign, Middle Grade

Fiction and headed back to the circulation desk to set Miss Prim straight. "I'm a new kid. I just got the list today." It didn't seem to make any difference to her.

"We close in five minutes," She tapped her wristwatch with her fingernail as if she was a hen-pecking seed.

Tommy meandered back to the fiction aisle, slowly finger-tracing book spines. He glanced to mom hoping for a rescue if he dawdled long enough. No luck. Then he saw it on the shelf... but left it there. *No book, no homework*. He grinned. His plan was almost flawless until Mom stood over him with folded arms and a frown.

Little fish caught again. A mischievous smile crossed his lips. "Got it right here, Mom." He slid it from the shelf.

"Miss Prim is ready to bust a gasket. Sign the book out and let's get going."

Adults always rushed him. "Hurry, Tommy. Finish your vocabulary. Hurry, Tommy... you're the last test paper." He could hear his reading teacher; Mrs. Black's scolding tone blaring in his head like a car horn. He felt beads of nervous sweat dampen his underarms. He dreaded reading class and school hadn't ever started yet. He jogged to the desk with the *Time Wheel* in hand.

She examined his card curtly in her bony fingers, softening just a bit as she caught his eyes in hers. "Interlibrary loan will work just for today. Come back for our *official* Hope Branch card during regular hours *after* the holiday weekend." She scanned in the book and handed him a due date receipt.

They left the library and he stepped in the car. He wondered how he'd ever finish reading a whole chapter, much less an entire book. She pulled up onto the gravel driveway in the back of the shop. Set the key in the lock and opened the door.

"Hello spiders, I'm home!"

"I want to show you what I've accomplished while you were at Orientation." She shoved a box aside, sneezed, and brushed a dust bunny from her jeans palm. "Dust bunnies everywhere."

"Maybe we can buy some carrots for them," he added. "Get it?"

"I get it." She jiggled the lock and opened the door.

"Seriously, a guy needs his own key, Mom."

Tommy eyed a clearing where a big pile of junk sat the day before. "I like what you've done with the place."

"I thought you might. I've wiped and picked through boxes all morning. Do you have any *other* suggested homework you forgot to mention?" Mom's brows lifted.

"No. Just the first chapter." Caught again, a little fish dangling on a hook. "Ahhh." He waved his hand at her. "That joke is so two hours ago."

Mom pulled the car up to the back of the shop. Tommy lugged his backpack in and set it on the wooden sales counter with a grunt. There sat the prayer wheel.

"Mom, why did you bring this down? I left it up in the Crow's Nest this morning."

"You probably forgot you put it here." Tommy's brows knit in a little V. "No...I didn't," he mumbled in quiet protest.

"It can't get legs and walk there."

"I'm not so sure."

CHAPTER 7

Woozy

He took the prayer wheel in his hands and twirled the barrel with his index finger. He heard a buzzing-bee hum inside his head as he watched the barrel spin. It made him dizzy. Then he heard the same sweet singing voice. The one that called his name. His vision blurred, his hands tingled, his head went fuzzy, and he swayed side to side. He lost feeling and the floor dropped from under him.

Mom saw him wobble and swift as an eagle, grabbed his arm to brace his fall. "Are you feeling ok, Punkin?" She shoved a wooden stool under him right before his knees gave way. "Maybe you're hungry...or ill." Her concerned hand touched his forehead. "Hmm, no fever."

"I'm ok, Mom."

"What happened?"

"I got woozy... like the time I went on the teacup ride at the fair." Tommy gave her a weak smile so she wouldn't worry. "I heard the buzzing sound."

"Maybe you have an ear infection. Do your ears hurt?"

"No."

"I'll schedule a visit with Dr. Jones just in case. This is the second time you've been dizzy like this and I'm concerned."

Tommy said, "I don't need a stinkin' doctor. Doctors make people sick, and dead.

Dad was fine *before* he went to the doctor."

"He was sick. That's why he went to the doctor. Doctors help people."

"They didn't help Dad."

She shook her head. "It's not the same thing."

Then Tommy thought of the benefit of a doctor visit. "Maybe you're right... I'm too sick to go to school."

"Now I know you're fine, but I'll call the doctor just to cover all bases."

Tommy stood up and touched his toes. "See? I'm all better. No doctor needed."

She checked her phone and called the doctor's number. "Ugh. The office is closed except for emergency visits until tomorrow morning. I'll see if I can get an appointment as soon as the office reopens."

Tommy looked at the artifact, but was hesitant to touch it. "I wonder what the squiggly words mean on the barrel."

"Maybe if we shine the barrel with a cloth, we'll see the markings better." She handed him a clean polishing cloth.

Tommy hesitated. "How 'bout you do it, Mom." He lifted it with care and handed it to her. A warm electric tingle tickled his fingertips. This time, he knew for sure it wasn't static electricity. In his heart, he believed it had magical powers.

"Mom, can you bring this thing back to my room? It does weird stuff when I touch it."

She watched him curiously. "Sure. For now, sit and read. If you feel ill again, tell me right away."

Tommy took in a breath. "Could we get take out tonight? I always feel better when I eat ribs. I'm wishing for baby back ribs from itsy-bitsy-piggies." He oinked a few times.

"Sure. Porkies Pork Palace. Take-out it is."

"Speaking of piggies, when will I get hair on my chinny-chin-chin? Time is running out. My face is as smooth as a piglet's bottom."

"Puberty happens in its own time." She walked up the staircase.

Half an hour later, Mom headed back down. "How many pages did you finish?"

"Two pages."

"It's a start. Are you feeling better?"

"I feel good enough to help you clean up."

"If you're sure." She handed him a spray bottle and a rag.

"Can I use the computer?"

"Not yet. I'm loading in the sales program in and making a sales roster."

Tommy wiped the shelves under the counter for next hour thinking of how much he missed his dad. The thought made his stomach knot like an old shoe lace. He walked back to the counter. "Can I use it yet?"

"Yes. I'm heading upstairs. Safe sites only. Try searching for prayer wheel. I'm sure you'll find lots of information."

Tommy pulled a stool up to the counter where a new computer sat. He watched pictures fill the screen. "Cool. There's a whole bunch of them in this page."

Mom headed back upstairs with the artifact in her hand.

CHAPTER 8

Creepy Purple Lights

"Any more woozy spells?" Mom leaned in with a concerned face as she examined him.

"I'm fine, Mom."

She kissed the top of his head. "Alright. I'll be upstairs if you need me."

Tommy sat in front of the counter twirling on the high stool next to the computer. He heard shuffling and rolling noises behind him on the counter. He whipped around and stared at it and his jaw dropped open. There was the prayer wheel on the sale's counter moving back and forth on its own. He continued to stare in awe trying not to move a muscle. "How did you get here?"

Sparks flew from the copper metal and a large purple circle of light cracked open. His mouth gaped open and he felt as if a giant magnet pulled his body toward the circle. "What the…" was all he could say before he was whooshed inside the rainbow of light. He grabbed his stomach. The vortex spewed him out on a white tile floor in another place.

When he stood up, he grabbed his head and almost puked. A strong smell of rubbing alcohol filled his nose. He stood up, shaky and weak in the knees. He found himself in a room he knew too well and never wished to see again… the hospital next to his father's bed. "Dad? Dad! How'd I get here?"

"Hey, Sport. Glad you stopped in for a visit."

"But…you're…*not alive*. How'd I get here?"

"Looks like the prayer wheel brought you here, Son."

Tommy burst into a flood of tears. "I miss you, Dad."

"You've been carrying this heavy memory around with you. Let it go. Can you do that for me, Sport?"

Tommy nodded his head, 'Yes. "No! I miss you too much." He held his father's hand in his.

"I miss you too, Sport." The next thing he knew, he and his father were transported in a bright beam of light right to the Yankee baseball stadium in NY. By magic, a hotdog appeared in Tommy's hand and a black baseball mitt and ball in Dad's hands.

"Sport, this is a sweet memory good enough to carry around with you. Chose this one instead of the other one," Dad said.

"We had the best day here! " Tommy recalling the fun day they had before dad got sick.

"When you're sad, throw your worries into the outfield." Dad threw a ball far into the field. "You try." He handed him a ball to throw.

Tommy tossed it as far as he could.

"When you're sad, replace the memory with this happy one." He hugged Tommy tightly. "Get going, Sport. Mom needs your help at the shop and you have research and reading to do."

Tommy felt his head rocking and reeling. He had so much to ask Dad, but he gripped his stomach as his body sucked back through a rainbow tunnel of light spinning as wildly as a teacup ride at the State Fair. He found himself face down, nose to floor, his stomach doing flippity-flops and whirly-gigs. He lifted his head up, stood on shaky legs, and then puked into the metal garbage can near the computer. He perched on the stool just as Mom jettisoned down the staircase to check on him.

Tommy glanced at the counter. The prayer wheel was gone.

"You're as white as a ghost! That's it. We'll call for an emergency visit."

"Mom, how long were you upstairs?"

"Less than ten minutes, Tommy."

"Impossible. An inning takes more than ten minutes."

"Oh dear." She twisted her mouth to one side and looked concerned.

It was no use. How could he explain he'd been to the hospital and saw an inning of baseball with his dead father in matter of ten minutes? He went along with Mom without complaint to see Dr. Jones.

They arrived at the office and Dr. Jones took his temperature. She hit his knee with a little hammer, and shined a flashlight into his eyes and throat. She asked the easiest pop quiz questions ever. "Who'd be dumb enough not to know their name and the date?"

"A+," Dr. Jones winked and turned to Mom. "He's just fine, Mrs. Delo. No fever, throat looks good." She turned to Tommy. "Take it easy tonight. Looks like you had a bad case of the jitters. And you take it easy, too Mrs. Delo."

"Yeah… jitters," *Not.* "How can I fix them?"

"Peppermints can help to ease an upset tummy." Dr. Jones smiled and gave him a handful of wrapped candies. "Just in case you need them."

"Will they help with gas?"

"They will."

Tommy unwrapped one and shoved the handful of extra mints into his jeans." Thanks, Dr. Jones." Mom paid the lady at the desk and they left the building.

They drove back to the shop. "See? I'm good as new," Tommy insisted popping a mint in his mouth.

"I don't want to go to school. Nobody will even miss me. They'll be looking for a short fourth-grader with a bare-assed face."

"Language, Thomas James Delo."

Tommy wrinkled his nose. She always used his proper name when she was ticked-off. "You don't get it. Being a short kid with no chin stubble gets a kid beaten up in sixth grade. I'm a prime target for gorillas. You wouldn't want that on your conscience. Would you, Mom?" Tommy wheedled. "If Dad were here— *he'd* understand." He kicked his toe against an empty box and sent it flying. It wasn't fair to make her feel guilty, but he did it anyway.

"One fine morning you'll wake up with chin hairs and new friends. You'll see." Mom sighed, then grinned. "When I was your age, I had braids and freckles— a killer combo, for a hamburger girl poster."

Tommy giggled as his mood lifted with the mind image. "I get it, like the girl on the sign, right?"

"The very one," She kidded. "Speaking of..." She held up an old metal object with joined two halves that opened and closed. "Guess what this is."

"Torture device?" Tommy made his face wrinkle in mock fear.

"Yes, but only for torturing chopped meat." She opened the two sides and pointed to the middle. "It's an old meat press. The chopped meat goes here. You press the top down and *voila*, the burgers are all uniform in size. Grandma owned one of these."

"Gram couldn't make 'em right either, huh Mom? Dad's burgers were *always* a perfect size without torturing meat." Tommy looked down at his shoes, lost in thought, he pushed cemetery day out of his mind.

"Yes, I remember." She hung her head low and closed her eyes.

"Are you praying again?"

"Yes. It can't hurt."

Tommy gave her a quick hug. "It'll be alright, Mom. I'll take care of you."

"You don't have to. I'm the mother." She gave him a tight squeeze anyway.

After dinner, Tommy flipped through the required reading book. "Twenty chapters, 100 pages. Let me do the math... I'll be thirty-one and three quarters when I finish...too old to have a life." Tommy groaned and gripped his stomach with his hands and doubled over. "Mom, I think I'm getting a tummy ache. You're right, I should stay home from school...just in case I'm getting sick."

"Nonsense. Doc Jones says you're fine. Remember? You even told me you were as good as new. You have School-ite-is"

"Harv's mom had the same thing. She couldn't stop pooping for a week! Harv told me so."

"That's *colitis*. Dr. Jones says your well enough to attend school, so keep reading."

CHAPTER 9

Whizz-pop-bang!

The last time he saw the artifact, Tommy had placed it next to the sleeping bag in the Crow's Nest. "Not again." Tommy scowled in frustration. "Where are you?" He plunked down in his makeshift Galaxy sleeping bag with every intention to read a few more pages of *Time Wheel*, but all he could think about was where did the artifact go? Nestled between an overturned box, nightstand, sat his stuffed bear, Teddy. He sighed, then grabbed Teddy, turned out the lamp, His eyes, heavy as sacks of sand, closed.

Hummmmm, whizz-pop-bang!

The unexpected noise startled him awake and his eyes shot open. He tried to block out the sound by pulling covers over his head. He hugged Teddy tightly, regretting his insistence to sleep in the room so far from Mom's. He hunkered down until the buzzing ceased, then drifted back to sleep.

The insistent hum, *whizz-pop-bang* jarred him awake again.

Unable to ignore the din, he sat up, flipped on the lamp, grabbed a flashlight, beaming it into every dark corner of the room. "No ghosts or monsters here, Teddy."

Whizz-pop-bang-hummmmmm

"There it is again. I think it's downstairs. I have to go look, Teddy. You stay here." Once he found his courage, he shot up and cupped his hand to his ear, listening for the direction of the humming sound. He gripped his metal bat in his free hand and braved the journey to the lower levels. He followed the sound down the five steps through the kitchen on the second level. He tiptoed passed Mom's room. Satisfied she was safe, he edged further toward the locked door separating the shop level from their living quarters. "Oh great." He muttered. As quiet as a mouse, he turned the silver dead bolt until it clicked. He jiggled the doorknob into his hand and it creaked open He gritted his teeth. As the man of the house, he'd need to investigate.

Hummmm, whizzy-pop-bang-bang!

He stood at the top of the step and cupped his ear to listen, playing a question and answer game with no winner. *What's worse, facing a burglar or a ghost?* He set his bare feet on the top step starting a slow and careful descent to the shop level. His breath increased, his heart thumping as if he'd ran a mile. When he got to the second to last step, he shined the beam from the flashlight into the room. And then he saw it.

An eerie purple-green glow swirled in a misty dance in the center of the room, an Aurora Borealis of light performing a ballet. Then with a crackle and a pop, it snapped like a whip. The hum grew louder as if it noticed him watching. A sweet voice called out his name. His eyes opened wide with terror. He dropped the flashlight from his shaking hand and the room turned pitch black. He wanted to run, but his feet froze to the spot. He willed his legs to unfreeze. Terror shot up his spine. He flew back up the staircase, his feet pummeling the wooden steps. He slammed the shop door, dashed up to the Crow's Nest on rubber legs, and dove under the covers.

His mom peeked out of her room, but Tommy had already jetted to the third. "Tommy? What's that racquet? Are you ok?" He heard her call, but pretended to be asleep. He shuddered, wishing his buddy Harv was around for a sleepover instead of many states away. Tommy fought sleep for hours keeping watch until his lids succumbed to sleep.

He dreamed of a young girl near his age. She was a pretty Asian girl being instructed by a bald-headed monk who wore a scarlet robe. "Very good, Choden. If only Yeshe studied as much as you do."

As sun streamed in from the small attic window, Tommy felt his mother's insistent shake to wake him out of a pleasant dream.

"Tommy. Get up. Practice run."

With the coverlet tossed over his head, his muffled voice said, "I have two more stinkin' days of summer. I'm so tired." He dropped the covers down so he could peek at the alarm clock. "Mom, 6:30? Seriously? Wake me up at trillion o-clock." He plunged his head into his star covered pillow.

September wake-up time is now official." She turned the knobs on the clock. "The alarm will go off at 6 am tomorrow and we'll see how you do on your own."

"But Mom...two more days," he groaned in protest.

She lowered his Solar System coverlet to examine the dark circles underlining his eyes. "You look exhausted. Didn't you sleep well last night?"

"No. I heard whizzy-bang noises."

"It's just the old heater making a fuss. Did you get up last night? I thought I heard you, but you were in bed when I checked."

"I don't want to scare you... but I think we may have a ghost in the shop. I went down to look for it." He could tell from her face, that she doubted there was a ghost.

"You should've come to get me. I don't want you wandering at night. It's not safe. We need to keep the debolt locked."

"Now that you're wide awake, how many pages did you read in *Time Wheel* last night?"

Zero. "We weren't even *speaking* about homework. We were speaking about ghosts. Geez, Mom."

"We're speaking about it now —so how many pages did you read, kiddo?" Mom squinted her eyes.

Tommy couldn't wiggle out it it. "I'll read more tonight."

"Remember our talk about doing your best this year?" Thump, thump went her foot on the wood flooring. "Remember you promised me and the counselor?"

"Read, even if you hear whizzy-bangs. No excuses. Your sticky apple-juice-smutched agenda clearly states to complete chapter one by week's end." She shook her finger at him.

Nothing worse than her lectures, except when the counselor pried into his brain asking how he felt every second.

"Good habits start with good choices, Tommy. Come down and have your breakfast. Practice run starts now. Get dressed. I'm setting the stop watch."

"Really? The stopwatch?" Tommy moaned.

He listened for her footfalls as she headed to the second floor. "September Bossy Mom, at it again." He threw his clothes on and trudged down to the second floor.

He drank the milk and downed the grainy muffin. He set the empty glass on the kitchen card table. "Done." He burped loudly and rubbed the sleep from his eyes.

She hit the stopwatch. "Twenty-five minutes. Too slow. I want you dressed, and fed in under twenty tomorrow. Grab a clean cloth and help me get through this mess, Tommy."

"I'm tired and now you're making me *work*?" The sympathy whine worked when Dad was in the hospital. But not anymore.

"Get cracking.'" She tossed him a clean cloth. "Help me clean up the shop, then finish reading."

He banged down the small staircase wary of the ghost. But since it was morning, he figured it was safe since ghosts don't like daylight.

Mom turned her body in a wide arc. "We're making fine progress. Tommy, start on that green shelving unit over there, and I'll work on this blue one. Use the stepladder again if you need to get to those upper shelves clean. But be careful."

Whiz-pop-bang!

He ran to the main desk. "There's that sound again. Did you hear it *this* time?" Tommy gasped and his voice hushed.

"We don't have a ghost." She smirked to dismiss his worry.

"Never mind." She didn't believe him so there was no use trying to convince her.

Out of view, the cylinder whirred wildly somewhere in the room out of sight.

Tommy followed the sound to the same shelf where he first saw the sparks. He gawked as the colorful sparks rose up from the top shelf. He dropped his cleaning rag transfixed by the mesmerizing colors. He saw the glint of the prayer wheel drop on the top tier of the shelf and became hypnotized by the white-hot glow of shimmers dancing before his eyes. A lightning crack sounded like a whip as it arose and disappeared into a brilliant circle of light. His heart raced. It was the same sound he heard last night.

He dragged a ladder over to the high shelf and felt around for the prayer wheel. It was gone.

CHAPTER 10

Bell's Treasure Trove

Tommy had almost forgotten about the purple lights and hide and seek prayer wheel, when he spied a large box marked *Comics*. He knelt down and rummaged through the stack of plastic covered treasures he was eager to explore.

Mom came down with a pad and pen in hand. "I see you found the comics."

A smile brightened his face and lit up his eyes. "This Hulk comic is ancient!" Energized by his find, Tommy just about dove head first into the pile, pulling out copies. "And this one is Superman from 1974!"

"Vintage copies aren't ancient, but they'll fetch a good price once we value them. Be careful with them, Punkin. I'm sure we can get $100 each if they're in mint condition," Mom tapped on her cell. "Tommy, the Hulk is listed for $110.00, and Superman is listed for $115.00!"

"Are you going to buy some mints for the customers?"

"Mints? Why do you ask?" She cocked her head in confusion.

"You're the one talking about *mint* conditions."

She smiled at him and shook and smirked. "*Mint* condition means it's untouched or in the original packaging, like in those comics in the plastic wrappers."

"Oh right." Tommy hated missing stuff other kids understood easily, like sarcasm and words with too many definitions. Last year, Fred said, "Nice tee shirt."

Tommy said, "Thanks!" But didn't realize Fred was making fun of his Zoo-bedo cartooned tee shirt. He never felt so dumb as when Fred laughed at him.

In reading class, he learned 'based on' isn't the same word as *basting* a Thanksgiving turkey. Vocabulary words were a confusing jumble. In a few days, he'd be basting in gallons of new words he'd most likely confuse. Worse yet, Mom didn't even care about his pretend stomachache, or the whizzy bang sounds. Mints wouldn't make school or his gassy stomach go away no matter what condition he was in.

He looked up at Mom. "Can I open just one comic book? There're bunches of mints in this box— Superman, Spidey, Batman and Flash. Tommy's nose wrinkled. "Just one?"

"An open copy is worth far less." She waved her hand.

"How can I *read* one if it's sealed in plastic?" Tommy wheedled.

"Collectors buy them and don't read them."

"That's the dumbest thing I ever heard. Why buy something and never open it?" He clasped his hands. "Pretty please with sugar on top?"

"Sure, what the heck. I'm thrilled you want to read— even if it's speech bubbles."

He pulled the plastic sleeve back. Happiness lifted him and his mood lifted like a hot air balloon.

"Just like before, three boxes —sell, donate, and trash. We're almost at the end of these boxes. If you aren't sure, ask."

"I think the boxes should say 'Trash' or 'Treasure'. Hey, that would be a great name for our shop! What do you think?"

"Hmmm. Keep thinking. No one wants to spend good money to buy trash."

"No one wants to buy fleas, but people still go to flea markets," Tommy burst out.

"And people go to white elephant sales, but they don't buy elephants."

"Good one, Mom." Tommy imagined a wrinkly blue-haired old lady walking an elephant on a leash. Just then, he had a funny feeling rise up his spine and tickle the back of his neck. He whipped around. There on the main counter the prayer wheel spun in a slow circle, as if he tapped it with his finger. Tommy shook his head in disbelief.

"Mom, why did you move the prayer wheel down here? You said you wouldn't sell it."

"And I won't sell it. You have to be more aware. A place for everything and everything in the right place."

"Ugh. The right place is everyplace," Tommy muttered.

CHAPTER 11

Last day of Freedom

Tommy heard the 6 am alarm ring. "One more day of freedom." He groaned and slammed the snooze button with his fist. He lifted his shirt to inspect his armpits with a sniff and made a face. "PU. What do you know?" He noticed one tiny black underarm hair sprouting. "It's not a chin hair, but it's a start." He dragged himself from his sleeping bag, clothes in hand, ran to the second floor to splash water on his face and armpits. He stomped down to the second floor.

Mom hit the stop watch. "Much better. Did you wash your face and underarms?"

Water counted, so he said, "Yes."

"Deodorant?"

"No, but I'll put it on tomorrow. Can I use the internet? I'll help you look up prices."

"Yes, if you'll remember to stay on safe sites. That miscreant, Petey was a bad influence on you."

Tommy recognized Mom's ticked-off face, second only to September-Bossy-Mom face. *Did miscreant mean finding naughty pictures? Probably.* "Geez. I told you, it wasn't even my fault. Petey tricked me. In Petey's defense, he had weird man stuff happening to his junk, hairy armpits, and smelled like a wet dog after gym class. He couldn't help himself."

"Likely true, but that's no excuse. If your dad was here, he'd…." She stopped as tears flooded her eyes.

"Are you ok, Mom?"

"Allergies," she fibbed.

"It's a great excuse, Mom. Petey isn't a bad kid, just curious about lady stuff. Besides he probably lives on pirate ship and is growing a full beard in by now." Tommy re-checked his bare chin with his idle hand.

She pulled herself together and wiped her eyes.

"I know it's hard with your dad gone, so if you have any questions— about junk and otherwise ask me," Mom replied. "Not the Internet...or Petey."

"Yuck, Mom." Tommy twisted his face and held his hands over his ears.

"Seriously, I'm sure you'll have lots of questions about puberty very soon."

Tommy wished Dad was alive. He'd have so much to ask him. But how would Mom know any of those things? She was always married to Dad.

That night Tommy's eyes stayed wide open. Tomorrow would be the first real day of school, a reality scarier than a ghost, whizzy-bangs, or a horror movie. After last night, he regretted convincing Mom to allow him to sleep in the Crow's nest alone. He'd never admit it and have her think he was a baby. He was the man of the house now. No use telling Mom he was scared of a purple ghost or whizzy bang noises. His stomach made twirly-loop-de-loops as if he was riding on a roller coaster. His gut complained, aching for his attention.

Before sleep, he scanned the room corners with a flashlight and said a prayer ending with "I miss you, Dad." He set the flashlight and metal bat next to the sleeping bag, and then dove into it. "Teddy, you keep watch over me. I'm too big to sleep with you."

First, he dreamed he was an explorer in an ancient land with a tall building topped with gold turrets. He saw an oversized, carved, red, shiny door. Outside the temple, rows and rows of brass canisters secured to a long wooden frame spun and whirred with an unmistakable sound— the very one he heard in the store. One cylinder stopped turning just long enough for him to see the strange writing on its barrel. Men dressed in long scarlet robes wore spiral tipped hats on their heads. The word 'prayer wheel' whispered into his ears. Then he heard singing, and the word, *Choden*, which floated as soft as a feather into his mind. He had no idea what the word meant, but somehow, he knew it was a clue.

His dream continued; he saw his father. Dad stood with a huge smile plastered across his face. He watched Dad twirl the row of prayer wheels watching them spin in unison. Tommy's dream-self ran to him, wrapping arms around his waist. "Dad, you're better!"

His dream outburst jarred him wide-awake. He shot up in bed wild-eyed breathing as if he ran a mile.

Frustrated, that he interrupted his father's dream visit, he punched his stuffed bear clear across the room and screamed, "Why did you leave me!" He pummeled his pillow with all his might until white feathers popped out like snowflakes.

He retrieved Teddy and sobbed into his fur. "I miss you, Dad." He rubbed hot tears from his eyes. Teddy bears were for little kids, but it didn't matter. Tonight, he'd cry like a kindergarten baby and wouldn't even care.

Mom barreled up the steps from the second floor. "Honey, are you alright? I see you have Teddy." She hugged him.

Her touch made him sob even more. "I had a stupid dream." He pouted.

"Do you want to come downstairs and sleep in the other bed near mine?"

"Yes, but only because I don't want the whizzy-bang noises to scare you." Tommy grabbed his pillow, flashlight, and bear. He followed her down the narrow attic staircase and headed to the second floor where his regular bed was set up.

"I appreciate that." She tousled his hair.

He tried to get into bed and sleep, but he didn't want to be alone so he walked to her room and tapped on the door. "Maybe I can even stay in your room, just for a while until I fall asleep."

"Sure."

He entered her room and did a customary ghost and under-the-bed-alligator and closet monster check. "You're safe, Mom."

"I feel better now. Sleep tight, don't let the bedbugs bite." She planted a kiss on his forehead. "I'll see you at 6:30 am."

Restless, he dropped back into a new dream where he walked through a vivid purple ring of light. Mom's alarm rang out and Tommy woke. His stomach rumbled like a volcano. Today was the first day of school.

CHAPTER 12

Cool Kid Jake Stanton

School Begins September 5 Tuesday

7:00 am

Mom hit the stopwatch. "You did it." She smiled as if he won a race.

"I even washed my monkey sweat and used the piney deodorant." He grabbed two peppermint candies and stuffed them in his pocket. "I want to be in mint condition today." He shoved a few more mints into the front pocket of his backpack.

He recited each item, a trick that helped him get out the door last year. "Schedule, pen, mechanical pencil, notepad, notebook, pocket tissues, peppermints, and combination lock." The jitters were making his stomach rumble and ache. He popped a mint into his mouth. He ran up to the third floor, grabbed his Galaxy Wars backpack and tossed the copy of *Time Wheel* into his bag. The prayer wheel sat by his sleeping bag. Even though it made no sense to talk to a piece of metal, he said, "I can't bring you with me. Wish me luck." He imagined the prayer wheel answered him and said, "I'll see you later."

He barreled down the stairs.

"Mom, I think I have gas, but I'll know in a second."

He let one rip.

"Try not to do that at school." She waved her hand back and forth.

"Sorry. I didn't want to hold it in and explode myself." He smirked.

"I hope that's the last of your air biscuits for the day."

"Me too."

"This was Dad's lunch bag. He'd want you to have it." She handed him a black lunch bag embroidered with T.D., his dad's initials on it.

Tommy hugged the bag in his arms and his eyes teared up. "Thanks, Mom."

She spit on her hand and pushed a stray lock of hair away from his eye.

"Mom-spit is not hair gel." Tommy twisted his face.

She ignored his insult and kissed his cheek. "You look so handsome. Are you ready?"

"You mean for the gallows? Sure." Tommy fake gagged and wiggled his tongue.

"Let's get a move-on." She tapped her watch.

"Bossy-Mom's favorite time of year." Tommy mumbled.

"Bossy-Mom's chariot awaits you, Sir."

Tommy wore his saddest expression as they walked through the store level to the outside parking lot. He slowed his feet. "I'm walking the plank and you don't even care." He pretended one hundred-pound weights shackled his ankles as he trudged to their car.

"Keep walking, Matey."

She unlocked her small red car with a click of the key fob.

Tommy climbed in and pulled the blue hoodie down over his eyes pretending to be a masked avenger. He peeked out under the hood as they approached the school.

He passed a gas bubble and smirked. "Jitters…"

She rolled down the window.

"Pull your hoodie down. It's messing up your hair."

Reluctant, Tommy dropped his hoodie and glared at the ominous entryway looming dead ahead.

A new block lettered sign hung above the portico. "Welcome to Hope School! Hope begins here." He read it aloud. As the car entered the circular driveway, Tommy mumbled, "It should say Tommy's *Hopeless year begins here.*"

"You are so dramatic. Turn that frown upside down and have a good day."

Tommy flipped the car lock up and down to delay his exit. He batted his big brown eyes at her.

"Last chance Mom."

"Love you. Be cheery!"

"I should've eaten *Cheer*-oats instead of sad oats." He shot a forlorn look her way. "K, I'm going to the gallows. Last chance to save me." He snail-paced to the front of the building as if he walked an imaginary plank to certain doom. He glanced back to her to see if she'd feel guilty about leaving him.

She blew him a kiss, which he didn't return. Too many judging eyes would see him. Instead, he pulled his ear, their secret sign for "I love you."

The crossing guard waved his mother on with frantic gestures and whistle blowing.

The car edged away. He was all alone.

The glass portico swallowed Tommy up whole, like being in the belly of a whale, or a minnow in an ocean of sharks. The throng of children moved behind him like a wave. He struggled to get a last gulp a breath of fresh air before drowning in a sea of students he didn't know.

Tommy mulled around the foyer which burst with children. Hope housed grades Kindergarten through eighth grade. He recited his own version of school prayers. "Let there be no homework today. Amen." He was a pirate in *Davy Jones'* locker suffering a watery death. Lost in a world of thought where he was invisible and safe, he recognized a tall boy with the TV commercial smile and jet-black hair he'd seen at orientation. Surely, he was older than Tommy.

The boy waved in Tommy's direction, his white teeth gleaming with confidence. Tommy glanced behind him assuming the tall boy was greeting an old friend.

The lanky boy swept the air with his hand and strode over to him. "Hey, New Kid." He held out a hand.

"Me?" Tommy pointed to his chest in surprise.

Jake jutted his hand out, a friendly expression glued to his face. "Yes, you. Shake, Dude. I was about to officially introduce myself at Orientation when Mrs. Lars interrupted my spectacular intro. My name's Jake Stanton. Spill—what's your moniker?"

Tommy squeezed his hand hard, just like Dad told him to do when you meet someone new. "Oh. I'm Tommy Delo." He cracked a lopsided smile and focused on Jake's chin where a few dark hairs peeked out. Absentmindedly, he touched his own chin. Tommy sized Jake up and down. "You're awful tall. What grade are you in?"

"Sixth. My dad is giraffe-tall." He lifted his hand above his head. " I take after him."

"My dad's hamster short." Tommy lowered his hand to his knees just to be funny. "I take after him." No use spilling his guts to admit Dad was gone.

Jake laughed. "You're a funny dude. I have a special greeting for would-be friends." Jake extended his hand then did a special finger wiggle. "Shazam! I bet you feel like a fish out of water. Am I right?" He clipped his thumb in his belt loop and shifted on his right leg. He brushed a lock of pitch-black hair from his face.

"How'd you know?"

"Deer in the headlight face—dead giveaway, Dude. All new kids have it." Jake arm punched him.

"You're right. I'm drowning in a sea of new faces." Tommy noticed a pack of giggling girls ogling Jake and whispering. Cool Kid offered them a head nod and nothing more. Tommy's gut was performing first day headstands. He mopped an unruly cowlick of brown hair from his eye that mom-spit didn't fix. *Was cool kid being nice just to stuff me in a locker?* He wasn't sure, but the name Jake sounded familiar, but he didn't know why.

"I miss my old school, even though I didn't like it much. Lame, huh?" Tommy hoped Cool Kid Jake wouldn't agree.

"Not lame. I get it. Leaving close buds behind I'll bet," Jake stated.

"Yeah, like Harv," Tommy answered, "I'm gonna call 'em later even though he's in California. I have a friend, Petey, too—but my mom calls him a Perv."

"News flash—all guys are pervs in sixth grade. My dad says it's our horny-moans. Get it?" Jake winked.

No. "Oh yeah, sure, I get it." Tommy winked back as if he understood the joke, which he didn't. Tommy wondered why Jake sounded older than his years. He didn't sound like kids he knew from Erie, PA.

"You'll like it here soon enough. I'll show you the ropes. Lucky for you batty Mr. Brown retired last year. I hope you're in advanced math with me. You'll love Mr. Taylor. He's the shit."

Tommy couldn't believe his ears. Cool Kid Jake cursed and didn't even apologize.

"Mr. Brown was a dead ringer for Mr. Bean. Dad and I rent Bean movies and superhero movies for our guy's night." A peal of laughter left his mouth.

"Guy's night? Sounds fun." Tommy's mood dropped like a rock and rolled into a ditch. *Ker plonk*, when a twist of jealousy knotted his gut. Glum, he stared down at his sneakers.

"You ok?" Jake studied him with a curious gleam in his eye, like a puzzle he had to solve.

Tommy nodded. "Yeah. Just had a thought."

"Good times, Bro. We watch flicks 'till late and eat junk food on Friday nights if my dad doesn't have a date. Maybe you can join us sometime?"

Tommy wrinkled his nose. "Your mom doesn't mind if your dad dates other women?"

"Dude, I don't have a mom. Haven't seen her in years."

Tommy watched a dark cloud drift over Jake's happy-go-lucky face. He wanted to ask him where his mom was but it wasn't any of his business. "Oh, sorry."

"Just me and Dad, two hapless bachelors." Jake dropped his news like a boulder in a lake.

Tommy could tell Cool Kid's mood changed from lighthearted to sad.

"No prob-lem-o. What about you, new kid?"

"I have a dad, but not an *alive* dad," Tommy's voice was barely audible. "You can call me Tommy."

"Sorry, Dude. That's rough. Foot in mouth—changing subjects." He tossed a hand on Tommy's shoulder. "Miss Bell was our smoking hot student teacher last year. The Bean, couldn't stop staring at her and I say props to him. We all did our share of gawking, too. Lucky for us, Miss Bell was hired for grade 6 this year. Fingers crossed we're in her homeroom and maybe one of her classes. Let me have a look-see at your skedge, Lil Dude." He tapped Tommy playfully on his back.

"Skedge?"

"Schedule," Jake clarified. "Remind me to teach you the Hope lingo."

Tommy shifted up on his toes to appear taller. Little Dude was a friendlier nickname than Shrimp, or Shorty. He unrumpled a paper from his nervous sweaty palms and handed it to Jake. A new friend? He hoped so.

"We're in homeroom and first period for history/ social studies. Stellar luck for both of us. Lil Dude, you're in advanced math with me, too. Mr. Taylor's class."

"Advanced math?" Tommy's heart thumped double time. There'd been a huge mistake. He was sure didn't belong in anything advanced.

"Says right here," Jake pointed to the schedule. "Miss Bell's name isn't on the skedge, but here's hoping." Jake crossed his fingers and kissed them. "I'll introduce you to my buddy, Jeff or as I call him, the Human Torch."

"Cool. Why do you call him that?" Tommy tailed after Jake, reshuffled his loaded Galaxy Wars book bag from one shoulder to the other.

"You'll see." Jake laughed.

"Helloooo, Jakey," Jennifer's long black hair bounced around her shoulders. She smiled and batted her dark lashes. Her overly short cheerleading skirt revealed shapely legs in dazzling white sneakers. "Adopted a stray puppy, Jakey?" She jut out her hip.

"Did it pee on your shoe yet?" She looked at Tommy with a snooty glare.

Tommy growled at Jenny like an angry dog. Bad choice. Why did he act so dumb? He should have just thought of a smart comeback instead.

"Hilarious, Jenny...not. New kid's name is Tommy. Give him a break from your evil ways, Woman." Jake turned his inky black eyes to Beth and softened his voice. "Hey Beth."

Timid, Beth's cheeks blushed cherry red. "Hey, Jake."

Tommy studied Beth's pretty freckled face and realized Jake possessed some sort of magical powers over girls. If he did believe in magic, he'd believe Jake cast a spell on them.

"Would your pet like a dog biscuit?" Jenny mimicked using a little girl voice. She whipped around to see Lana paced down the hallway. She called out, "Lana, did you meet Jake's new puppy?"

Tommy caught a whiff of strawberries and vanilla cookies as Jenny skirted by him.

Lana walked over. "You got a puppy, Jake?" Lana's voice lilted like music. "I'd love to see it!"

Jake interrupted. "Ignore Jenny. She's insulting Tommy, the new kid."

Jenny snickered and pointed to Tommy. "He's a stray who wandered into our school hungry for a biscuit. Am I right, Beth?" She elbowed Beth to agree.

Beth didn't play along.

Lana made a disgusted face in Jenny's direction. "I'm Lana. Nice to meet you, Tommy."

"I'm Tommy Delo." He shook her hand and smiled.

"Don't let Jenny bother you. Some of us are nice people."

Beth nodded as blotchy spots eked up her neck like giraffe spots. "My name is Beth, Tommy. You can call me Lizzy if you'd like." She whispered, "Sorry about my friend."

"Whatever. Let's go, Lizzy-Beth, before we get rabies." Jenny's nose flared. She grabbed her baby pink lip-gloss out of her pink backpack pocket to re-shine her lips. She puckered and blew a kiss at Jake. "See you later, Jakey-poo."

Beth shrugged and gave a timid wave to both of them.

Beth seemed shy and kind. Why was she friends with the mean cheerleader girl? Beth was pretty, but in a simple sort of way. Her metal framed glasses made her look smart. "What's with her?"

"Jenny's a mean snake," Jake whispered to Tommy. "Don't let her fool you; inside that pretty face lurks an evil troll. I'm sorry I ever made out with her."

"You mean you kissed her?" Tommy swooned, in disbelief. "For real?"

"Yeah. No big deal-e-o. It was last summer. Now she thinks I like-like her. I don't-don't." Jake rolled his eyes. "But I still can't smell strawberries without—well you know…"

"Have you kissed other girls, too?"

"Just one, Sally Andrews. Make that two if I count Dina's cousin, Lu. She moved out of state last year. I plan to kiss a few others before I turn 13, just for practice."

"I'll be old and gray before I get my first kiss," Tommy quipped.

"Girls like funny dudes. Besides, hamsters are cuddly-wuddly. Don't sell yourself short. Get it?" He fist bumped Tommy's shoulder.

"I get it." Tommy gave him a lop-sided smile.

"Beth follows the lipstick demon everywhere, her personal pet poodle. I suspect she keeps Beth around to do her homework. Jeff told me Beth did all of it last year."

"How does Jeff know?"

"Jeff is Jenny's cousin. She comes to school for cheer, jeer, and leer, but not much else."

The morning bell blared.

"Here goes nothing. Stick by me."

"Like gum on a sneaker." Tommy followed behind Jake to room 10. A giant smile stole Tommy's face when he saw Miss Bell for the first time. Her shiny black hair tied in an emerald ribbon just like Snow White. Her skin, like vanilla ice cream, and her lips, the color of summer cherries. She looked like a Disneyland princess.

"The planets have aligned in our favor."

"Maybe sixth grade won't be so bad." Tommy blushed fifty shades of red.

"I'll say. Maybe I'll plan to fail sixth grade this year," Jake kidded.

"You're in luck! Failure is my specialty."

"See? You're a funny dude. Come on, Tommy. Let's go in."

CHAPTER 13

Grade 6 Day one

September 5
Tuesday First Day of Grade 6
First Bell: Homeroom

On the way in, Tommy noticed only the lower grade kids dared to carry backpacks with Superheroes cartoons on them. He should have known better. Embarrassed, he removed his Galaxy Wars backpack and crossed his arms over the cartoon on the front pocket. Tomorrow he'd be sure to unload the backpack into the locker before anyone saw. He didn't have a locker assignment yet, so he carried his backpack covering it with his sweatshirt. He'd attempt to convince Mom to buy him a plain black one, just like Jake's. She'd say it was perfectly good condition and he didn't need one. She'd be right... but also wrong.

A large banner hung above the doorway in room 10 had the words, *'One giant step for Mankind.* It showed a photo of the Apollo 11 moon landing with Neil Armstrong taking his first step on its surface. Tommy's perpetual grin lit up as he stood in the threshold of room 10 pretending to be an astronaut. He felt like an alien on a foreign planet in his new school.

He couldn't believe his luck. Miss Bell was as gorgeous as Jake said she'd be. His heart skipped beats and went pitter-patter. He hoisted his heavy Galaxy Wars backpack higher on his shoulder and shifted up on tippy toes.

Miss Bell beamed brightly at each incoming student. "Don't be shy. Take one giant step into room 10, boys and girls. Clear the doorway and enter with a stellar smile."

Here goes nothing. Tommy clipped his thumb into the belt loop of his jeans to mimic Jake's stance. His stomach did acrobatic flip-flops and he held in a gas bubble waiting to shoot out and ruin his morning.

He stepped on the shiny lunar surface of room 10. There was no turning back. His dad always had said a smile goes a mile, so he plastered on a mile-wide smile and hoped it was stellar.

Jake grinned a set of dazzling teeth and tossed his hand forward for a vigorous shake. "The eagle has landed. Miss Bell. Welcome back!"

"Hi Jake. Welcome to room 10," Miss Bell answered. "By your quote, I can tell you know your history."

"Or the Buzz...Aldrin, that is..." Jake laughed at his pun.

Miss Bell's eyes gleamed. "I see you've made a new friend with Tommy."

"I have, Miss Bell." Jake shifted on his leg smiling a perfect row of white teeth. "I'm sure glad you're back this year."

She extended her rose-petal hand toward Tommy. He paused to wipe his clammy digits before shaking her soft-as-butter hand. "Pleased to meet you, Tommy Delo." Her face sparkled with fairy dust and her delicate movements were like a graceful butterfly. "You know my whole name, Miss Bell?"

"I sure do!" Her mouth lifted like a melon slice catching his eyes with hers. "Being new is not always easy, but hope starts here, Tommy."

"I know. I read it on the sign." It was a stupid thing to say, but he couldn't think of a clever remark. Miss Bell smelled like gingerbread and spice cookies. The scent reminding him of Christmas wafted around her making his head spin in circles. Tommy was airborne floating onto a cloud of happiness. He must have had a stupid grin on his face, since Jake poked his side and said, "She has that effect on all of us, Lil Dude." Even though Tommy hadn't asked him a thing out loud.

Other teachers always had strict seating charts. Tommy didn't want to break any rules on the first day, so he checked the whiteboard for clues. All he saw were the words, 'Welcome to School! My name is Miss Bell,' in fancy cursive writing with a heart over the lower-case letter i. His feet glued to the ground as he viewed the neatly lined up chairs with the desk part attached to the seat in one piece. His last school had real desks, not one-piece torture chambers. He bit his lower lip and tried to get Jake's attention.

Jake was chatting with everyone. He didn't notice Tommy's distress.

Tommy was relieved when Jake turned to him. "Come on. Let's claim our territory. Head for row three... two end seats. Best vantage point. Not too close yet not too far."

Tommy sighed, "Got it." He wriggled into the vacant righty's chair, but Tommy was a leftie. Once he sat, the attached desktop captured him, like a prisoner in its grip. He didn't want to ask Miss Bell for another desk, so he sat wondering what to do.

"Find your seats quickly. I have to take lunch count and attendance before you head to your respective classes for the first session which begins at 8:40. You'll get locker assignments. After announcements, head out, find your locker, and secure it with your lock. Drop off all belonging except for your school supplies and return here before the bell. History section will begin. Some of you are assigned here, so I'll see you soon."

The group headed out to claim lockers.

Jake's locker was a few down from his. Tommy took out a notepad and pen, then closed his locker. They headed back into room 10.

Tommy glanced up at the digital numbers 8:20 am—clock watching was a hard habit to break. Last year, time bored into his head like an inchworm on a football field, second by second. No use rechecking the clock but he couldn't draw his eyes away from the changing numbers on the digital display.

Jeff sat down to the left of Tommy and greeted him with a nod. He gave a special finger wiggle greeting to Jake, showing they had a close bond. Tommy studied the tall thin boy with the shock of copper hair. "Jeff Dent, Human Torch, this is a new kid, Tommy Delo, or I like to call him, Lil Dude. Tommy, this is my best bud, Jeff."

"Pleased." Jeff lurched forward and pumped Tommy's hand as if he was campaigning for votes.

Tommy noticed Jeff's friendlier greeting once Jake introduced them. This kid was evil Jenny's cousin. They seemed so different. He tried to wear a stellar smile, like Miss Bell said. "I get your nickname, now."

"I thought you would." Jeff smirked. "It's better than the last nickname Joe gave me."

But he didn't say what the last one was. Tommy figured Jeff was too embarrassed to repeat it.

Tommy made a wish Joe and Jenny wouldn't return. His stomach churned, an ocean storm of

Time Wheel Book 1

movement. He held tight to a thundering air biscuit ready to rumble. Then he remembered the mints in his backpack. He forgot to put some in his pants pocket. He raised his hand. "May I use the lavatory?"

"Certainly. Take the hall pass, Tommy. Hurry back."

Tommy got up and grabbed the wooden room 10 pass and headed toward his locker. When he opened it, he couldn't believe his eyes. There sat the prayer wheel, as innocently as if he brought it to school with him...only he didn't. He glanced around to be sure no one would hear him. "Why are you here? I told you to stay put."

The prayer wheel lit up, turned, and disappeared in a crack of light right through the back of his locker. Tommy whipped around to be sure no one saw what happened. His heart pounded a mile a minute. He grabbed a mint and shoved it in his mouth. Since no one was around, he let an air biscuit rip, and headed back to class. Did he just imagine what he saw? He'd check his locker again after class.

When he returned to class, Jake and Jeff were knee deep in first day conversation leaving Tommy to float into a daydream.

Once again, odd man out. Tommy was adrift in a sea of new faces. He ran down the list of new people. *Tommy, lost at sea ready to walk the plank of the pirate ship at any minute. Jeff? Safe. Jenny? Mean. Joe? Scary. Were his old friends, Harv and Petey lost at sea just like him? Or did they manage to stay afloat in their new schools?*

Tommy watched Jeff toss a wide smile in Lana's direction, the girl who liked dogs. Tommy guessed Lana was a friendly girl since she didn't tease him. She was dressed plain without hair ribbons or make-up.

He watched as Jeff dove into his cargo pant pockets unleashing a fury of activity. He unearthed mechanical pencils, eyeglass case, and an assortment of pens and mechanical pencils in a matter of minutes. Jeff snapped his eyeglass case open with a click and set the wire frames on his nose.

Tommy decided glasses made everyone look smarter. He'd have to convince his mom he needed a pair. Students filled in the seats in front of him. Tommy tried to stand up to wiggle his legs. The desk top smacked his thighs. In a foolish awkward moment, he sat back down, prisoner of the 'righties' desk's steel embrace. A tall girl in a gray sweat suit sat right in front of him, stealing the view to the front of the room. He grunted in frustration.

Jake turned to him. "Dude, what's going on?"

"I need a different desk, Jake. I'm a fun-sized leftie." He wiggled his left hand. "Do you mind switching seats with me? I can't see over the tall girl's head." Tommy pointed ahead of him. The tall girl turned around and looked right at him with a reddened face showing she overheard him.

"Sorry!" She said. The girl got up and moved one seat over so she wouldn't be directly in front of Tommy.

"Oh, thanks." Tommy didn't mean to make her feel bad. It was almost a compliment He wished he was just as tall, and not a fun-sized short kid.

"My desk is a rightie too. I'll be back in a jiff." Jake walked to the back of the classroom and returned and set down a leftie desk. "This should work. Slide before you try to get up."

Tommy slid out of this desk seat and stood up with a grateful sigh he said, "Geez, thanks, Jake." He sat in the leftie desk. "Much better."

Jake pushed the other seat-desk to another row.

The first wave of homeroom students had already flooded into room 10 wearing the dazed first-day expression.

Tommy wondered why some kids were popular and some weren't. Maybe the smart kids were popular and dumb kids were always butt of jokes. Or maybe it just seemed that way, since he was the one teased. This year, he was determined to change his fate. He'd pretend to be smart, just like Cool Kid Jake and maybe he'd fool everyone. He'd study the smart kids and copy what they did.

Beth shifted her wire-framed glasses on her pert nose. She set her notebook on a desk top in the second row and her purse on an empty chair next to her. A quiet dark-haired girl approached her.

"Hi Dina," Beth said.

"Hey Lizzy Beth," Dina greeted and pointed to the seat next to Beth. "Is this seat taken?"

"Yes. It's saved for Jenny. She's *always* late. Sorry, Dina."

"Oh, alright." Dina frowned and set her notebook on the desk top one spot over and sat down. She turned abound to greet Jake. "Hi Jake. Hey, New Kid."

Tommy studied the way Dina's finger toyed with a lock of her curly brown hair.

Jake grinned and nodded. "Hey Dina. This is Tommy."

Tommy's voice squeaked. "Tommy Delo." His face blushed and he got lost in her dark almond eyes.

Dina's dark-lashed eyes glinted. A little dimple formed in her cheek. "Hey, Tommy Delo. Welcome to Hope School."

Tommy liked the way her nose crinkled when she smiled. He watched King Kong enter the room. The wide-bodied boy lumbered wearing a number 25 football hoodie cloaking his head and face. To his right, Jenny bounced in sporting a red and white cheer outfit with florescent white sneakers that almost shined.

Jenny waved to Beth and took the saved seat. "Thanks, B.F.F. Could you save me a seat in the next class, too? I plan to be late to every class. I just hope we don't have assigned seating. That would mess up *everything*."

If she wasn't so mean, Tommy might have admitted he thought Jenny was pretty.

Miss Bell nodded her head to acknowledge the late comers.

Beth pushed her glasses on her nose and asked, "Will we have assigned seats, Miss Bell?"

Joe bellowed, "Give it a rest, goodie two shoes. There's no A+ for sitting your butt in a chair."

Beth hung her head low, too afraid to respond to Joe's taunt.

Miss Bell smiled at Beth with kind eyes. "I don't believe in seating charts, Beth. If you like the seat you have already chosen, you can stay there."

Tommy wondered why she didn't discipline Joe for saying the word "butt".

Joe grunted. He passed Tommy's desk and muttered, "I saw your stupid backpack this morning. Did you buy it off a five-year-old?"

Tommy was smart enough not to poke a stick at a rattle-snake, so he continued to study the interactions of the other students.

Joe headed for the last row and slammed his backpack with a purposeful thud. "I believe I'll sit here."

Miss Bell strode toward Joe. Tommy's eyes followed her.

"After class, you'll need to put your backpack in your locker. You should have done it already, but you smell of smoke. You're at locker 28. Miss Bell's voice was barely audible when she said, "You know the rules, Joe. Hoods down, hats off." But Tommy heard her.

Joe turned pushed his hoodie down and moved a hand to cover a bruised cheek.

Tommy strained his voice to hear her.

"Accident?" Miss Bell raised a concerned brow to Joe.

"Yeah, I got hit with a football," Joe said. "And dad's flying fist." He mumbled. Tommy almost didn't hear him.

"Sorry to hear it, Joe." Miss Bell said.

"Sorry it happened," he answered.

"Did you have a good summer?" Miss Bell asked. She lifted the corners of her mouth into a pleasant smile.

"Sure," Joe said dismissively.

"Good morning, Jenny. I see you're on cheer squad with Sally this year."

"Good guess." Jenny wore a plastic smile.

Tommy caught Jenny when she rolled her eyes the minute Miss Bell turned away from her. Sally giggled.

Miss Bell jotted a note on a book on her desk. Was it about Joe or Jenny? He hoped it wasn't about him.

Tommy studied his classmates for clues about their personalities. Joe was a big nasty iceberg with treachery right under the water waiting to sink him. Beth saved Jenny a seat even though Jenny ignored her. Dina was pretty. Jeff was serious and studious with tons of school supplies. Would the Human Torch be friends with him, too? He hoped so.

Miss Bell's patent leather heels clicked-clacked on the floor tiles as she glided like a Disney princess across the room. Her shiny black hair neatly secured with a green silk ribbon.

"I trust you found your locker assignments. Greetings students of room 10. Wonderful to see you all again." Miss Bell grinned like a Cheshire cat. She arched her brows and surveyed the twenty youngsters in her charge. "Some of you I know from last year and many of you I haven't officially met." She tossed a manicured hand onto her black pencil skirt and sashayed to the third row. Tommy's heart leaped when she neared him, her sweet scent of gingerbread and vanilla teased his nose as she approached. She stopped in front of him. Miss Bell's mouth curved like a bow. "I've been waiting to introduce you to the other students, Tommy. Since we're both new at Hope School, we can help each other acclimate."

Tommy blushed red. "Sure," he said.

When she turned, Jake said, "Dude, your face is blooming like a rose."

Tommy's red-hot cheeks were a dead give-away to his embarrassment. He drew his hands up to his warm, red cheeks. His crush on Miss Bell must have showed all over his face.

Tommy turned around and followed Miss Bell as she floated across the room on graceful legs.

"And Beth, I see you have new eyeglasses. They're so becoming on you," Miss Bell said.

Beth said, "Thank you, Miss Bell." She shifted her eyeglasses back on the bridge of her nose.

Jenny muttered, "Glad *I* don't need glasses. They're for ugly girls. Oh, no offense, Beth."

Tommy wondered if Beth was offended by Jenny's insult. Jake was right. Jenny was mean on-purpose, even to her friend.

Tommy drifted back into his world of daydreams as Miss Bell made her rounds to speak to each student. He pretended to be Captain Hook navigating a pirate ship through rocky waters of grade six. Joe, the alligator, a ticking time bomb, ready to explode at any moment. Jenny, a craggy rock, waiting to rip everyone apart with her sharp-edged words. Lizzy Beth, a quiet island. Dina, a nice lighthouse. Miss Bell, a beautiful mermaid who just might save him from drowning in Davy Jones Locker. Like a boat adrift, Tommy would need to anchor himself to a best buddy. Was Jake his safe harbor? *What would Captain Hook do? He'd be fearless. What would Tommy do? Hold on tight and tread water for dear life.*

Jake tapped Tommy on the arm. "Miss Bell is the bomb, right? Ten years, Dude. I'm asking her out."

Tommy was amazed at Jake's confidence. "Really?"

Jenny smirked and whispered something to her cheerleader friend Sally. Tommy watched Jenny exclude Beth from their conversation. Was it because she wasn't wearing a cheer outfit too?

Jenny eye-rolled, re-glossed her lips, then blew a kiss to Jake, who didn't appear to notice her.

Tommy glanced at the wall clock. *Fifteen minutes ticked away.* Last year, Tommy earned an A+ in torturous time watching. This year, he tried not to focus on the crawling minutes and seconds and to his surprise, time moved faster in Miss Bell's class. But, six hours loomed ahead of him and there was no telling what was ahead.

"Homeroom. Tommy Delo. Check." Miss Bell ticked names off on a roster using a feathery pen with a glittery barre. "After morning announcements and flag salute and your locker run, we'll officially begin *first period.* Check your schedule to know where you are going after homeroom."

Tommy didn't understand why Jenny and Beth giggled every time Miss Bell said first period. He didn't hear anything funny.

The loudspeaker crackled. "Welcome to Hope School. I am Principal Radling," Mr. Radling rapped the mike with his fingers. The speaker-box picked up the *thump, thump* sound and his comments to Mrs. Sweet, the secretary. "Mrs. Sweet is this newfangled microphone working?" *Thump, thump.* "You know I don't like this newfangled intercom system." Tommy realized the principal didn't think anyone heard him.

Tommy figured he was tapping on the microphone.

Mrs. Sweet piped up in a hushed whisper. "Yes, Mr. Radling. Every word is loud and clear. Just speak into the microphone like I showed you yesterday."

Tommy and the other students in room 10 erupted in peals of laughter hearing the distressed conversation between the principal and his secretary.

Laughter erupted like a volcano. "Children, please calm down," Miss Bell donned a Mona Lisa smile and cast a finger to her lips. In a hushed voice, she said to them, "It's a two-way intercom. The

Time Wheel Book 1

office staff can hear you just as you hear them." She pointed up to the ceiling where the black intercom box hung.

Tommy stifled his urge to join in the revelry. He wanted to make a good impression on Miss Bell.

Tap, tap. "Students, I trust you've had a restful summer." *Tap, Tap, thump.* "Welcome back. Just a reminder to keep your cell phone in your locker at all times. No chirping or typing is allowed during class time... L.O.L."

Right then, the whole class laughed-out-loud at his incorrect use of text speak.

Miss Sweet whispered, "It's *tweeting and texting, sir.*" Her voice audible as she coached the principal on popular vernacular.

"Oh, right," he muttered. "No texting and twerking allowed."

Explosive laughter filled the rooms of Hope. Jenny and Sally mopped wet tears from their eyes. "Twerking. Good one." Jenny sassed.

"Tweeting," Miss Sweet repeated in a soft voice.

Even Jeff couldn't hold it together any longer. Tommy thought Jeff looked like a Human Torch more than ever with his face matching his hair.

Tommy buried his head in his elbow, crying with tears of laughter he couldn't hold back.

The announcement continued. "I don't know why I'm hearing all this ruckus. Teachers, please calm your students so I can continue vital morning announcements."

"Shhh, boys and girls, please." Miss Bell held a finger to her lips.

Tommy saw her turn as if she was coughing. To his surprise, Miss Bell stifled a laugh.

Tap, tap. "The lunch choice today is mac 'n cheese, or pizza. Teachers, I trust you passed out the appropriate forms. Our student announcer, Jeff Dent, from Miss Bell's homeroom will report here Friday morning for instructions."

Miss Bell pressed a button and spoke up near the intercom. "Will do, Principal Radling."

Mr. Radling voice rumbled through the speaker. "As we like to say in Hope School, Hope starts here! We will now rise for the pledge to the flag."

Miss Bell motioned graceful hands for all to rise.

As the students stood, Tommy noticed that everyone, including the girls, towered above him. He shifted up on his tippy toes and wished he'd grown taller.

"Boys and girls, please make your lunch selections on the paper at your desk tops. Drop them in the basket as you leave homeroom. If you have room 10 on your schedule, stay put. You're in my history Section 1. If not, you can head to your class now," Miss Bell announced.

Ten students got up and left for their next session. Tommy hoped that Joe and Jenny would leave for good.

Tommy rechecked his schedule. "Nice! I'm still in room 10 for first period." He said to Jake.

"Sweet. Miss Bell is our history teacher," Jake couldn't stop smiling.

Tommy congratulated himself on making it through the first 20 minutes of homeroom. As luck would have it, he could stay put for Miss Bell's history class. He slid back into the leftie desk.

CHAPTER 14

Miss Bell

First Period: Miss Bell-Social Studies
First Period History Room 10

As soon as the homeroom students filed back in, Tommy view shifted to the wall clock. After history class, he'd make a dash to recheck his locker for the prayer wheel. Would it return to his locker before the dismissal bell? Maybe he imagined the whole thing. His stomach rumbled. Was school-itis making him lose his marbles?

His stomach was still doing flippity-flops. He was glad his spot was near the door. If an air biscuit escaped, he'd make a quick getaway to the lavatory and save himself embarrassment. His tummy growled, "feed me," even though it was a full two hours before he could eat lunch. Mom said he might be going through a growth spurt, but he doubted it. He was still short.

Miss Bell called out to Beth, "Would you bring the selection of papers from the basket and bring them to the cafeteria?" She turned toward Jake. "Jake, please bring today's attendance to the office."

"Sure, Miss Bell," Jake answered. "Happy to oblige."

Beth nodded and her lips pursed in a tight-lipped smile.

Tommy watched Beth's face flame up fifty shades of red. Did Beth like Jake?

"Ass kisser." Joe made kissing sounds on the back of his hand.

Jenny giggled.

Beth, mesmerized, followed Jake's hand as it swept his raven hair away from his dark eye. Her feet froze in place. "Now, Miss Bell?"

"Yes, dear. Now," Miss Bell clapped her hands, "Chop, chop. Run along, Beth. First bell rings in eight minutes for first period."

Sarah and Jennifer giggled. Tommy didn't hear anything funny.

More students shuffled into History class with sleepy first-day expressions.

"Welcome to first period social studies. Take a giant leap into room 10! For those of you who just arrived, my name is Miss Bell and I recognize some of you from last year."

Sally's strawberry blonde curls bounced each time she laughed with Jenny. She tugged at the bottom at her navy cheerleading skirt, crossing her legs at the ankles in a little X.

There they go again, laughing at nothing. Tommy thought.

"Is something amusing, girls?" Miss Bell asked them.

"Nothing at all Miss Bell. We're just thrilled to be in your class." Jenny smiled like a cat with a mouth full of feathers.

"I see." Miss Bell raised a brow and didn't say more.

Sally snorted and covered her mouth to cover up her laugh.

Tommy saw a tall boxy girl from homeroom, Reese, had left her desk to return with a rectangular flute case and a notebook. Her big gray sweat suit swallowed her up. Joe huffed like a gorilla when he saw her approach. Tommy noticed how Reese hung her head low after Joe teased her.

Miss Bell greeted her. "Hi Reese. I'm glad you're in my history session." She ticked off names in her roster. "I think everyone is here."

Her name sounded like Halloween candy.

Reese looked for an open seat after she returned from her locker. She saw an open seat near Beth.

Jenny said, "It's taken."

"It's empty."

"I'm saving it for Sally. She'll be right back."

Reese turned to find a spot.

Tommy saw Jenny intentionally jut her foot out, but it was too late to warn Reese.

Reese lurched forward and her notebook flew from her hands flapping like an angry bird as it fell.

Time Wheel Book 1

Jenny snickered. "Oops, sorry. Nice sweat suit, Reese. Not." Jenny's sugarcoated tone had a poisonous bite.

Tommy didn't want Jenny to get away with it. He slid from his seat and got up to help Reese. "I'm Tommy. Are you ok?"

"Yes. I know your name since I'm in your homeroom. I'm Reese. Thanks for helping me, Tommy."

"I think you look nice today." Tommy whispered, even though it was a little white lie.

Miss Bell didn't see Jenny trip Reese. "Are you ok, Reese?"

Reese nodded. "I'm fine. I just tripped."

Jenny's eyes seared a hole into Tommy with intent so evil he was scalded by her glare.

Tommy felt his stomach rumble and he was out of peppermints. He waved his hand. "Miss Bell, may I be excused. I left something important in my locker."

"Sure, hurry along. History is about to begin," Miss Bell said.

Tommy dashed to his locker and pulled out his backpack. No prayer wheel in it. He convinced himself he'd imagined it. He took a handful of mints from the front pocket of his backpack, but he felt something lumpy inside. He unzipped the top of it. "What?" His heart pounded. The prayer wheel lit up like a flashlight and shined in his eyes. "You have to go home," he whispered. He shoved the backpack into the bottom of his locker. He looked around, sure that no one heard him. He dashed back to class. Why was the prayer wheel at school?

He returned to room 10. Reese was attempting to fit a rectangular flute case on top of a square wire shelf under her chair. Tommy watched her frustration. She was boxy and tall and just the size he'd hope to be by now. Reese seemed embarrassed by her size, bending her shoulders to shrink her height, wearing gray so no one would notice her. None of the girls even bothered to save her a chair. Reese wasn't wearing a special new-day outfit. He decided Reese must be lonely.

Tommy leaned in to whisper to Jake. "I found a cool artifact in the shop. It's in my locker."

"You brought it to school?" Jake asked.

"Not exactly," Tommy said. "I'll show you…if it's still in my locker later on."

Jake gave a non-committal, "Whatever, Dude."

Jake must have thought he was lying, but he couldn't explain without sounding crazy even to himself.

Tommy guessed Jake's friend, Jeff must be smart, judging by the amount of school supplies appearing like rabbits from a magician's hat. Jeff also wore glasses. Tommy squinted his eyes. Maybe he could fake an eye test at the nurse's office.

Lana scooted past Jenny's acid stare. "Hi Reese. Is this seat taken?"

Reese shook her head, "No."

Lana claimed the seat between Reese and Dina. She placed a dog notebook on her desktop. She turned to give a cheery wave to Tommy, Jeff, and Jake.

Tommy supposed he wasn't the only person who'd been teased. He could only guess why Lana folded her arms over the front of her body as if she hid something precious.

Jeff opened his binder and wrote the date and the word 'homework' before Miss Bell even told him to write it. Jeff lined his school gear up like soldiers ready for battle. Tommy noticed a shiny gold pin with an H on Jeff's collar. Dina and Beth had an H pin on their lapels too. Were they in a secret club? He'd have to ask Jake about it later.

Jake and Beth headed for the office.

"Alvin, would you please pass these agenda papers out?"

"Sure, Miss Bell."

Jeff was busy jotting down every word Miss Bell uttered. The only thing that made school bearable was Tommy's new friend Jake and Miss Bell. So far, there were lots of directions to remember but no history lesson, which was fine with him. So, he let his mind wander.

"Jake and Beth, would you please deliver these the office and the cafeteria?"

"Sure." Jake got up and took the papers.

"Hurry along, Beth," Miss Bell said.

Beth got up and left with Jake.

Tommy watched as Jake's lazy-eyed grin to Dina, a thumbs up to Jeff, and a smile to Reese all in a matter of a minute. *Impressive use of time.* Tommy guessed no teacher ever asked Jake to hurry up. It's like he was immune to rules that other kids had to follow. But why? Jake never seemed to rush anywhere, including heading back to his seat after passing papers. Right then, Tommy was convinced, Jake was smarter than he let on. More students filtered into first period filling the empty seats that weren't yet taken. "Thanks for saving my spot, 'Lil T," Jake sat down and grinned ear to ear.

"Hey, what happened to your head?" Tommy asked.

Jake leaned in and whispered. "Ah, this big lump on my noggin? Got hit by a sweet peach."

"A peach?" Tommy's eyebrows lifted. "Did you go to the lunch room?"

"No, Dude. My dad calls pretty girls Peaches; sweet and ready to pick. Get it? Beth and I slammed heads in the hallway when I tried to kiss her." Jake dropped his news like a sugar bomb.

"You did *what?*" Tommy's hand flung to his mouth.

"You heard me right. She's really pretty without her glasses." He gave a thumbs up to Tommy.

Tommy made a mental note to ask Jake how he found the opportunity to kiss Beth in school right near the office.

Breathless, Beth entered the room as if a swift breeze blew her in. She held an ice pack against her forehead and looked shaken up.

Tommy knew she hid an egg-shaped lump blooming purple on her brow.

Beth avoided looking in Jake's direction.

"What happened, Beth?" Miss Bell asked.

"Some lower grade kid ran into me by accident," Beth stammered. "And I dropped all the papers in the hallway so I had to pick them up."

Jake winked at Tommy.

Tommy knew Beth fibbed. He sent Jake 'the look' and Jake returned it with a smug smile.

By now, Tommy surmised Jake was catnip to females judging by the hyena giggles each time Jake walked by them. His new friend also knew big words, so must be intelligent. In no time, Jake became Tommy's hero. In the short time he knew him, Jake tossed words like *acclimate*, and *renovate*, as easily as a baseball... and Jake smelled like men's aftershave and had the nerve to try to kiss Beth.

Beth glanced over. Tommy smiled.

Jake smiled at Beth.

Beth's neck bloomed blotchy patches that eked up her neck like a spotted giraffe.

Jenny's face lit with infuriation as she watched the interaction. She tugged Beth's sleeve and whispered something in Beth's ear.

Beth frowned and shrugged, then fumbled to open her notebook.

Tommy's new mind movie began. He called it *Lost at Sea* and he was neck deep in it when Miss Bell called out his name.

"Good morning, Tommy Delo." She smiled and tapped her fluffy pink pen on his shoulder. "Earth to Tommy? Are you present?"

"Yes." Tommy blushed crimson. He realized Miss Bell's question was to jog him out of a daydream. He gave her an apologetic frown. "Present."

Jenny joined Sally in a mocking laugh at his expense.

Tommy sunk back into a daydream, inventing mind pictures, when he heard Miss Bell's voice chime like a bell. This time his chin shot up and he paid close attention.

"Some of you just shuffled in to history, so, we'll start by introducing our new student, Tommy Delo. Let's give him a Hope round of applause!" She motioned toward Tommy with a slender hand dip. She rotated her arms in a circle while she clapped her round of applause. "Would you tell the students about yourself, Tommy?"

"Oh, sure." He fumbled to talk, but the words stuck to his tongue like peanut butter with no jelly. "My name is Tommy Delo. We moved to Hope this summer. Mom bought Treasure Trove on Main Street. We used to live in Erie, PA, then moved to an apartment one town over before we came here." Tommy's voice cracked at the worst possible time.

Joe stuck his top teeth over his bottom lip. He crossed his eyes and mimicked Tommy loud enough for everyone to hear him. "Der, I'm from Erie, Pennsylvania and I'm a hillbilly."

Tommy felt a hot rush of blood fill his cheeks.

Jake whipped around and spat, "Cut it out, Joe."

Jenny blew a kiss of appreciation in Joe's direction.

"Yeah, make me." Joe challenged Jake with a tightened fist.

Miss Bell whipped around. "That's enough, boys." She winked at Jake and shifted her gaze back to Tommy. "Thank you for your share, Tommy. Did you know that my grandfather owned Treasure Trove? I have such fond memories of spending summers with my grandfather." Her face was wistful. "Grandpapa was a world traveler! He had wondrous adventures. You're one lucky fellow to own the store."

"I'm not sure how lucky we are. There's a ton more junk to sort before we can open." *Should I ask her about the Prayer wheel? He thought.*

Some children giggled. Did they mock him?

Miss Bell smiled brightly. "I'm sure there is! Grandpapa collected all kinds of trinkets. Admittedly, some of it was pure junk. The saying goes *one man's trash is another man's treasure!*"

Tommy waved his hand. "Hey, that's the name I wanted for the shop."

"It's an old cliché. This repartee brings me to my Segway. *Time Wheel* chapter 1 is due by Friday."

Tommy's stomach flipped in distress at the new word he didn't know, but other kids did. He sank in the ocean unable to take a breath. He waved his hand like a flag in the wind. "Where's the segway?"

Some quiet laughing ensued and Miss Bell heard it.

"No need to laugh. Tommy posed a good question. Asking when you don't know something is a mark of a smart student. A segway is the connection or bridge between one related thought and another."

Tommy nodded, relieved she threw him a life raft just before he drowned himself.

She winked at Tommy. "We'll use our text only as a reference guide and *Time Wheel* as a fun springboard to our class research about artifacts and history."

Tommy wasn't ready for spring-boarding. He barely knew how to segway.

Jake nudged Tommy in the ribs as soon as Miss Bell turned around. "I'm jealous. You're the

Teacher's Pet."

Tommy's spirits soared. He'd never been teacher's pet, only the teacher's problem.

Jeff furiously jotted in his notebook. Tommy wondered what he was writing and if he should be writing something too.

Tommy rode on a merry-go-round of new faces. The day was a blur until 3:20— last bell. He had only checked the clock two bazillion times, but one bazillion fewer times than last year.

"Hey, wait up Lil T!" Jake yelled. "I'd love to see your shop. Do you mind if I tag along?" Jake pushed his mid-length dark hair off his handsome face. "I'm totally into old junk."

"Really? Sure." Tommy couldn't believe Cool Kid Jake wanted to be his friend. "But first, tell me what happened with Beth and you."

"We were talking about how Joe is such a bully. I asked Beth to remove her glasses so I could see her pretty eyes... a Clark Kent and Superman thing if you catch my drift."

Tommy nodded yes.

"So, I moved in real close to her. She smelled nice and soapy. Then I got close enough to kiss her. I think I startled her. She dropped the folder and the papers scattered all over the hallway like autumn leaves. I knelt down to help her and we banged heads— hard."

Tommy doubled over laughing.

"Beth bolted like a scared rabbit. I feel kinda' bad about it. She covered for me with Miss Bell, but you'd have to be an idiot not to notice we both have matching egg- sized lumps on our heads. I'm sure Jenny noticed." Jake exploded into a full-on laugh.

"So, you didn't actually *kiss her*?"

"Naw, but I got this close." He pinched his fingers to show an inch.

Tommy trailed behind Beth and Jenny.

Beth left her locker with Jenny hounding her for answers. "So, what gives with the lump on your forehead?" Jenny prodded.

"I told you. A kid ran into me." Beth studied her pink sneakers.

"I don't believe you. Rock Star Jake has a huge lump on his head, too. Why would you lie about it?

Makes no sense...unless...." She tugged on Beth's arm. "I called dibs on him, Beth."

"It was just an accident. I dropped the papers and Jake wanted to help me pick them up. We bumped heads, is all." Beth defended.

"You know that Jake *kissed me* this summer. And... no offense...but I'm way prettier than you are, Beth."

"Jake told me I was pretty," Beth mumbled under her breath. "In fact, he said I should get contacts."

"He just feels sorry for you because you wear glasses," Jenny sneered. "Jake drops sugar bombs on *all* the girls. But he only means it when he says it to me. You should know that by now." In a huff, she joined with Sally leaving Beth behind them.

Tommy realized no one was safe from Jenny's venomous tongue.

Dina caught up with Beth. "Are you ok, Beth?"

"I have huge secret to tell you about Jake. Promise you won't tell Jenny." She leaned in to whisper.

Tommy couldn't hear any more, but he guessed Beth told Dina the real story about the giant lump on her forehead.

CHAPTER 15

Worst Class Ever

Language Arts Class

The prayer wheel nipped his fingers like a badly-behaved puppy, followed him to school like Mary's Little Lamb, and then dragged him back in time without his permission. Worse yet, it would go off on its own and he'd have to search for its hiding place. He couldn't tell Mom about losing it. It was maddening. She'd just repeat her famous saying, "A place for everything, and everything in its place." Mom would assume he'd been careless with it, like a forgotten homework assignment, or lost lunch money. Guilty as charged —but that was *last* year. *This* year he was responsible. The prayer wheel had its own agenda and he had his. He needed to find the darned thing. What else could it do?

Maybe there was a clue to the missing puzzle piece in the squiggly writing on the barrel he couldn't decipher. With school starting, he needed time to research the artifact before homework ate up his life. His mind was full of questions with no answers.

When the dreaded reading class arrived, he already had a bad taste in his mouth for it, like mushrooms and stinky blue cheese combined. He didn't look forward to those confusing questions and hard vocabulary words he was sure to muddle up. He plopped down next to Jake as if life had been sucked out of him.

Jake saw his face and was ready to ask him what was wrong when Mrs. Otter started her lesson.

"Boys and girls, we'll begin our unit with a study of the great classics."

Tommy dreaded every word she spoke. He grabbed his forehead with both hands. He was a trapped rat on a sinking ship. He gulped for air. As Mrs. Otter's voice droned on, Tommy palmed his forehead and leaned forward. His face was hidden from the teacher. He struggled to pay attention in class, but his head buzzed and vibrated. His eyes felt gritty and heavy. Soon, he dropped into a daydream about the great pyramids he'd recently watched on TV. He imagined he stood in the center of giant-sized triangle of stone as son of the great pharaoh. He imagined he wrote in pictures instead of words, so spelling didn't matter. Mom wouldn't have to worry about money because he was tremendously rich. And best of all, he never had to attend school where kids could laugh at him for making mistakes. Then he heard the sweetest voice call out his name. Was it Miss Bell?

"Tommy...It's Choden." Was this strange word a name? He'd never heard a name like Choden before.

Jake poked him on his side to wake him.

Tommy sat up just in the nick of time just as Mrs. Otter passed by his desk and gave him the stink eye.

He yawned and blinked his eyes to stay alert.

Once Mrs. Otter's voice droned on while Tommy's attention rode away atop a camel in the Sahara Desert. Many servants attended to him. Beads of sweat formed on his brow and he felt the scalding sun beat against his skin. He swallowed hot and dusty air and his mouth was pasty dry. In his daydream, he ordered a servant to get him a drink, but instead his servant poked his ribs.

Jake prod was insistent. "Lil' T, snap out of it before the Otter sees you."

Too late.

Jenny, Sally, and Joe all fake-snored drawing attention to Tommy.

Mrs. Otter stood right near Tommy's desk thumping her sturdy black shoe on the tile floor. "Mr. Delo, wake up and pay attention!"

There it was; the phrase he'd heard time and time again. He considered saying, *"I'm so poor I can't even pay attention."* But knew it would get him in hot water. So, he gave a sheepish smile and fake-apologized, "Oh, I'm sorry." He sat up and willed fuzzy cobwebs to clear from his mind.

Her flaming dragon eyes glared at him. "Well, you should be!"

Mrs. Otter's thick black heels smacked the tiles as she walked toward Jenny, Sally, and Joe. "Enough insolent behavior from you three *troublemakers*." She spat it like a bad word.

Tommy's mouth was parched, gritty, and desert-dry. Against his better judgement, he raised his hand.

"What is it now, *Mr. Delo*?" Her mouth cemented in an unhappy frown.

"May I get a drink of water, Mrs. Otter? I'm dying of thirst."

She pointed to the clock with her bent index finger. "You'll have to put up with a dry mouth for fifteen more minutes."

Was the Sahara a desert in Africa? All he could think about was water… oceans of it. But oceans were salty. He smacked his paper-dry lips together. Urgent to leave the room, he waved his hand.

"Yes?" Her eyes bored into him and she didn't smile.

It was no use asking to leave the room, so he came up with another question. "Mrs. Otter, will we ever read about pirates?"

Mrs. Otter snapped at Tommy like a hawk ready to snare a defenseless mouse. "Unlikely. Pirate stories serve no purpose. Why do you think we read classic literature instead?"

She sounded like a squawking parrot to his ears. He imagined prodding Mrs. Otter overboard with the Classics tethered to her chubby ankles. *Ker-plop*, right into Davy Jones Locker. He grinned.

"Answer, please." She tapped her heavy shoe on the tile floor with a thump, thump, thump.

The stench of carnations filled his nose and reminded him of Dad's funeral day. He squirmed in his seat and held his breath. Not even Jake could rescue him. "Beats the heck out of me, Mrs. Otter." Tommy didn't mean to sound rude, but his stupid grin made her think he was.

A peal of laughter erupted around him. If this was his old school, Petey and Harv would have congratulated him for the interruption. This year, embarrassment engulfed him.

Exhausted, Mrs. Otter took in a long breath and zeroed in on him. Her lips were tight and angry. "Let's talk *after* class young man."

Tommy watched the clock for fifteen torturous minutes. The tip of Mrs. Otter's ugly black shoe ached to push him off the edge of the plank. Even worse, his water fountain trip was now delayed. His stomach dropped 1000 meters clear to his feet, just like on the Tower of Terror ride at Disney World. It was no use. Tommy was captive until Mrs. Otter booted him into to the hallway. He wet his parched and sunbaked lips with his tongue.

Jake leaned in with a surprised look. "Dude, you have a bad case of sunburn on your face, or you have a rash. Do you have any allergies?"

"Just to Mrs. Otter." Tommy's hand drifted up to his cheeks. "Weird." He felt the burning sensation flamed his cheeks. It was definitely sunburn, but it made no sense.

The Prayer Wheel

While Tommy was in reading class with Mrs. Otter, the prayer wheel had already transported out of Tommy's backpack. She was on her way back in time. Her connection with the boy was getting stronger by day. He daydreamed about her journeys, only he hadn't realized it yet.

She sped through a portal, floating through the time-space continuum to arrive at the Pharaoh's chamber room. She whirred through the ceiling and zapped through a brilliant light. She landed inside of the Great Pyramid of Giza in the year Cairo, Egypt 2490 BC.

Pharaoh Khafra addressed the Prayer wheel in a soft

murmur. He held it in his hands like a rare and delicate bird. "The sacred spiral has returned to me! Praise Osiris!" He addressed the object. "Where have you been these many years my sweet?" Pharaoh spun the barrel. Khafra was drawn inside a blinding flash of purple light which encircled his body.

The Prayer wheel spun Pharaoh several centuries forward in time to present day Egypt.

"Why do you show me our great kingdom's fate?" Khafra asked the Wheel.

The wheel spun speaking to Khafra like a forgotten melody.

He understood. "I see."

Pharaoh placed the Prayer wheel on a gilded stand near his bed. Downtrodden and sorrowful, he knew that the wheel was no longer his alone to enjoy. Khafra's son would be the next guardian, but only if she found him worthy and less prideful. Pharaoh's travel felt like hours, but he'd only been gone for minutes.

He called out to his son. "Khafra Khaf, please come here."

Pharaoh's twelve-year-old son entered and bowed respectfully to his father. His head was clean-shaven, except for one long braid of hair hanging to the right side of his body, a sign of royalty.

As if in pain, Pharaoh held the sides of his head in his mahogany-brown hands.

"Father, are you ill with head pain? Should I call the High Priestess for you?"

"I am well, but sad of heart. I have a secret to share with you, son."

"Secret? Is it about that shiny object you won't let me touch?" He pointed curiously at it. "I'm twelve, I won't break it."

Pharaoh nodded. "This Prayer wheel appeared to me right before my twelfth year of life. And many years later, she has returned to me."

"She?"

"The wheel is enchanted," the Pharaoh explained.

Khafra walked closer to examine the barrel. "What magic does it do, Father?"

"She adjusts karma. Our actions matter in the fabric of time. She will help you rule the land when I am gone. Long ago, a wise young girl named Choden merged with the wheel. Her Ka, her soul essence, lives within it. Before I was a Pharaoh, she and I have traveled to faraway lands and she revealed my character flaws."

"You are the great pharaoh and ruler of the world. You have no flaws. I am your son, therefore I have none either." The boy puffed out his hairless chest.

The Pharaoh shook his head. "None are perfect. My Ka shall walk amongst the stars in the sky with the great ones soon. I am old and near the end of my life. But you will be able to travel with the prayer wheel and gain wisdom so you can be a fair leader." Pharaoh hung his head low.

"Why are you sad?"

"I could have been a better Pharaoh. When I was a young Pharaoh, Choden and I time-walked into future Egypt. I learned about our land. In the future, people gawk at our pyramids and culture as a curiosity. Our treasures are robbed and looted by greedy people. Our bodies… desecrated, displayed in cases as clear as water. In the future, Pharaohs will no longer rule." His face creased with sadness.

"You had a perilous visit, Father. It can't be true!" Khafra Khaf said.

"The wheel never lies."

"I will demand she show me the future!" he said.

"She chooses us. No one owns Choden and she is not at your command, Son." He held it in his hands. "She told me all people need to be free; not just the royal house."

"I don't believe it!"

"Truth is truth. My heart is heavy with guilt." Khafra cast his eyes down. "When Jackal God weighs my heart, I wish it to be as light as a feather, not heavy as a stone."

The cylinder spun away from Khafra 's hands like a bird taking flight. The wheel landed in his young son's hand.

"Son, Choden may chose you as her next guardian. Ask that she return to you and that you be worthy of her," Pharaoh said.

Khafra stamped his foot. "She must be worthy of me!"

"No. You must be worthy of her. Only then will she return."

The boy held the wheel and bowed his head. "Please return to me." He felt the wheel warm and spark in his hands. It lifted and dropped through a portal of light.

The bright circle of purple light stunned Khafra. The whites of his eyes were as big as the moon. "Father, where did she go?"

"She travels forward and backward in time to the next one who needs her," Pharaoh answered.

"But I need her, Father." Khafra Khaf's lips pouted.

"She lives in many portals of time."

"Pray she returns." Pharaoh bowed his head in reverence and clasped his hands together.

The prayer wheel spun back to Tommy's Crow's Nest.

CHAPTER 16

Prayer Wheel disappears

After School Same Day
3:45

Tommy dashed to his locker half expecting to see the prayer wheel sitting on top of his school books... but it hadn't returned. Disappointed, he loaded an English text in his backpack. What would he tell Jake now that the artifact was gone?

Jake stopped by Tommy's locker. "So where is it?"

"It's gone now," Tommy said.

Jake had a funny look on his face. 'Where'd it go?"

He was right. Jake thought he lied to him. "Once I find it, I'll show you. I promise.

"Whatever. It's no big deal." Jake shrugged like nothing mattered.

Tommy could tell Jake was disappointed. Did Jake still want to be his friend or did he think he lied to him? His stomach his dropped to his feet.

"Lil T, can I hang after school? My dad's working late tonight."

Relief flooded Tommy. "Sure can, if you don't mind a two hour wait while I finish Mrs. Otter's 'thirty-minute reading assignment'." Tommy air quoted with his fingers and lolled his tongue.

"Jake, vocab wiz at your service." He bowed like a gallant knight.

Tommy's nose wrinkled. "Really? You'd help me?" Tommy felt the knot in his gut untangle.

"No prob-lem-o. Words are my super power."

Tommy wondered if he had a superpower. He bit his lip. *Probably not.* "Did you know that Mrs. Otter is tiring?"

"Yeah, I saw you sleeping in class," Jake teased.

"No… I mean she's leaving for good this Friday. She told me so after class."

"Oh, she's *retiring*. Good. Maybe we'll get someone who likes kids."

Tommy walked to the shop with Jake side by side with him. They passed the stone bridge then headed up Main Street toward the shop. Tommy took the key from around his neck and unlocked the door securing it behind him. The bell above the door tinged when they entered.

"Lil' T, I heard you met my dad about a month ago."

"I did? When?"

"He checked on the electric sparks you saw when you first moved in," Jake said. "He's says your mom's a fine peach. I'm looking forward to meeting her myself."

Tommy's jaw dropped. It was like a giant rock hit him in the head. "The big guy with the tattoo is *your dad?*"

"Yeah. I thought you knew."

Tommy's heart chugged like a freight train trying to recuperate from the awful news. "No wonder your name sounded familiar." The big bad man with the movie star good looks was Jake's dad. Somehow, it made perfect sense. Why hadn't he realized it sooner? Jake and his dad had the same good looks and super power with females.

Jake pointed toward him. "Your face looks funnier than usual. What's up with that?"

Tommy gulped down his distress to say, "I'll bet your dad dates lots of women."

"Sure, but they're vapid and not future mother material."

"Vapid?"

"Dumb, airheaded— and way too young for him. Why do you ask?"

He tried to be nonchalant. "No reason." But Tommy had every reason in the world because he was protecting Mom.

Jake swung in an arc and examined the room. "I see what you mean about the shop. It's crammed ceiling to floor with merchandise."

"You should've seen it *before* we filled the dumpster. We tagged almost everything with prices, but we're still not finished with all of it." Tommy paced to the bottom of the second-floor stairwell.

"I'd be happy to help, once we finish the HW, my lingo for homework."

"Really? Sweet." Tommy pounded up the steps and called out to Mom.

"I'm home and I have a friend with me."

"Come on in so I can meet him!" Mom called back.

Tommy beckoned to Jake with a hand wave. "Follow me up. She'll tell you her name is Mary, but call her *Mrs*. Delo because she's old."

"Got it." Jake laughed.

They bounded up the five stairs to the second floor and entered the kitchen.

"Mom, this is my new friend Jake."

"A pleasure to meet you, young man. I'm Mary Delo." Her eyes were level with Jake's. She extended her hand.

"Nice to meet you, *Mrs. Delo*." Jake's voice cracked when he said her name, and his eyes checked in with Tommy. "Name's Jake Stanton. You've already met my dad, Jackson."

Mom's face registered with recognition. "So, I did. You're in sixth with Tommy? You're quite tall." She lifted a curious brow.

He swiped jet-black hair from his brow then held his hand out to shake hers. "I have my dad's tall genes," Jake said.

"You're wearing his *pants* already?" Tommy was incredulous.

Jake smirked but didn't tease. "Not jeans you wear, but *genes*— like in DNA."

"Oh, yeah, right." Tommy realized that Jake was kind to him. Last year, Petey loved to tease him anytime he made a mistake.

"Quite a lump you have on your forehead, Jake," Mom said.

"It was *almost* worth it." He poked Tommy in the ribs with his elbow and winked.

"Well then, pleased to meet you, Jake Stanton. Remarkable resemblance to your father." Jake's white teeth glinted at her and he shook her hand. "People say the same, Mrs. Delo."

Mom laughed lightly and drew her hand back from Jake. "I'm sure they do. No wonder Tommy keeps checking for chin stubble. You appear older than your years."

Even with her hair pulled back, dusty jeans and sneakers, Tommy realized Jake was gawking at Mom. Jake couldn't hide his goofy grin; the same one all the boys wore when they looked at Miss Bell.

Jake shifted on one leg and gave her a toothy smile. "My dad was right, Mrs. Delo. You're very pretty."

Mom arched her brow. "Oh, he he say that? My goodness, it's a rarity to hear such glowing compliments."

"I tell you you're pretty *all the time*," Tommy grumbled and kicked his toe into the floor. Tommy sent Jake an acid stare.

Jake ignored Tommy's stink eye and dazzled a smile. He thumbed his belt loop and said, "I have to say it because it's true, Mrs. Delo."

Mom tousled Tommy's hair and changed the subject. "How was school, Tommy?"

Jake snickered and elbowed Tommy. "Tell her, 'Lil T."

"We have a real pretty teacher. Get this... her grandfather *owned* our shop. You never told me."

"Sure, I did. *Bell's* Treasure Trove. Miss Bell is his lovely granddaughter I met at the lawyer's office when I contracted to buy the shop. Do you like her?"

"I'll say I do!" Tommy grinned. "She is my homeroom and history teacher."

Jake said, "Miss Bell is sweet on Tommy."

"Is not." Tommy bloomed scarlet hoping it were true.

"How about your other teachers?"

"Mrs. Otter teaches reading but she's tiring."

"Retiring?"

"Yes. And tiring." Tommy pretended to snore.

"Do you have homework?" She asked.

"I do, but Jake's going to help me with it. He's a word wizard."

"Ok, then," She knelt by the old desk. "I'll be arm-wrestling this beat-up desk if you need me." She grunted, forcing a stuck drawer in and out. "Snacks are on the counter. Take some up with you." She tugged at the drawer. "Ugh."

Jake turned toward her. "Mrs. Delo, if you rub a bit of candle wax on those drawers, they'll slide really easy. That's what my dad does."

"Great idea! I just came across an old candle in the top drawer. I'll bet that's what it was used for."

Tommy took two bags of cookies and two juice boxes.

"Let's get to it. We'll be done in no time," Jake said.

With a glint in his eyes, Tommy said, "Follow me up to the coolest hidden room you'll ever see. Watch this." He tapped on the panel near Mom's room and pushed on it. The secret entrance creaked open.

"Woah, nice digs!" Jake's head bend down to clear the five-foot door jam.

Tommy climbed the five steps to the hidden room with Jake behind him.

"Sweet digs." Jake glanced around the small wooden paneled room and climbed the steps to the third floor. "Maybe we can do a sleep over some time. This is a perfect clubhouse."

"My thoughts exactly. I have an extra sleeping bag. Welcome to the Crow's Nest." Light streamed into the room through the circular window even before he flipped on the lamp.

Jake smirked. "I'd like to stay over sometime. Do you think your Mom would mind?"

"Really? Sure!"

Less than an hour passed and Tommy had completed all his homework with Jake's assistance.

Mom walked up the steps into the Crow's Nest. "How's it going, Tommy?"

"Just finished *all of it*." Tommy smiled.

"Record time! Jake, the candle trick worked. Thanks to you, the drawers slide easily and I didn't even break my nails. Tommy, did you ask Miss Bell about the artifact yet?"

"Not yet." They clamored down to the first-floor shop level leaving Mom to finish tidying the desk drawers on the second apartment level.

"Is the artifact the disappearing one you claim to have had in your locker today?" Jake lifted a brow in challenge.

"The same one. My mom thinks it's an old prayer wheel. It has squiggly writing on the barrel part. It does weird stuff...like today. You've no idea the trouble it's given me," Tommy said.

"Such as?"

"Such as nipping at my fingers. When I touch it, my hand tingles, kind of like electricity."

"Static electricity. Interesting."

"... and it hides on me just like it did today. It's never where I put it." Tommy paused and checked Jake's face for judgement.

"Maybe you just forgot where you placed it."

"You don't believe me, do you? You sound *just* like my mom." Tommy checked the top of the old wood counter top pushing aside empty boxes. "

"You have no reason to lie to me, but it does sound a tad preposterous, moving on its own...but I suppose it's not inconceivable."

"That means *silly*, but maybe *possible*, right?"

Jake nodded.

"Well it's true. All of it." Tommy folded his arms over his chest. He called from stair loft, "Mom, did you see the canister thingy? It's not up here." Tommy barreled down the steps with Jake behind him.

"Did you, Mom?"

"I didn't touch it, Tommy. It can't get legs and walk away," Mom said.

"Are you sure?" Tommy wrinkled his nose, then clattered to the shop level with Jake trailing behind him. "I'm going to check the shelf where I first found it."

"You know you're talking about an inanimate object, right? Come on, Dude. This is a joke, isn't it?" Jake folded his arms over his chest.

"I don't lie. You'll see." Tommy pulled a ladder over and climbed up. He felt around. "Not here."

"We need to check the Crow's Nest again. I have a hunch. Follow me." They reached the second floor. Tommy cupped his ear. A low tapping and humming vibrated the air. "Come on." Tommy climbed the hidden stair case to the Crow's Nest and stopped short. The buzzing grew louder. "The humming can drive me batty sometimes. Do you hear it?"

Jake laughed. "I do. Fluorescent lights buzz, in case you didn't know."

"In case you didn't notice, there's no fluorescent lights in the Crow's Nest." Tommy felt an electric shock shoot up his spine. Out of the corner of his eye, he caught a glimmer of light. He pointed to the corner of the Crow's Nest. He lowered his voice. "Hey Jake, how do you explain the creepy purple lights?"

Jake cocked his head in amazement and stared at the unearthly light. "Geez, I have no freaking idea. My apologizes for doubting you." He backed up slowly and headed down the stairs.

Tommy did the same.

Goosebumps prickled Tommy's arms. "I think it's a ghost."

"Ok, I believe you. Maybe your artifact is haunted or maybe it's your room We're going to have to figure out how to ghost bust."

"It's the same thing I told my mom, but she didn't believe me."

"Hey, can I come by tomorrow. We'll figure this out and get rid of it, whatever it is."

The brass canister materialized and hid on the uppermost shelf, nestled out of sight behind the school globe.

She'd been playing Hide and Go Seek with Tommy, but he didn't know the game.

Jake left at 6:00 pm.

Tommy didn't hear Mom's cell phone ring, but saw the familiar unhappy frown on her face. "We have to talk, Tommy."

Tommy watched her brows push together like two fuzzy caterpillars. Talk meant she'd talk, and he'd listen.

She crossed her arms and the corners of her mouth dropped at the edges. "Mrs. Otter called me to tell me you fell asleep in reading class."

"I was tired from all those words." It was a lame excuse, but also true.

"Try again." Her voice was a bad lullaby.

"I didn't mean to…"

"Early bedtime tonight, Tommy. You need more sleep to pay better attention at school."

"I'm so poor I can't even pay attention," sat on the tip of his tongue, but it would make matters worse, so he just said, "Ok, Mom. I will."

"Were you outside for PE today?"

Tommy nodded. "Yes, why?"

"You have sunburn on your nose. Tomorrow morning, slather sunscreen on your delicate skin. Skin cancer is real threat!" She shuddered.

"Aww, Mom. You worry too much." But Tommy worried even more. PE class was inside all week. He ran to the bathroom to take a look at his reflection. Could imagination give him sunburn?

CHAPTER 17

Joe-rex-it-all

September 8

Tommy touched his sunburned nose and winced. He said, "How did I get sunburn during reading class?" He could have sworn he heard the prayer wheel giggle at him. He glanced over to it, sitting innocently on his nightstand. Tommy saw a bottle of sunscreen Mom left right next to it. He didn't bother to put on since there was no point to it.

Tommy headed down to the second floor and had breakfast. With a few minutes to spare he felt an urge to walk down into the shop. His head buzzed.

Just as he reached the bottom of the stairwell, he heard the voice softly calling his name.

"Helloooo, Tommy!"

Even though it went against every caution from every scary movie, he needed to investigate. The disembodied voice didn't scare him as much as it darn well should've.

"Over here!" It said.

He twirled around to find the source of the female voice. He threw his palm to his aching head.

"I'm up here, Tommy!"

The voice emanated from the shelf where he first found the artifact, but he was too short to see anything without the ladder.

Tommy dragged the ladder over and climbed up the metal rungs. He shoved his hand back and felt a gritty surface on the cool metal barrel. "No freaking way," he mumbled. "It's you? You can talk to me?" He rolled it forward and wrapped his fingers around it. It heated up, responding with a warm tingle and soft giggle. He climbed down to examine the metal object with a gritty coating of sand on its surface. "Where have you been? On a beach, I bet." His fingers tingled, but she stayed silent.

He ran the artifact up to the Crow's nest and set it on his pillow. "Please stay put. I need you to be right here after school so I can show Jake, ok?" Tommy wondered if he imagined the whole thing. But he knew for certain, he'd seen the artifact next to his bed not more than fifteen minutes ago.

Mom called up to the Crow's Nest. "Tommy, it's time to leave for school. What are you doing barreling up and down the steps like a charging rhino? You're going to be late!"

"I forgot to put sunscreen on." He crossed his fingers. How could Mom understand why sunscreen wouldn't make any difference? He bounded down the stairs and boarded the car pretending it was sea worthy vessel and he was a pirate. "Arrg, Matey."

Mom said, "Arrg, you ready for school?"

"Yes, Captain. Can I walk home from school if Jake walks with me? You wouldn't have to pick me up."

"Are you sure he'll walk with you? You're not to walk the busy street alone." Tommy groaned. "Geez, I'm a fearless pirate and almost twelve."

"But not ready to sail the seas alone just yet."

He wondered why three short months could make such a difference to her.

"Can Jake and I have a sleep over sometime?"

"As long as it's not on a school night."

"Rules, rules, rules," he muttered.

Mom turned into the school parking lot to let him off, pulling right next to the curb in front of Hope School.

Tommy stepped out and waved goodbye. He entered the glass portico and headed down the hallway behind Lana. He watched the fluffy dog-ears on Lana's backpack bob up and down. Lana didn't mind that her backpack a cute dog on it. Apparently, girls had different rules for sixth-grade backpacks than boys did. His mind drifted to Dad's words before he got sick: *We'll get a dog someday*. But it never happened. Tommy sighed and pushed the ache away. Last year, the counselor told him not to stuff up his feelings like a Thanksgiving turkey. The counselor said his feelings could explode out. But he stuffed them anyway. Maybe that's why he got diarrhea after dad died, and so much gas when he felt anxious.

Lana scampered toward her locker. Tommy wondered why she was moving so fast until he checked the hallway behind him. Joe sailed down the narrow corridor like an ocean liner. Jenny rode the wake at his side and students parted to allow him clear passage. Tommy saw him coming and fumbled to recall the combination on his locker. He twirled the lock until he heard a click. He took a breath, shoved his jacket and backpack in the locker, grabbed a folder, notebook, and history book, and slammed it shut for a quick getaway.

He glanced to Lana who unloaded a doggie backpack into her locker and detach a doggy-eared little bag which she slung over her shoulder. In her hand, she held a copy of *Time Wheel*.

Joe was approaching fast.

"Drat." In his rush, he forgot Time Wheel. He spun the dial but it was too late.

With an evil grin, Joe slammed his meaty fist on the metal locker next to Tommy's ear. "Bam! Did I scare you, Ass wipe?" Joe bellowed a foghorn laugh.

Tommy startled, but was determined not admit Joe scared the daylights out of him. So, he said, "Nice try, *Gorilla*." Tommy grabbed the book, shut his locker, and dashed away double time before Joe's fist could fly at him. Once he was safe, Tommy mumbled an insult that could've gotten him detention if anyone heard it. Detention didn't scare him more than Joe punt kicking him through the goal posts of kingdom come.

Jenny witnessed the locker slam incident and couldn't stop laughing. She followed down the hallway next to Joe. "Good one, Joey-woey. The widdle-puppy and almost peed himself."

Tommy winced at her annoying babyish tone she was fond of using near boys.

Joe bellowed, "Maybe next time he'll actually pee himself."

Tommy jetted up to Lana and headed into the safety of homeroom.

Homeroom

8:45 am Period 1 History

A clutch of students gathered by the entranceway as Miss Bell greeted each arrival. Joe's loud voice echoed in the hallway. He shoved through the crowd, with his elbows ramming anyone unlucky enough to be in his way. Jenny surfed the tide behind Joe's massive frame.

Tommy imagined himself to be like James Bond, stealthy and fast. Jenny was a sly, deadly, assassin; secret agent 00-hate with her stupid dog-faced bodyguard. Joe was more than willing to stomp happy people wherever they lurked. Tommy's imaginings helped him feel brave and in control.

Miss Bell stopped Joe at the entrance lifting her delicate hand in the air. "Stop and say good morning, Joe." Miss Bell prodded with a raised eyebrow.

"Good morning, Joe."

Miss Bell let him pass.

"Good morning, Jenny," Miss Bell said.

"*Whatever*," Jenny mumbled and rolled her eyes.

"It's *Good morning*, Jenny. Not *whatever*," Miss Bell corrected.

"Morning," Jenny mumbled with fake sincerity. "Whatever," she muttered as soon as she entered the room.

Tommy swam in behind Lana's floppy dog-eared purse. Lana turned to him. "Oh, good morning Tommy!"

Tommy thought he'd been invisible until she greeted him. "Oh. Hi Lana." He scooted in expecting to see Jake seated. He hadn't arrived.

Jenny whipped around to target Lana as soon she sat down next to Dina. She barked-coughed and said, "How's the new puppy, Lana?"

Lana shrugged and looked confused by her question. "I don't have one, Jenny."

"Sure, you do. I saw you talking with the widdle-piddle-puppy, Tommy Delo." Jenny pointed toward Tommy and panted like a dog.

"You're not funny at all," Lana spat.

Jenny snickered. Her friend Sally pretended she had pom-poms in her hands and said, "Rah, rah, Jenny! I think you are hysterical."

Jeff strode into room 10 like the mayor of sixth grade. "Miss Bell!" He edged between students to greet his teacher.

"Jeff," Miss Bell cast her glowing smile in his direction.

Tommy saw the Human Torch's face flame scarlet red to match his hair.

As he waited for Jake, Tommy amused himself taking inventory of his classmates. For instance, he noticed Lana's eyes stuck to Jeff and she studied his every move. So, he guessed Lana must like Jeff. Next, he watched Jenny, who shared secrets with Sally and laughed… even though nothing was funny. Joe-Rex-it-all is a giant-sized pea-brained dinosaur with deadly fists and huge arms and zero manners. Other kids avoided him. Tommy considered the other students in the room. Who are they? Are they lost at sea with him? Or are they happily afloat?

Jeff handed Miss Bell a note from the office. "I'm in charge of morning announcements starting next week, so I'll be a few minutes late for homeroom…if that's alright," Jeff said.

Miss Bell didn't even open the note, but smiled. "Of course, Jeff." Miss Bell's lips turned up in a crescent moon.

A rush of red splotches bloomed up Jeff's neck.

He drew his hand up to cover it. "I have allergic hives. Thanks, Miss Bell," Jeff wiped his damp brow. He sat in a front-row seat claiming a spot near Jake and Tommy. Jeff sat down and dug an arsenal of school supplies from his cargo pants pockets.

Tommy imagined Jeff's pockets were as big as a magician's hat. He almost expected him to pull a white rabbit out by the ears. He watched in amazement as Jeff unearthed an assortment of notepads, mechanical pencils and pens, lining them up like soldiers ready to do battle. As swift as an eagle, Jeff opened his notebook, clicked his pen, a sword of truth, and was ready for action.

Jake sauntered into the room as leisurely as if time didn't exist. He greeted Jeff and Tommy with a lazy grin. No one rushed Jake. On his way in, he winked to several girls, then sat down next to Tommy. "I got a ghost busting book. We can try it out afterschool."

"Guess what. I finally found the artifact," Tommy whispered.

"Where?"

"It was back on the same shelf we checked after school yesterday," Tommy said.

"Totally weird…I can't wait to see it close up."

Miss Bell walked over to Dina. "Dina, you were in Miss Cree's last year, weren't you?" Miss Bell inquired.

Joe let out a low wolf whistle at the mention of Miss Cree's name.

Miss Bell zeroed in on Joe's face. "Air leak Joe?"

Caught, Joe flinched and shrugged his shoulders. "Just gas."

"Yes, she was our student teacher," Dina stated firmly. "But *someone* made her quit last June." She tossed an accusatory glance in Joe's direction. "*Someone* made her cry."

Joe stared at his mud-caked dirt bike boots slamming the them on the tile floor.

"I was so disappointed to hear she left Hope. Students don't know how good they had it. Miss Cree was a *wonderful, and creative* teacher." Miss Bell clicked her tongue. Her eyes zeroed in on Joe.

Joe kept staring at his boots.

"I agree," Dina stated. "Miss Cree was so nice."

Miss Bell's eyes lit on Jenny. "*Too nice*, perhaps."

When Tommy turned around, Joe appeared to be studying the laces on his oversized boots. Joe stomped his feet together. Bits of caked mud drop on the tiles to mark his territory in the back row.

Tommy watched Miss Bell scroll the word 'homework' on the white board with a cherry red marker. He followed her graceful hand doing a ballet as she created fancy bubble letters, turning the 'o' into a heart with a smiley face inside of it.

Tommy held his head in his hands. "Homework," he muttered. Fancy letters didn't dress up the fact he'd have work to do after school. He finally understood dad's funny expression, "You can put lipstick on a pig but it's still a pig." Homework was a time hog.

She drew a big red balloon and wrote, "Part one of your project is due 9/27. You'll have two other due dates before the oral presentations in early November." Mark the due date in your agendas, please. Chop, chop!" She clapped her hands to move the slow pokes along.

Tommy watched Jeff jot every word Miss Bell uttered. Jake was writing too, so he figured he'd do the same. He wrote: *Tuesday partner report due*. Like a good detective, he stopped writing to listen for important clues.

"This is a long-range study. You'll have ample time to research before you present your findings," Miss Bell said.

Tommy wrote, '*research*'.

"Start early— finish *on time*," Miss Bell suggested.

Tommy wrote, 'on time.'

Miss Bell gave a nod of approval at Jeff's intense concentration.

Tommy waved an anxious hand.

"Yes, Tommy?" Miss Bell paused.

"What are we going to research?"

"Glad you asked!" Miss Bell heard the groans. "Why the sad faces? History is an exciting adventure where the past and the present collide. Your first assignment is to research an old object, family possession, or heirloom. Old items tell a story of the past. *Her story, or his story*, as it were, is our '*History*'." Miss Bell wrote the word *History* in squiggly cursive writing. She laughed at her own joke, which fell flat on most of her audience.

Tommy jotted the word, *History*. He got her joke!

His eyes glimmered and he grinned, encouraged. He waved his hand. "Miss Bell, what's a hair-loom? Is that like a weaving thingy? Or a hair clip?"

Jake shot him the 'you're about to say something stupid' warning face, but it was too late.

"Neither," she said. "That's an excellent question, Tommy."

Muffled laughter ensued. He was used to asking dumb questions. Only he didn't know they were dumb until *after* he asked them. How would his classmates ever believe he was smart if he couldn't figure out what not to ask?

Jake leaned in and whispered, "Vocab error dude."

Miss Bell held up an old metal pot. "This is an old pot passed down from my grandmother. An *heirloom* is an old object that a family owns or passes down through time. Any object older than 50 years would be suitable for our purposes. The object you select is your choice."

Jake leaned forward as if he didn't know the word either, but Tommy knew he did.

"Any questions?" Miss Bell asked.

No one raised a hand. Tommy had lots of questions, but decided not to risk embarrassment. He'd wait and see if he could catch on.

"Now then, let's refer to last night's paragraph passage: Please answer the following question and pass it back to me. Do you think Pharaoh Khafra was a fair leader? Support your answer with a reason."

Various moans filled the room.

Tommy did his homework so he finished his answer and passed it in. He wasn't done last this time —Joe was.

Miss Bell stacked the homework papers in a neat pile. "Visit Mrs. Reed in our media center as soon as you've decided upon your subject of study. I've informed Miss Prim, the town librarian, of our study theme as well."

Tommy's mind spun like a wheel. He leaned in toward Jake. "The artifact would be perfect if it stays put."

Jake made a funny face, like he didn't understand what Tommy meant by it.

"Study buddy, Lil T?" Jake gestured a shazam finger wiggly handshake.

"Study buddy." Tommy returned the handshake in agreement. Tommy waved his hand like a pirate's flag.

"Yes, Tommy?" Miss Bell tipped her perfect jaw his way. Her red apple earrings swung and danced on her earlobes.

"Jake and I would like to partner up."

"Jake, is this partnership amenable to you?" Miss Bell caught Jake's dark lashed eyes.

Jake lit with enthusiasm. "Yes, Miss Bell. It would be great."

Tommy was thrilled. Cool kid Jake wanted to be his partner. This time, he wasn't last picked, like in basketball, volley ball, or baseball. This time he was picked first.

Jenny crossed her arms and placed a pout on her rosebud lips.

Joe raised his hand. "Can I study my gym socks? They have a great story to tell."

Miss Bell smiled, "Smelly socks will earn a smelly grade, Joe."

The children laughed at Miss Bell's answer to Joe.

Tommy heard Joe stomp his boots on the floor like he was angry.

Jenny turned around from the second row pursed her strawberry pink lips like a flower bud and blew Joe a kiss.

Miss Bell ignored Joe's boot slamming and said, "That's a fine idea. Yes, Tommy, you can pair up with Jake."

Tommy's joy bubbled up all over his face. "I found a special hair-loom on top of the shelf at our shop."

"How exciting!" Miss Bell's eyes glimmered, "That *heirloom* will make a fine research. I'll be thrilled to know what you find out about it."

Miss Bell turned back to Joe.

"Joe. Let's meet after school to hash out a suitable idea for you."

Joe tightened his fists. Anger rose up in his voice like a tidal wave. "I can't. I'm not missing football for a dumb report."

"I agree. It would be a shame to miss practice due to your stinky sock dilemma. Perhaps you'll think of something before class ends today. How about it, Joe?" Her voice was light and airy, as if she said, *have a nice day*. Miss Bell won the battle.

Tommy couldn't help but turn around and look at Joe. It was kind of like when you pass a car accident. It's wrong to stare and shouldn't, but you do. He had to admit, he felt a bit of satisfaction from Joe's distress.

"Sure." Joe knocked the heels of his boots together and dropped bits of dirt on the floor.

Miss Bell's lips curved like a melon slice. "Joe? Please bring the dustpan back to your seat to clear up the dirt you left with your boots."

Joe's stomped his feet to the front of the room like giant ogre. He grabbed the dustpan in his meaty fist and glared at Tommy as he passed by him.

Jenny turned her head and barked a "Woof" to Tommy.

Miss Bell must have heard Jenny because her eyes leveled at her and she said, "Do you need a gulp of water, Jenny? Seems you have a *bark* stuck in your craw."

"No, I'm fine, Miss Bell. Just a nasty cough." She put a breath mint in her mouth as part of the pretense.

"Nasty it is, dear." Miss Bell said, folding her arms over her chest.

Lana threw a hand over her mouth to muffle a giggle.

Jenny whipped around and sneered at Lana.

Tommy thought Miss Bell got her point across very nicely.

Jenny waited until Miss Bell turned from her. If looks could kill, Miss Bell would have been dead meat. "Miss Bell? Isn't it *cheating* to let the new kid have a partner, and not the rest of us?"

Tommy turned to Jenny to ask, "Why do you care so much about what I do?"

"I don't." She shot Tommy eye daggers. A twinge of jealousy pinched like new party shoes. She wore a fake innocent smile said to Miss Bell, "Maybe Jake will do *all* Tommy's work and that's unfair." Jenny turned to Jake and her eyes flashed a red warning signal.

Tommy realized she was out to get both of them.

"Would you like to partner up, too Jenny?" Miss Bell asked with a lifted brow.

"I would like to partner with Beth, but only if it's not *cheating*." Jenny's false sincerity dripped like honey from her lips.

"Are you amendable to this?" Miss Bell asked Beth.

Tommy heard Beth's soft voice say, "I'm not sure, Miss Bell."

Jenny clasped her hands and raised her voice. "Bestie? How about it? Come on, Beth, please?" She batted her eyelashes and pleaded.

Tommy wondered why Jenny wanted to be Beth's partner so badly. She wasn't even nice to her.

"I guess so...." Beth muttered.

Girls made no sense. Did Beth hope Jenny's glittery stardust of popularity would rub off on her?

Miss Bell's heels clickety-clacked against the tile floor as she headed toward Tommy.

Her eyes danced with delight. "Grandpapa told the strangest stories about the artifact. I have vague memories of them, since I was young."

Tommy wondered what her grandfather knew about the artifact.

After the class ended, Tommy glanced at Beth's heart shaped doodle. The initials J.S. were hiding in the flower blooms, but he saw them. Beth swiped her hand over the design to hide it from him, but it was too late. He already saw it. "Nice doodle."

Beth looked guilty, as if she just swiped a cookie. She snapped her spiral notebook shut. Then left the room leaving Jenny and Sally to whisper together.

After class, Tommy walked behind Jenny and Sally. He overheard them talking.

Sally said, "Miss Bell is super mean to poor Joey. I wouldn't miss *my cheer* practice for *anything*. Cheering is *my life*."

"I agree! I'll never miss cheer practice. You-know-who will do the report for me, just like last year." Jenny flung her arm over Sally's shoulder and giggled.

Then it dawned on him, Jenny accused Tommy of being lazy because Jenny wanted Beth to do the report for her. It was just like Jake said. Jenny was not Beth's true friend.

Sally raised up imaginary pom poms. "Cheering is our life, Bestie. Rah, Rah, Rah."

Jenny repeated her. "Rah, Rah, Rah. Cheer or die!" She glanced back at Tommy. "What are you staring at, Mutt?"

Jake walked up behind Tommy before he could come up with a comeback answer.

He tapped Tommy on the shoulder.

Jenny blew Jake a kiss which he blocked with his outturned palm.

Jenny huffed, insulted, and turned around.

Tommy leaned in. "What's with her?"

Jake waved his arm. "Who knows, Lil T. She must have some convoluted reason only making sense to her and brainless Sally."

"I guess." Tommy thought, if Jake didn't understand girls, how would he ever figure them out? "I'm glad Miss Bell let us work together."

"Me too."

CHAPTER 18

Friends

After school

Tommy glanced at the wall clock— 3:00 pm, twenty minutes left before the dismissal bell. He watched Jake and Jeff pull out notebooks and start homework. Last year, he would've wasted time telling dumb jokes with Petey, but not this year. This year, he was smart.

He opened his notebook and jotted answers to the math equations. "Super easy," Tommy murmured. He put the completed homework into the new red folder Mom bought him, then stuffed it into his backpack. He bubbled with anticipation for the dismissal bell. Today he could prove to

Jake he actually owned the artifact before it spun off somewhere. He crossed his fingers and wished it would still be in the Crow's Nest after school. Tommy leaned over to Jake. "You're coming over after school, right?"

Jake closed his notebook and looked up. "That's the plan, Lil T. Are you sure it's alright with your mom?"

Relieved, he sighed. "She's fine with it."

"I'm anxious to see the artifact." Jake said.

"If it didn't fly away."

Jake raised a brow. "Fly away?"

Tommy waved his hand. "Awww, just kidding." Not.

The dismissal bell sounded at 3:20. Tommy jetted to his locker with Jake on his heels.

"See you at the double doors in five, Big J." He turned the padlock dial and opened his locker. "What the heck." Confused, he checked the number outside of the locker to see if he opened the wrong one. But it was his. He pulled an old leather journal with an embossed cover from the shelf. He untied the leather string, and peeked inside. It said, *Visit*

Mr. Bell in fancy cursive. He stuffed the journal into his bookbag and ran to meet Jake at the door. The words sunk back into the pages and disappeared from view.

Jake tapped Tommy on the shoulder.

"T, what took you so long?"

"I'll show you." He unzipped his bookbag. But the journal was gone. "Never mind." He hoped Jake couldn't hear the disappointment in his voice.

They left the building. The crossing guard tooted her red whistle and waved them on. Tommy furrowed his brow and cast his eyes around.

"I have to be honest—it would be classic Joe to follow you home and punch you into a new time zone. But he won't try if you're with me. I had plans to follow you home."

Tommy stuffed in his fear down into his belly. He hoped he wouldn't explode from it. Joe wouldn't dare hurt him with Jake at his side... at least that was what he hoped.

"You seem worried. How long has the Neanderthal been after you?"

"Since day one. But it's no big deal." He lied and

shrugged his thin shoulders.

Tommy edged closer to the stone overpass bridge, walking single file with Jake behind him and he in the lead.

"I got your back, Lil T…literally."

"Geez, thanks." Relief washed over Tommy like a cool wave on a hot day.

After they passed over the bridge, Jake moved up next to him. They continued the uphill climb on Main Street heading toward the Trout Alley path and Walnut side street. "No prob-lem-o. That's what good friends do." Jake turned to give the secret shazam finger wiggle handshake.

Jake pulled closer to Tommy. "I knew it. T, don't panic but Joe is hiding in the bushes near the Trout Alley sign. He must be waiting for you since he lives in the opposite direction."

"Let's make a run for it," Tommy felt his stomach rumble. His feet double timed to Bell's Treasure Trove. "Safe." He said.

"You're fast." Jake said. He pointed to the shop sign. "When are you getting a new name for the shop?"

"Mom asked me to come up with a better name than *Trash or Treasure*. She says no one wants to buy trash. I suggested *Timeless Treasures*. What do you think?"

"I'd have to agree with your mom. Trash is an offensive term. I like *Timeless Treasures, or Curio for the Curious*. Hey, how about, *It's Better Than Online?*"

"How do you know so many words, Big J?"

Jake tipped his chin in thought. "I'm an avid reader, but I never advertise it at school. I study on my own terms, when I choose— not before. I learned, way back in third grade; fast finishers get tons of busy work. I coast, enjoying the ride."

Tommy pondered. "I can give you great pointers on being done last." He gave a nervous laugh. "Aren't there special classes for smart kids like you? I know there's classes for dumb kids... *like me*." Tommy's voice quavered, hoping Jake wouldn't agree.

"For the record, I don't think you're dumb. You're in advanced math, just like I am."

"I guess I'm pretty good at math. You're also really popular with girls."

"It's true. My dad shows me the ropes." Jake

grinned his white teeth. "My trusted circle is reserved for you and Jeff, which is high praise since I'm very *discriminating* with friendships."

Jake said discriminating like a compliment, so Tommy smiled. But his math placement was surely a mistake. He'd have to confess it to Jake, who was already becoming his closest friend. He sucked in his breath and said, "I'm pretty good at math, but the office must have made a huge mistake with my placement."

"Did the office tell you they goofed? How do you know?"

"No, but I'm not smart enough to be in advanced *anything*, unless they give out awards for vocabulary screw ups, poor spelling, or asking stupid questions."

"You finished all the worksheets, right?"

"They don't count, since they were easy and from the substitute."

"How'd you do on your state tests?"

"I have no freaking idea. Dad was in the hospital for months. School stuff wasn't on my mind...and truth... I had trouble at school even before he got sick." Tommy didn't want to mention the counselor, his anger outbursts, gassy stomach, or the bad thing he yelled to Harv right before his best friend moved away to California. How could Harv ever understand? He just couldn't bear one more person leaving him. So, instead of "Good bye, Harv, I'll miss you. Enjoy California." Tommy yelled the most awful thing he could think of. "Good riddance. I hate you." Then, he just let Harv move away. He didn't mean to be so terrible to him. Harv must have been hurt and steaming mad at him. He couldn't even tell Mom.

"I'm sorry about your Dad, T. That's a lot for a kid to handle."

"Do you think best friends can ever forgive each other?" Guilt sucker punched Tommy in the gut. He didn't want to lose Jake by saying or doing something hurtful.

Jake tossed an arm over Tommy's shoulder. "I know I could."

Tommy waved his hand to change the subject. "Does your dad know you're coming over?"

"He's working late, as usual. Can I borrow your cell to call him? I ran out of minutes chatting it up with Felicity, a college girl I met last year."

Tommy shook his head. "A college girl? You call a college girl?"

"She thinks of me like her little brother. Hey, whatever works. I still get to call her." Jake high fived Tommy and burst into a laughter.

"Whatever works!" Tommy repeated. "If I had a cell phone, I'd let you use it. Maybe I'll get one for my birthday."

"When's your birthday?" Jake asked tipping his chin.

"November 4th."

"We'll have to celebrate, T."

"When's yours?" Tommy asked.

"August first. I turned twelve this past summer."

Jake stood a head ahead taller and was only three months older. It just wasn't fair. Tommy took the key from his backpack and unlocked the door. "We're hoping to get the shop up and running in a month or two. You can use the cordless phone on the counter."

Tommy and Jake walked in the cleared aisle right down the middle of the shop. It led to a central desk and the stairwell leading to the second floor. "Maybe we can head to your place sometime?"

Jake said, "It's lonely at my place, T. Dad works all the time. Pizza is good, but I'd like a home cooked meal once in a while. Dad's not much of a cook."

"I'm glad I can share my mom with you. She says home cooking is healthier for me, but I think fast food is way more fun."

Jake hit the numbers into the keypad. "Yeah, Dad. Treasure Trove on Main. She's good with it, Tommy said. Pick me up here. Uh huh. Sure. Ok. Thanks." He turned to Tommy. "Is it ok if I ask Dad to pick me up after 6:00?"

"Sure!"

"After 6:00 is good." Jake placed the phone in the upright stand.

A chink of metal to metal rang out from the front of the shop. The globe tipped over, crashing from top tier of the shelf. It hit the floor with a bang. "What the… " Jake paced toward the shelf. "T, do you have a ladder? I'll put the globe back on the shelf for you."

Tommy threw a hand to his forehead. "Again?"

He pointed to far corner of the shop. "Sure. Against the wall." He helped Jake drag the tall metal ladder over to the blue shelf. Jake climbed up the rungs with the globe in hand. "I don't believe it! Your artifact is sitting on the shelf. I can see it!" He pushed his arm back to retrieve it. His fingers grazed the metal. "Got it! Geez, it's burning hot!" Jake drew his hand back and turned to Tommy. "I'm going to try again." He pushed his hand back. "Ouch! What the… It nipped my fingers." He climbed back down.

"Told you so." Tommy folded his arms and raised a brow.

"Maybe I can try to get it down with a broom handle."

With a snap of light, the wheel spun up to the ceiling and disappeared through a crack of light.

Jake whipped around. "No way! Did you just see that?"

"I've been trying to tell you. Every day, I put it in the Crow's Nest, but it moves around on its own. Once it even turned up in my locker at school and then it disappeared by the end of the day."

Jake gave Tommy a side eye as they walked around the shop. "Is that why you couldn't show it to me when I asked you at school?"

"It is. But I know it sounds crazy."

"Do you mind if I look around at the shop for a few minutes until I calm down?" Jake said.

"Might as well. You believe me now, right?" Tommy shoved his hands to his hips. He toyed with telling Jake about the voice, but held back.

"I do…completely." Jake took a few deep breaths. He picked up a few items to examine them. "Ok, better now."

"This way," Tommy motioned. "I'll introduce you to my mom." They climbed to the second level. "Mom, I'm home! My buddy Jake's with me."

She held out a tray of cookies. "Hi Jake. Hi Punkin. Help yourself. I just made them.'"

"See? Your mom makes snacks." Jake smiled.

"Mom, I told you not to use my baby name!" Tommy grumbled.

Jake waved his hand. "No worries, 'Lil T. My dad calls me Squirt, which is way worse than Punkin."

Tommy's hand covered his mouth to cover a giggle. "Sure is!"

"Pinky swear we keep our baby names a secret." Jake gripped Tommy's pinky in his.

"I swear." Jake took a cookie and was ready to take a bite.

"Be warned— my mom hates gluten, sugar, and junk food. She calls them Frankenfoods." Tommy laughed.

"Noted." Jake took a bite.

"He's right, you know. The body is a temple for the soul." Mom added with a finger shake.

"If that's true, my soul is made of Doritos, pizza, and cola." Jake grinned and stuffed a cookie into his mouth.

"I'm literally made of junk food."

Mom's questioning eyes caught Tommy's. "Homework?"

"Got it handled, Mom. I already finished my super easy math sheet from the fake math teacher. Mr. Taylor is not off leave yet," Tommy said.

"I'm impressed," she said with a smile.

"Hey, Mrs. Delo, my dad renovates historic buildings. I'll bet he'd work wonders here."

"I'm on a shoestring budget, at least 'till we get the shop up and running." Her voice trailed away.

Tommy cast his eyes to his sneakers. "We can't even afford shoelaces and I'm too old to wear Velcro."

"You're a funny kid," Jake chuckled. "Good play on words, T."

Tommy didn't know what was so funny about his shoelaces or what words Jake thought he played with.

"I'll be here or on the shop level sorting trash from treasure if you need me," Mom said.

"See? It would have been a *great* name for the shop," Tommy insisted. "Mom, how about Tommy's Timeless Treasures?"

"Hmmm. I'll think on it!" she said.

"I wish I had a mom to bring me cookies —even ones that taste like sawdust with brown pebbles in them." Jake took a swig of juice. "But I ate them, anyway."

"Gluten and taste free. Yum." Tommy grinned.

"I'm dying to see the mysterious object up close. Will it come back?"

"It always does, once its ready. In the meantime, follow me up to my secret hideout on the third floor."

Tommy touched the rim on the door frame and it opened with a click. He headed up the narrow and hidden staircase. "It hasn't returned. Sometimes it's on my pillow or the nightstand."

Suddenly, a bright glow filled the room. Jake's eyes widened and he took a few steps back. "T, I think I found your artifact." He pointed to the copper object whirring in the air.

Tommy watched the object spin then blast into a beam of white light and disappear again. "No way! I never saw it do that before!"

Jake flung his hand to his forehead. "I don't believe my eyes."

"Told you so."

"What now?"

"We have to wait for it to come back here. But that can take a while."

"I'm stunned. Sorry I doubted you. I might as well take a load off." Jake sat in the blue bean bag chair, and Tommy plopped down on the sleeping bag. They placed a round of cards.

The prayer wheel jettisoned through the ceiling of the shop. She couldn't get much rest with the boys so interested in studying her. So, she spun away to a great stone castle in Old England. She'd find a way to help Tommy with his Joe problem. She'd need to convince Tommy to bring her to school, then get Joe to take a time trip. But how? Tommy would have to think it was his own idea. She could feel his fear of Joe. She considered another option. She could enter Jake's mind and have him come up with a plan to share with Tommy. She was sure Tommy would agree with any idea Jake gave him. Satisfied, she spun back to the 3rd floor room so Tommy could show her off to Jake. It was the perfect time to send her message to Tommy's friend.

An eerie glow filled the room. A snap of light cracked and the artifact dropped down on the box next to the sleeping bag. A soft glow emanated from it.

"It's back!" Jake exclaimed.

Tommy's face wrinkled up "Told you so." Tommy asked the artifact, "Where have you been?"

Jake reached over to grasp the artifact then dropped it. "Damn! You're right. It bites, like a static shock on my fingertips. I'd like to examine it. How about you hold it. Bring it to the window where's there's more light."

"Good idea." Tommy held it and it warmed in his hands like melted butter.

"Turn it slowly so I can see each side."

Tommy rotated the barrel. Sunlight glinted off the copper surface.

"Interesting writing. Lucky for us, I just happen to know a prof at the college who can assist us. He'll translate these inscriptions. Put this thing in a safe place."

"I do —every stinking time and I still have a daily scavenger hunt." Tommy took the pillow from this bed and propped it under the artifact. He laid it on the box near the sleeping bag. "Stay here." Tommy spoke to the object. "There's more, Jake. Sometimes, I think I know where it goes. I have visions so real it's like I'm there with it. Do you remember when I got sunburned in reading class? I was daydreaming about being in the desert!"

"Maybe you're linked to it mind to mind," Jake suggested. "Hey, wouldn't it be something if you can zap Joe through a time trip? It would teach him a lesson."

"Yeah, that would be something," Tommy said. "But you're kidding, right?"

"I'm not sure that I am."

Tommy turned to Jake. "How do you know the professor?"

"He's friends with my dad. When I chose to do a personal enrichment study at the Cathedral College last summer, Prof said to feel free to contact him. This would be one of those times."

"You took a class at real college?"

"Sure did. The buildings look like old English castles… and then there's the girls…so many pretty girls…" Jake gestured an hourglass shape with his hands. "Stacy interned last year. It's how I got to know her."

"Oh yeah… girls." Tommy winked and played along, but didn't have the same obsession Jake seemed to have. He wished his dad was around to ask about puberty. When would it happen for him?

"Nice of him to help us for free," Tommy muttered.

"Naw, Dude, the college pays him when he works. *Feel free* means he'll help us because he wants to, you know, *gratis, pro bono*. He's offering his time."

Tommy locked his new words away.

"Let's head downstairs. I'd like to look around at the stuff you're going to sell," Jake said.

"Sure. If you want anything, let us know. I'm the co-manager and Mom's ordering business cards with my name on them." They headed down to the store level.

"Nice." Jake walked to the shelf tagged *1700-1800* toys. "Hey, look at this old steel penny bank." He lifted it up to examine it.

"It's a bank? I thought it was just a toy." Tommy leaped over a full box of garbage to investigate.

"Watch this." Jake pulled a coin from his jeans pocket. "You insert a penny in the dog's mouth, then you crank the dog's tail up and down. The penny shoots from its mouth to the back of the bank, then the dog plops the penny into the bucket. Watch this!"

Tommy bent over laughing. "That's awesome. Mom *can't* sell this."

Jake stopped and lifted the acoustic guitar. He ran his hand over the flower painted around the hole of the instrument. "Weird. I've seen this before." He picked the guitar up and traced the edges of it with his hand. He strummed a few chords. "It's a beauty!" He peered into the center of the guitar. The initials S. R. scratched inside the guitar's hole. "I didn't notice this before." Jake's skin prickled. His mother's name was Sunshine. Was this just a weird coincidence or something more?

"Geez, you even play guitar? You could be a rock star."

"I just fool around with the strings a bit. I was really little, but I still remember the songs my mom played to me." His face was wistful and sad.

Tommy assumed Jake was thinking about his mom leaving him. "Do you have any sisters or brothers?"

"Naw, it's just dad and I... two lonely bachelors."

Tommy watched a cloud drift over Jake's face. "That's what I thought." He didn't want Jake to feel so sad. "I get lonely sometimes without a sister or a brother." *Or my dad,* he thought.

"I know what you mean. Mom took her guitar and left us when I was two. Dad raised me by himself. He did his best, but he's not a mom. He says it wasn't my fault she left us— but who knows? Maybe she didn't want a screaming kid like me on her hip. She never did come back home, so...."

Tommy saw Jake's face torque as if he swallowed a rock by mistake. Jake quickly hid behind an 'everything's fine' smile. His mother wore the same lie on her face when Dad was ill, so he wasn't fooled by Jake's pretense. "Mom says bad things happen to good people sometimes."

"Thanks, 'Lil T. Water under the proverbial bridge." Jake perked up a bit. "What happened to your dad, Tommy?" Jake's eyebrows furrowed with concern.

"He was really sick for a year. One day he went to the hospital, and... he didn't come back home. You and I...we're kind of the same, aren't we?"

"Appears so," Jake looped his thumb into his pocket. "We have each other now, 'Lil T."

"We do." Tommy couldn't believe Jake understood him so well. "I wish I could talk about my own dad in an alive-way instead of the *gone*-way.

Let's head up to the Crow's Nest."

"My dad likes you, T. You can borrow him any time."

"You can borrow my Mom too, but don't try to kiss her," Tommy warned.

"Don't worry, I won't. You know, my dad could work miracles in this old place." He waited for Tommy's smile in agreement.

Tommy frowned and knit his brows. "We don't have much money, not even for shoe strings. Mom said so."

Jake smirked. "T, a shoe string budget means your mom is careful with her money. It's an old saying."

"Oh. So, I don't have to worry about wearing shoelaces?"

"Not unless you want to," Jake laughed. "My dad offered to help her."

Tommy ran the word in his mind. *"Pro boner?"*

Jake burst out in laughter. "The correct word is pro bono, but pro-boner works too."

When Tommy heard the words in his own ears, he realized his obvious error. His hand flew to his mouth and he giggled. "I didn't mean it the way it sounded."

Jake joined in laughter. "Your mom's *really* pretty. Haven't you noticed me gawking at her?"

"I did and it's gross." Tommy gagged and lolled his tongue.

He placed a hand on Tommy's shoulder. "Don't get your tightie-whities in a bunch, Lil T. I have my sights set on the formidable Miss Bell." Jake made an uncharacteristic silly face just to make Tommy laugh at him.

"It's six-o-clock already. I hear Dad's horn. Gotta' go." Jake grabbed his backpack and dashed out the door of the shop.

"See you tomorrow!" Jake waved goodbye and hopped into the Ford pickup truck.

"Hey Dad. What gives? Why didn't you come in?" Jake asked.

"I'm filthy and I smell like a goat. Next time, Squirt."

"Don't wait too long, Dad. Mrs. Delo is really pretty."

Jake's dad gave him a sideways smile. "I remember."

CHAPTER 19

Sasquatch foot

11:40 am Media

For the first time in his 11 ¾ years, Tommy surprised himself because he wanted to visit the media center. Armed with a secret mission —he'd pretend to be a detective searching for clues. If the artifact was haunted, he'd need to know how to fix it and pronto.

Tommy dashed in to the large book filled room. He glanced up at the blue poster hanging from the ceiling. Big red letters advertised *Imagine*! Tommy was a champion imaginer, but it always got him into trouble. Teachers used code letters, like A.D.D. to describe his imagination. Mom said it meant he had trouble sitting still. But here, right in the media center, a poster celebrated it like party balloons on his birthday. Right then, he decided he liked the media room.

Tommy wandered through the maze of shelves. *I should have paid better attention to the Dewey Decimal System, then I'd know what to Dewey.* He laughed at his clever pun. He drowned amongst the ABC's on the shelves, gasping for air. His classmates had only been there a short time and they already toted book selections to the main desk. But here he was, still struggling for a breath of air. He checked the wall clock ticking away time and his pun was no longer fun.

Tommy watched in awe as Jeff headed to the counter. Each one of his books sported a colorful tag hanging out of the pages like bird feathers. Tommy grunted. Jeff not only found books in fifteen minutes flat, but he had enough time to mark the important pages. He wished he had colorful tags so he'd look just as smart as Jeff. *Last done Tommy, at it again*, he grumbled. He gripped his churning stomach and released an air biscuit, silent but deadly. He dashed into the next aisle to avoid being discovered as the culprit.

Joe bellowed, "Dude, who laid a fart?"

Tommy heard a girl answer Joe from behind a tall shelf. "Whoever smelt it dealt it."

Then he saw Dina and Lana peer around the corner, each hugging an armful of books. "Hi Tommy," Dina said.

Lana waved.

"I'm trying to find the right book," Tommy said, trying to excuse his empty hands.

"Do you need help?" Dina asked.

Tommy wanted to shout out, Yes! But he was determined to appear smart, especially to her. "No. I can find it."

"Ok." Dina and Lana headed away.

He wished he asked Dina for help, but it was too late. Time slipped away like sand through his fingertips. *I have zilch, nada, nothing, a big goose egg.* He scolded himself. Last year, the counselor told him, "Don't be your own worst enemy, Tommy. Be patient with yourself." How could he be patient when bells and clocks rushed him. Plus...it was dumb to tell a kid who just lost his dad to be patient... when his dad was a patient. Tommy skirted the aisles to avoid Joe-Rex-it-all lumbering around the corners like a brainless dinosaur. In a strange way, he felt sorry for Joe.

Beth trailed behind Jenny with her purple wireframes peeking out over the high stack she carried. Jenny pranced ahead of Beth, freehanded, swinging a fluffy pink purse. She opened the catch, re-glossed her lips, pursed them, then ordered Beth around with a Miss America hand wave, "Follow me, Beth."

Beth huffed and set a heavy pile of books on the counter with a thud.

Tommy passed Beth and gave her a sympathetic smile. He still had no selections of his own. He walked back into the aisles drowning in the sea of titles. He pretended to read the spines with great interest, treading water, hoping for a life raft to save him from a watery death. If only Jake was in the same media class, he'd rescue him. He didn't know Jeff well enough to ask him for help. He was just about ready to beg Dina for help when Mrs. Reed strode over.

Mrs. Reed's must have recognized the lost-at-sea look on his face because she said, "May I assist you, young man?" Her face crinkled with grandmotherly concern.

Time Wheel Book 1

Tommy sucked in a relieving breath of air. "Yes, I'm trying to find a particular subject about my artifact from a faraway place. I'm just having trouble finding it." Tommy tried to sound as smart as Jake by using big words, like particular. He hesitated. "And for leisure reading, I'd enjoy a book on ghost-busting." There, he said it.

"I see. Follow me," Mrs. Reed walked ahead of him. Her sturdy heels moved in silence upon the ocean blue fish designed carpet runner.

Tommy noticed the pirate poster waving above him. Printed on a big ship were the words, "Arrg you ready to read daily?" He remembered the last trip to Disney when Dad was well. He loved the pirate ride. Dad bought him a black eye patch and hat. Tommy pretended he rode on a creaky pirate's ship cresting mighty waves and being fearless. Pirates had no need for books. He counted the starfish on the carpet runners and walked heel-toe, heel-toe behind Mrs. Reed. *One, two, three, four, walk the plank. Five, six, seven, eight, Kerplop into a sea of books.*

Mrs. Reed stopped short.

Tommy plowed right into the back of her.

"Oh, my goodness!" She lifted a brow.

"Oops." He dug his sneakers into the carpet runner and tipped his head sideways like a puppy begging for forgiveness.

Mrs. Reed smiled like his Grandmother used to do. "Tommy is it?"

"Yes, Mrs. Reed. I'm Tommy Delo." He held his hand out to shake hers. "I'm sorry I bumped into you."

"I know you didn't mean to. Are you enjoying Hope School, Tommy? As they say... Hope starts here."

"I guess so. I met a new friend and I like Miss Bell a whole lot."

"What type of heirloom are you researching?"

Tommy's face wore a lopsided grin. "If I knew, I wouldn't need to research it."

"Good point. That's paradox of sorts. Describe it to me so I can narrow your search." Mrs. Reed prompted.

Tommy tried to visualize the artifact. His attention drifted. His raised his chin up to the overhead sign 'Make Time to Read.' He saw a black pirate's flag with skull and crossbones on cover of a giant book.

Mrs. Reed waited for Tommy's attention to return to her. "Tommy?"

Her voice jolted his attention back to the room. "I like pirates. I wish we could study those."

"I can suggest a factual book about Black Beard, the famous pirate of the seas."

"Really? Mrs. Otter says reading about pirates is a waste of time."

"Did she now...." Mrs. Reed looked as if she was holding back words she couldn't say.

"Can you describe your artifact for me?"

"It's metal. Mom thinks it's copper or brass and it might be a prayer wheel. I saw a picture of it on the Internet. I guess it might be from Tibet. It's a can-shaped thing-a-ma-bob with squiggly writing all around it and a little piece of metal attached by a chain. The can part is stuck on a stick, like a lollipop. I twirl the can part on the stick part."

A sparkle lit up in her eyes. "Marvelous! My guess is you have a Dharma or prayer wheel in your possession."

"What's Dharma?"

"It means cosmic order… the right actions. There are many types of prayer wheels used for different purposes. Some are singular, and some are in a group outside of temples." She handed him two heavy bound books. "Is there anything else I can help you with?"

Tommy considered telling her the prayer wheel was probably haunted, but bit his lip and held his secret. "No."

"Jake Stanton was in media earlier today. I take it you're partners with him?"

"I am and we're buddies, too."

"Wonderful. Let's try searching Tibet or Asia. "Please share your findings with me once you are done with your research project. I'd love to see what you find out."

"Sure." He lifted his eyes to the overhead sign displaying the words, 'Time Travel with a Book'. He gave a little giggle. He time traveled with the artifact.

Mrs. Reed tipped her chin trying to capture his eyes and attention once more. "Where did you get it from, may I ask?"

"Mom and I own Bell's Treasure Trove on Main Street. I found it there. I'm thinking of a better name for the store. Mom didn't like Trash or Treasure. We spent all our shoestring money on it…that means we don't have a lot of money."

"I see. I'm glad the shop will be back in business. I loved to browse Bell's place. The owner was such a kind man." She un-shelved a few books and stacked them in his arms. "Here are several book selections to peruse." She tapped the R on the bookbinding. "This R means it's a reference book, so you can't sign it out, but you can use it while in the media center."

"Thanks, Mrs. Reed." A sigh of relief escaped his lips.

"Come to the main desk once you're ready to sign the other books out. We have a good twenty minutes left of class. When you're done, put the reference books on the red cart in the 900's section and I'll find a nice home for them."

Tommy imagined little books drinking hot cocoa and wearing slippers. He walked back under the 'Time to Read' poster and headed to sit on the blue beanbag chair.

He didn't see him coming. Tommy's arms were full when he toppled over a big black dirty boot. Wham! He landed face down on the blue ocean runner. Books were strewn around him. He rubbed his sore nose and sat up.

Joe fake-apologized. "Sorry. Not." His snort sounded like a braying donkey.

Dina scooted by Joe and knelt next to Tommy to help him. She turned to Joe. "You're a major idiot, Joe."

Joe said, "Better a major idiot than minor shrimp." He cast a wary glance toward the circulation desk where Mrs. Reed was busy scanning books. "Don't dare tell." He pumped his fist to warn Tommy and Dina not to tattle on him.

"You don't scare me, Joe," Dina said.

Joe lumbered away and didn't say anything to Dina.

"He's a bully." Dina stacked Tommy's book selections in a neat pile next to the beanbag. "Are you ok?"

Tommy's face flushed red and he felt his armpits get wet and soggy. "I must have tripped over my shoelaces."

"Or a giant Sasquatch foot. You should tell on him."

Tommy studied her long dark lashes. She smelled like a fresh spring day. "Nah, I don't want to get Sassquashed later. Thanks for helping me, Dina." He felt a rush of heat rise up to his cheeks.

"Are you sure?" Her pretty brown eyes caught his. She smelled of soap and flowers.

"Yes." Tommy's face flamed again. Embarrassed, he bent down to lift the book pile and headed to the circulation desk.

Joe and Jenny sneaked out of class early. Tommy guessed Joe was afraid he'd tattle on him. Mrs. Reed was too busy see them leave. Sally tossed a quick look at Tommy and mouthed "Don't tell" as she put a finger on her lips. She sneaked out next.

Mrs. Reed finished checking out a few students and then handed Tommy two books. "Try these."

Tommy read the titles. *It's Only a Ghost and Ghost Clearing 101*. You and Jake must have similar interests. It's no wonder you're friends. He signed a ghost book out earlier today." Mrs. Reed's pink lips curved up in a crinkly smile.

"Thanks a bunch, Mrs. Reed. Do you make apple cobblers?"

"Why do you ask?"

"My Nanny bakes them, but she moved to Florida last month."

She captured his eyes in her own. "I'm sure you miss her very much."

"I miss her a whole bunch. She lived with us when Dad… was sick in the hospital."

She touched his shoulder. "Sorry to hear it. Is Dad better now?"

"Mom says he's in a better place…." He stared down at his shoelaces and squeezed back tears.

"Oh, I'm so sorry, Tommy." Her eyes misted up and she touched his shoulder. "Come see me anytime you need to talk."

"Thanks, Mrs. Reed."

With five minutes to spare at the end of the class, Tommy plopped down on the bright blue bean bag chair and tried to forget cemetery day. He wished he could go home and cry when no one was looking.

He propped the heavy Asia reference book on his lap and flipped through the pages. He stopped when he saw a picture of a row of prayer wheels, just as he'd seen in a dream. Then he turned the page. His heart leaped when he saw a photo resembling his artifact. Tommy jotted the words *prayer wheel and Dharma Wheel* into his notebook and wrote the page number down from the reference book. Before the bell, he set it on the red cart, just like Mrs. Reed told him to do. Tommy checked the school clock. It was already 2:35 and only a few more minutes of media class before heading to Mr. Taylor's class. He was excited to meet the real teacher, who'd been out on leave. But then, it also made him very anxious. He was sure to be found out as a fake. He closed his eyes and made a wish. "I want to be smart."

CHAPTER 20

Advanced Math with Mr. Taylor

The ringer buzzed to signal the end of media class. "Boys and girls, our time is up," Mrs. Reed announced.

Tommy left the media room and scurried to his locker to unload his book selections. His eyes scanned the hallway for Joe. The coast was clear, so he headed to math class, the last section of the day. Today, Mr. Taylor was back from sick leave and he'd finally meet him. He'd be found out for sure. *What if* he was just a dumb kid with someone else's paperwork? *What if* a brilliant math student found themselves sitting in the lowest math class where he supposed to be sitting. The smart kid would complain at the office and Tommy would be kicked out of advanced math. His stomach flipped like an acrobat and churned like an old furnace. His butt cranked out rumbles of acrid steam. "Oh great. Now I have gas," he muttered. Tommy dashed down the hallway to catch up with Jake. "Hey Jake!"

"You'll like Mr. Taylor. He's a quirky dude with a corny sense of humor. Once you get his jokes, you'll figure out how they relate to his math lesson in some weird and convoluted way."

Convoluted. Tommy made a note to define the word. "Does the school ever botch up placements, like sticking a dumb kid in an advanced math class?"

"Not likely, T," Jake said. "I know you're worried, but stop obsessing about it. Trust me, you belong."

"Hey, Jake. Guess what? I found a ghost busting book and information on the artifact. Mrs. Reed thinks we have a prayer or Dharma wheel."

"Sweet! I found some books, too."

"Did you know Dharma means Cosmic order'?" Tommy asked.

"Impressive find. No, I didn't. Can we do research at your place after school?"

"That would be great!" Tommy and Jake slapped hands.

They entered room 24 not seeing the teacher.

Jake turned to Tommy. "I wonder what gives. Don't sit yet."

"Why?"

Students entered the room, mulled around, and glanced at the white board. No one sat.

"Why is everyone standing around?" Tommy asked.

"Mr. Taylor always had a specific seating chart on the board for us," Jake said.

Mr. Taylor's head popped up from behind his metal desk startling Tommy. His classmates giggled and shrieked, also surprised.

"Do I hear the carnival has arrived in town?" A shock of salt and pepper hair stuck up on his head looking like a scared porcupine. His black-framed glasses sat perched on his nose over a furry dark mustache that wiggled whenever he spoke.

"Hey Mr. Taylor!" Jake greeted. "Glad you're back."

"My old ticker is back to business and ready to rumble." He thumped a hand to his heart. "Jake, how-are-ya-doodley, doing?" He wiggled his fat mustache left and right.

Tommy imagined Mr. Taylor wore fake nose glasses, but his nose and mustache were real. He grinned a set of white teeth. His clothes were a menagerie paint box of colors. It was clear to Tommy— Mr. Taylor had his own unique style. He stared at the teacher's huge bow tie decorated with geometric designs and numbers.

Jeff stepped forward and greeted Mr. Taylor with a firm handshake. "Welcome back. Nice tie, Mr. Taylor!"

Mr. Taylor wore a mile-wide smile. "Glad you appreciate my flair for color and geometry." He clicked his tan topsiders together at the heels.

Mr. Taylor eyes crinkled with delight and he addressed the newcomers with a hand wave.

"Where's the seating chart, Mr. Taylor?" Dina giggled. "There's always a chart."

"But not this year." Mr. Taylor beamed. "This year, I'm breaking all the rules... living dangerously, like a trapeze artist with no safety net. Sometimes it takes a brush with death to live life fully."

Tommy wondered if Mr. Taylor had a heart attack.

"Yes, choose your seat ladies and gents. I'm trying something brandy-new."

Jake tugged on Tommy's sleeve. "You heard the man." Jake announced to his peers. "T, let's head over and claim our spots." Jake sat next to Jeff and motioned Tommy to claim a spot next to him.

"Really? We can sit anywhere?" Lana murmured. Her eyes followed Jeff. She wandered over and drifted to an open seat near Jeff and Dina.

"Oh hi, Tommy," Dina said.

Tommy smiled and sat down next to Jake.

"Hey Jake! Hey Tommy." Jeff, The Human Torch toted a spiral pad under his arm, sat down and as usual, pulled an arsenal of mechanical pencils and erasers, from his cargo pants pockets.

"Chill, Dude. Mr. Taylor didn't start class yet," Jake said.

"I like to be prepared," Jeff said.

Reese lumbered into the front row and sat down. Tommy normally didn't notice girl's clothing, but he did recognize Reese's gray sweat suit and sneakers. It was all he saw her in since school started. Most girls worried too much about hair and makeup. But not Reese. Reese turned back to say hello to Dina and Lana. Her eyes stopped at Tommy. The ends of her mouth turned up.

Maybe I should say something nice to her. "Hi Reese. I like your... flute case." It was a dumb thing to say, but he couldn't think of anything else to make her smile.

Reese's eyelashes fluttered. "Oh, thanks, Tommy."

Tommy looked down and caught a glimpse of Mr. Taylor's bright purple and orange argyle socks peeking out from his slacks as he walked toward him.

"And a fine how-are-ya-doodley-doing newbie? If you haven't already guessed, I'm the infamous Mr. Taylor." He extended his hand for a shake.

Tommy shook his hand like Dad showed him and craned it up and down.

"That's a good firm handshake, Tommy Delo."

"You know my name? I'm on your class list?"

Tommy bit his lip, angry for outing himself so soon.

"Darn tootin', young sir." Mr. Taylor tooted a red bicycle horn.

"That's the first time a teacher honked at me!" Tommy broke into laughter.

"But not the last." Mr. Taylor added with a quick left-right moustache wiggle.

Jeff turned to Lana. "Hey Lana." Tommy watched Jeff's face turn red.

Lana folded her arms over her chest and blushed like a ripe apple. "Oh, hey Jeff."

"Well, well, welcome and well wishes on this wonderous Wednesday! I see you've found the perfect seat. Ever since I met the lovely Miss Bell, I've leapt out of my comfort box— or was it Fluffy's litter box?" he muttered. "No matter." He paused for laughter.

"Him too?" Tommy said.

The students joined in with the merriment.

Tommy's ribs ached from laughing so hard.

"Life is too precious to waste. With my ticker healed, I've leaped back into three-ring circle of life and embraced my inner clown." He thumped his chest with his fists.

Tommy bit his lip and watched the door for signs of trouble.

"Dude, if you're worrying about Joe, Jenny, or Sarah—don't," Jake said. "They've never been in advanced math and never will be."

"Looks like the whole circus has arrived! Prepare your fertile minds for puns, funs, and numbers and a smattering of sumptuous, stupendous, sunny September where *angles and sinusoids* exist." He drew a squiggle on the board that looked like a wave.

Tommy breathed a sigh of relief. His *sinusoids* were perfectly clear, or was the word sinuses? More than ever, he wanted to stay out of the lower level math class. It was easy to fool a sub, but this was the real teacher.

"Good afternoon, ladies and gents. It's official. I'm Mr. Taylor, and this is *advanced* math, room 24. If you found yourself in the wrong hemisphere, you have two minutes to boogie on down the hallway to your correct longitude and latitude." He pointed a carved walking stick leaning against the door jam.

Tommy sat up straight and made a serious expression. He wished he wore glasses like Jeff's to appear smarter. He leaned onto one elbow and opening his eyes wide in order to suck up all the smart words he heard.

"Please sign your name on the attendance sheet which is heading in 360 degrees." He made a circle with index finger. "Or should I say, *a-round* the room." He paused to let his joke sink in. "You will work hard, but learn math from new *angles*. What do you call an adorable angle? *Acute* one!"

A good natured groan filled the room.

Tommy couldn't stop laughing at the knee slapping jokes. "I like him," Tommy whispered to Jake.

"I knew you would," Jake said.

"Students are hungry for knowledge at the end of the day. So, I ask you, what kind of meals do math teachers eat? *Square* meals!" He chuckled. "Follow me on this year's magic carpet adventure ride through gastro-math-ology! My punchlines are delicious and you'll eat them up."

Tommy soon realized that Mr. Taylor's riddles and jokes helped him to pay close attention. He laughed so hard, his eyes were teary and his stomach ached. He hadn't checked the clock—not even once. His peers were just as attentive. Mr. Taylor's style wasn't like the drudgery of last year's kill and drill math class. Tommy forgot all concerns and couldn't believe his stroke of luck. He was determined to convince Mr. Taylor he belonged, even if the office made a gigantic mistake.

Mr. Taylor kept cranking out the jokes. "Now then, where were we? Ah yes, what did the tree say to the math teacher? So glad I asked you. Gee-I'm-a-Tree! And my Segway…today, our discussion will be…" He air-quoted. "Quadrilaterals! For those who like to think outside of the box, you might be disappointed today. Today we will be *right inside* the box only, if you catch my *angle*."

"See what I mean?" Jake whispered.

Tommy nodded in agreement.

Mr. Taylor jotted geometric shapes on the white board. He wrote a number in the corners of several angles. "Before I go off on a *tangent*, please copy the shapes on your paper and supply the missing degrees for the remaining angles." He winked at Reese and wiggled his moustache just for her.

Time Wheel Book 1

Reese blushed and giggled.

Tommy copied the angles and quickly filled in the missing numbers easily.

Mr. Taylor wrote the missing numbers in a different color marker. "Check your angles against set A. If you're correct, complete set B. B sure you C if you are correct! It's up to U." He air-quoted again the pun with his fingers.

"Tommy Delo, what did you get for the first one in set B?"

Tommy crossed his fingers. "90 degrees?"

"Right! Or should I say, *right angle*," Mr. Taylor tooted a bicycle horn.

Tommy beamed. All his answers from A and set B were simple.

Reese raised her hand. "That's easy, Mr. Taylor, it's 45 degrees."

Reese's voice was more assured and confident than Tommy had ever heard her.

Mr. Taylor clapped his hands. "And the next one, Reese's Pieces."

Reese giggled at his nickname "I like Reese Peanut Butter cups better!"

"Then I dub thee Reese Buttercup, my smart lady." Mr. Taylor bowed. "Correcto-mundo! 45 degrees is perfect weather for a fall jacket," He pretended to shiver. "Please open your notebooks for today's lesson." Mr. Taylor turned toward his desk. When he whipped around, he was wearing a red rubber clown's nose. "Let's clown around with numbers, shall we?"

The class was in an uproar.

Mr. Radling opened the door and peeked in with a good-natured smile. "What's all the ruckus in here, Mr. Taylor?"

"We're just clowning around with angles."

"Proceed," Mr. Radling said, then shut the door and left. More giggling ensued.

Tommy checked the wall clock. He couldn't believe his eyes. He hadn't looked at the clock in a full 35 minutes, a new world record!

"What do you call more than one L? Big hint here." Mr. Taylor held his arms straight up in the air. "In case you haven't guessed from my arm-raising clue, it's *parallel* lines. In a parallel universe, two worlds exist and intersect at the same time, but in math, parallel lines travel side by side, never to touch. Ahhh, to admire such beauty and never possess it. Alas, I exist as a parallel line with Miss Bell." He swooned dramatically.

Tommy sat up at attention. *Parallel Universe.* He wrote the words in his notebook. This clue was important, but he didn't know why.

Mr. Taylor drew an example of two lines next to each other. "And that—boys and girls," he paused, "is how we have pun-fun in my class." Mr. Taylor bowed and waved his hand toward the door and tooted a bicycle horn twice to signal the end of the class. "Two toots till tomorrow!" Then the bell which ended Mr. Taylor's class buzzed.

Tommy checked the clock it was almost 3:15, time to head for his locker and wait for the last bell. He had to stay in this class no matter what.

Jake tugged on Tommy's arm. "So, what do you think?"

"I think he's the best math teacher ever! I might have broken my torturous time watching habit, too!" Tommy said.

"In case you didn't know, Mr. Taylor attended Clown College in the 70's. He's even crazier this year than last, which is freakin' awesome," Jake said. "He's a nut ball for sure, but we wouldn't trade him."

"I agree," Tommy chuckled. "I never laughed that much and didn't get detention for it. Big J? My place?"

"You got it, 'Lil T. It's no small feat to keep up with Mr. Taylor's rapid-fire lessons. You did great today."

"What's a sinusoid?"

"It's a wave pattern."

"Oh. I thought so," Tommy fibbed, because he thought it meant an infection in his nose.

CHAPTER 21

Choden, the spirit in the prayer wheel

Tommy began to suspect the artifact was going somewhere while he was at school. Ever since he found the artifact, his day dreams felt so real, as if he too had traveled. True to his guess, the artifact dipped through time portals. During Tommy's science class, the prayer wheel spun away from ancient Egypt then headed through a wormhole, dropping back in time to ancient Rome. While he was in Mr. Taylor's class, Choden spun to the mountain peaks of Tibet to visit the place where the artifact was forged with precious metals so long ago. When he was supposed to be solving algorithms, his mind drifted away.

There sat a pretty twelve year old Asian girl, Choden, playing with her twin brother, Yeshe. Tommy's mind merged with hers. He felt melancholy strike his heart. Choden missed her birthplace. There, high atop the snowy mountain peak in front of the temple with the red door and the golden dome far in the past, Choden sighed. Tommy watched Yeshe and Choden sitting on a boulder. "What's wrong, sister?"

"I'm not feeling well today. What are you holding?"

"This prayer wheel fell into my lap."

"It had to come from somewhere," Choden said. "You are supposed to be inside studying, Yeshe."

"I was meditating on the prayer flags." Yeshe defended.

"It looks like you're playing with the prayer wheel. Let me see it," Choden said.

Tommy had seen this same place he'd seen before. He watched the scene unfold before him. It was the day Choden first discovered the mysterious prayer wheel in her brother's hands— the artifact *she* now inhabited. He saw the row of silk prayer flags furl and snap in the bracing wind like colorful fish dangling on a rope line. monks. He felt the wind upon his own cheeks.

"Mr. Delo, where did you go?" Mr. Taylor tooted the bicycle horn and startled Tommy.

"Oh, sorry." Tommy touched his cheeks and felt the sting of windburn on them.

Tired from her journey, Choden tumbled through the vortex, landing back in the Crow's Nest in right on the pillow where Tommy placed her the day before.

After school, Tommy and Jake ran to the shop.

"Where were you during math class? You zoned out," Jake said.

"Believe or not, Tibet. I saw Choden and her brother. It was the exact same memory as when you and I traveled there."

"You must have seen it for a reason," Jake said.

Tommy and Jake ran up to the Crow's Nest. "Whew. You're still here."

He picked it up to examine it. "It's freezing cold!" It didn't vibrate or spark, it was icy cold to the touch. "Hey, I don't remember seeing an eagle yesterday."

"Let me take a look. I'm not touching it. You

hold it." Jake took a pen from his bag and turned the barrel with it. "Maybe I missed a detail, but it's highly unlikely. T. I'm wondering if it travels places without you."

"My thoughts exactly," Tommy said.

CHAPTER 22

Mr. Edwards, Science teacher

Science Class 3rd period the next day

Today was the first of the three-month cycle when class sessions change. He was hesitant about meeting Mr. Edwards, the earth science teacher. He was doubtful Mr. Edwards would think he was smart. He wasn't good at science last year.

Jake pulled Tommy aside right before they entered. "You look like you're going to barf, but it'll be fine. Mr. Edwards has a bad speech impediment. He can't say his R's and L's. Once you know that, you'll understand him better. He's not trying to sound funny, so don't laugh at him—even if you want to, and even if the other kids do."

"Got it." Tommy peeked into the room. Six tall long black tables faced the white board. Each table had two sinks with pipes sticking up out of them. Each table had a set of tall leggy stools. He calculated the number of students the classroom could hold. *Six times four is 24 students.* Just as he was concerned about where to sit, Jake tugged his sleeve.

"Follow me." Jake claimed the first table in the front. "We'll park it in the front row, so you don't have to see above the giraffes."

The faint sickly-sweet smell of rubbing alcohol and formaldehyde lingered in the air and made Tommy's stomach lurch. "Geez, it smells like an old fish tank in here. I think I'm going to barf."

Jake laughed. "I hate to tell you, T, funky stink is business as usual. It's left over from seventh grade biology dissection."

Tommy pinched his nose. "Gross. I hope all the frog guts are gone from the table tops. Here's goes nothing." He dropped the notebook on the high black table and climbed the rungs to sit on the stool. His feet dangled at a ridiculous twelve inches from the floor. Embarrassed, he said, "I feel like a five-year-old on a high chair."

Jake teased. "Don't fall off. It's a long way down."

Mr. Edwards stood behind a tower of glass beakers and jars. His balding head shined a full moon glow when it caught the reflection of the florescent lighting. He turned around just as the last student shuffled in and shut the door.

Tommy noticed that Mr. Edwards didn't smile or greet students. Was he shy? Or just unfriendly?

Mr. Edwards grabbed his grade book and squinted and cleared his throat.

"Welcome sixth *gwade* science students." He called each name with a deliberate pronunciation, still having trouble.

Tommy was thankful Jake warned ahead of time about Mr. Edward's odd speech pattern. In the back of the room, people burst out into laughter. Tommy guessed it was most likely Jenny or Sarah. Joe bellowed a fog horn snort at each mistake Mr. Edwards made and Tommy felt bad for the teacher.

"Our first unit of study is famous twentieth century scientists. I'm sure you've heard of Albert Einstein. "*Pweeze* open to page 70."

Jenny and Sally erupted in a slew of giggles from

the back of the classroom. Joe had parked his big body near them in the last row.

Tommy whipped his science text open to page 70 to demonstrate he was listening.

"Today I'll *pwesent a thee-wee* called The Time Continuum."

Jenny and Sally burst out in shrill mocking squeals. Joe joined in with desk banging.

Mr. Edwards' face flamed bright red. Tommy wondered why the teacher didn't discipline their outbursts.

After class ended, Tommy and Jake walked through the crowded hallway to the row of gray lockers. "Why didn't Mr. Edwards tell Jenny and Sally to stuff a sock in it?"

"I think Mr. Edwards is embarrassed about his speech impediment. They say we teach people how to treat us. He's too nice a guy."

"I felt bad for him. And Joe is obnoxious," Tommy said.

"I agree. Hey, T, I have to head to the head. See you in a few." Jake dashed off to the lavatory.

Tommy spun his locker dial and exchanged his science text for a math text. His mind buzzed with new ideas. He was so engrossed in thought, he didn't see Joe barreling down the hallway heading for him like a mac truck on a mission to destroy.

WHAM! Joe knocked him clear off his feet. "Oops, sorry *Shrimp*! Not."

Tommy hit the tile floor with a splat. His math text and homework sheets flew from his hands and plummeted upward. The papers scattered around him like fallen leaves. He lay there, splayed out and terrified, staring face to face with Joe's demon fist curled and ready to punch him into a new time zone. Students gathered around him, but no one helped.

Joe knelt down hovering over him with a death blow fist. Just as Joe's fist was ready to fly at Tommy's nose, Principal Radling showed up behind Joe.

"Break it up! Gentleman, is there a problem here?"

"No problem," Joe said. "The new kid fell. I was just giving him a hand up." Joe shot to his feet and extended a meaty hand to hoist Tommy to his feet.

Tommy ignored Joe's meat hook. He stood up, rattled, but unhurt. He retrieved his text and papers, and dusted off his pride, and caught his breath.

Mr. Radling eyed Tommy with concern. "Anything you want to tell me, Son?"

"No Sir. I slipped, just like the big oaf said I did." He insulted someone who could kill him with one punch. Tommy willed himself to grow one foot taller by Monday.

"Come by my office if you change your mind." Mr. Radling pointed to Joe. "I'm watching you, Mr. Carp. Don't let me hear you had anything to do with this incident."

"You won't hear a thing about it." Joe threatened Tommy with a glare.

Once the principal was out of sight, Joe pumped his fist and held it up. "Don't even think about tattling. Next time, Shrimp."

It wasn't bad enough that Joe almost killed him, but now he made him late for Mr. Taylor's class. The late bell buzzed his arrival. He dashed to his seat, red in the face and heart thumping double time.

Mr. Taylor added the last touches to his drawings of colorful geometric shapes. He put his marker down, whipped around, and tapped his watch, aware of Tommy's late arrival. "Glad you made it 'round' to class Tommy. The circus almost pulled away without you!"

Day two and he'd already managed to prove he didn't belong. "Sorry. I stopped at the lavatory, Mr. Taylor." Tommy's chest heaved in an out.

"What gives?" Jake whispered.

"Joe-rex-it-all gave."

"Fill me in about the dumb ape later. Are you hurt?"

"I'm still breathing." Tommy opened his notebook and copied the diagrams.

Joe's ugly mug and big hulk fist loomed in Tommy's brain. Worry times one hundred. Joe's image faded along with his classroom. Unexpectedly, Tommy' mind drifted away. There he stood in his daydream outside of a massive stone castle. In front of him, three knights in full chainmail, wielded spiked maces. They rode atop majestic prancing horses. The vision was so real, he could actually smell the earthy horse dung, burning fires, dust flying up from the horse's hooves. His mouth tasted gritty and acrid.

The prayer wheel spun back in time. Was Medieval England or ancient Rome a better choice to teach a bully a lesson? She considered her options. She'd bring Tommy to England. Then, she'd listen in for Tommy's next history lesson. Last, she'd convince Tommy to bring Joe along on a time trip. Tommy wouldn't like the idea, but he'd need to be courageous.

Mr. Taylor stood near Tommy and honked the horn startling him to attention. "Today we'll discuss crushed angles. You know, wrecked angles —rectangles, also known as parallelograms." He wiggled his moustache. "Mr. Delo, what do you call a four-sided shape with two long sides and two short sides?

"A rectangle?" Tommy was relieved to recall the answer. Joe tried to turn him into a wrecked-angle.

"Sir, the honk of success is yours." Mr. Taylor tooted a bicycle horn twice.

Jake leaned in. "T, you have some brown gunk on your cheek. Wipe it off."

Tommy wiped his arm against his face. He was safe, but he'd better stop daydreaming about castles and concentrate on math.

Jake shook Tommy's arm. "Snap out of it, 'Lil T."

Mr. Taylor drew two parallel lines on the board. "There's that word again. *Parallel. I'd like to draw a parallel* to yesterday's math lesson. When there's a set of *parallel* lines and we add one on the top and another on the bottom of it... bazinga. We have completed a rectangle. If you shift the lines sideways and lengthen one of them, the shape is also known as..." he paused to wiggle his moustache. "Anyone?"

Reese waved her hand, "Is it a rhombus, Mr. Taylor?"

"Good job, my Dear! The rhombus is correct, but not to be confused with the Rhumba—a spicy Latin dance developed in Cuba." He shoved a flower ended pencil between his teeth and twirled around the room. "But that's a dance for another day." He arched his bushy eyebrows up and down going for the entertainment factor.

He flipped on a Smart Board screen. "Speaking of Cube-Ah, notice this three-dimensional figure called a cube."

Tommy followed Mr. Taylor's roller coaster ride, dipping back and forth from math terms to puns and riddles. He almost forgot about his earlier brush with death.

"And tonight's assignment, page 90 and 99, do odd item number problems only...even if you want to do them all. TGIF, or as I like to say, Today — Grand Illusionary Friday!" He pulled a fake flower bouquet out of his vest pocket. "Ta da! Please have your homework finished for Monday's class so your good grades won't disappear!"

Every student left Mr. Taylor's class smiling. "Why can't every class be as much fun as Mr. Taylor's class?" Tommy said.

Jake said, "He's the shit."

"I agree." Tommy had the coolest friend in school, a kid who didn't even apologize for saying the s word.

Tommy mulled over the Joe problem. Why was Joe so mean to him? It didn't add up or have an easy solution.

"What happened before class?" Jake asked reviewing his face like it was a quiz question.

"He knocked me down for no reason at all."

"Joe doesn't need a reason. It's what he does."

"How do I stop him?"

"Joe is terrified of his dad. I'd feel badly for Joe if he weren't such a jerk to everyone on the planet. I had a run-in with Joe last year. He can do real harm if he's not stopped," Jake said.

"What'd you do about Joe?"

"I tried using my words, but Joe only speaks fist. Two years ago, he followed me home and whacked me a good one in the eye. I had a hell of a shiner. So, I punched him right back in his big potato nose. He didn't expect me to do it."

"Did you get detention?"

"Naw. It was late in the day and off school property. I'm sure Joe planned it so no one would be around to see him."

"No way I'm going to punch him. Got any other ideas?"

"My dad called Joe's dad, who happens to be a major bully himself... big surprise, right? Joe's stayed clear of me ever since. My dad will protect you, T. You just have to let him know. Did you tell your mom that Joe has been hassling you?"

"No way. She's already overprotective. After dad ...well you know...she's been even more nutsy with me. Besides, if she knew about Joe, she'd insist on walking me to school like a kindergarten baby." Tommy twisted his mouth to one side.

"I wouldn't mind holding your mom's hand." Jake slapped Tommy on the back. "But seriously, you have to tell someone, T," Jake said.

"I just did. I just told you," Tommy answered.

"I mean you have to tell an *adult*. Do you know Joe's been bugging Jeff since before the third grade? Seems it's your turn, being the new kid."

Tommy shook his head, No. "Does Joe still bother Jeff?"

"No. Jeff's older brother is on the same string in football as Joe. I guess there's a truce because of the sports thing. Otherwise I'm sure he'd still be at it."

"Then I'm in big trouble. I don't think I'll make the football team, unless they need a water boy." Tommy held up a skinny bicep to demonstrate.

They arrived at the shop. Tommy wiggled the door key and entered.

Jake took out a cell to call his dad. He touched the screen and said, "Dad, I'm at the store on Main with Tommy. Yes, ok, 6:00 ish. Hmmm, ok. See you later. Let's get to work, 'Lil T."

Tommy threw a cleaning cloth to Jake and said, "Let's get to it. These shelves won't wipe themselves."

"On it, T," Jake said.

CHAPTER 23

Jake and Tommy best buds

Two Hours later 5:45 pm Friday night at the shop

Jake held up a plastic Cupie doll and waved it. "T, this doll needs a price."

"I'll be right back." Tommy ran to the front of the shop and tapped on the computer.

Tommy called out, "Does it have blue wings?"

"No. Pink ones."

Tommy ran back to him.

"Since the wings are pink, not blue, it's from the 1950's making it newer and worth less to a collector. The blue winged Cupies sell for $1000?"

"Just for a dumb doll…impressive."

"Just one of my super powers. I just researched the item on Mom's computer." Tommy laughed.

Jake stopped. "How much for this old guitar?" He picked it up and strummed a bar.

"Not sure. We'll ask my Mom once we're done cleaning up," Tommy said.

They continued to wipe and organize the shelves. With Jake's help, they finished all of them.

Mom paced to the front of the shop. Her face lit up like a sunny day. "I am so impressed. You two young men have done an outstanding job!"

"Spic and *Spam*." Tommy tossed his shoulders back and thumbed his belt loop imitating Jake's confident stance.

"Spam is meat in a can. Span is the word you meant," Mom said.

Tommy noticed Jake never rolled his eyes the bad way his old friends did when he goofed up a word or asked a stupid question. Teachers always said, *There's no such thing as a stupid question*, but they were wrong. He'd asked loads of them. And kids laughed when he asked them.

"Now, all we need is a new shop sign. When do you think we'll open, Mom?"

"Right after your birthday. That'll give us a few more weeks."

"Mrs. Delo, did you come up with a shop name yet?"

"You'll see." Mom winked her sneaky I-have-a-surprise-but-I'm-not-telling wink.

Jake glanced at his watch. "6:15 already. My dad will be here any minute."

Mom took cash from her pocket. "I'd like to pay you for your help, Jake."

Jake waved his hand. "I won't take any money, Mrs. Delo... but I'd sure like to earn enough to buy the old guitar I saw. There's something... familiar about it. How much do you want for it?"

"Do you play?" She asked.

"I just fool with the strings. My mom played music for me."

Mom said, "I think you earned it already, Jake."

"Naw, I couldn't just take this for free, Mrs. Delo," Jake said.

"I insist. Consider it payment for your help. Bring it here. I'll be right back." She returned with a hard, black, guitar shaped case. "This goes with it."

Jake held the guitar in his hands. Tears gathered up in his eyes. "Geez, thanks, Mrs. Delo." Jake strummed a few chords. He adjusted the knobs on the neck of its arm and strummed a tune. He tapped the wood. "It has a good mellow sound."

"Geez, now you even play guitar like a rock star. It's not fair. Mom, can Jake stay over tonight?"

"Yes, if it's ok with his dad. Oh dear. Bad mother moment. I forgot to put the defrosted roast in the oven. We'll need to get take-out tonight." She ran up to the second floor.

Tommy snapped his fingers. "Oh darn." He laughed. Just then, Tommy heard a sturdy knock on the heavy entrance door.

"My dad's here." Jake set the guitar down by the counter and dashed to the door. "Nice! Thanks, Dad." He grabbed the two liter soda bottle from his dad. "Follow me, Dad."

Jake scooted with the soda and Mr. Stanton followed behind him.

Time Wheel Book 1

Tommy heard the stomp of cowboy boots on the wooden floor planks. Mom was sure to notice Mr. Stanton's movie star good looks and it worried him.

Mr. Stanton strode in carrying two boxes of pizza balanced on his muscled arm and set it on the counter near the soda. He smelled of aftershave and wore a mile-wide smile. "Hey, Tommy. Nice to see you again." He put his hand out toward Tommy for a man to man hand shake.

Tommy squeezed tight and craned his arm up and down feeling the man's strong callused hands. "Thanks for the pizza, Mr. Stanton. Mom forgot to put the roast into the oven."

"Any time." The tall man brushed a hand to his raven black hair and grinned a row of perfect white teeth. He turned around to look at the shop. "Where's your mom, Tommy? I wanted to say hello."

"She's *really* busy upstairs." Tommy looked away to hide his fib.

"Hey Dad, look at this sweet guitar Mrs. Delo gave me just for helping her out."

Tommy saw Mr. Stanton's face fall, as if he swallowed a rock and it got stuck in his throat.

Mr. Stanton cleared his throat and his voice choked up. "Let me see it." Mr. Stanton took the guitar from Jake and studied it. He ran his hands over the wood. "Jake, this was your mother's guitar. I suppose you were meant to find it here."

"*Mom's* guitar? For real?" A struck expression crossed Jake's face. "But how?"

"She must have pawned it for the cash before she left." He twanged the strings and played a melody. "Still has a good sound after all these years."

"I never heard you play, Dad," Jake said.

"Jake and his dad were like catnip to females. Tommy had seen how his old cat, Sadie would go crazy over a catnip toy, even though it made no sense at all. Mr. Stanton and Jake were mirror images of each other. No wonder the girls swooned over their good looks and charm. Tommy wondered about the mysterious magic they both possessed. He must have had a silly expression on his face because Mr. Stanton asked, "Does the cat have your tongue, Tommy? You're awful quiet."

Tommy tried to hide his worry with a half-hearted grin. "I was thinking how much you and Jake look alike."

"No denying he's my son." He and Jake grinned matching toothy smiles.

"No denying," Jake repeated.

"You play good!" Tommy said.

"I haven't placed since...." Mr. Stanton's voice trailed away and his eyebrows pushed together.

Tommy couldn't believe the weird coincidence. Was this synchronicity?

Mom headed down to the shop. "Oh, I didn't know you were here. Tommy, why didn't you call for me? I was just about to order food... but my nose tells me someone beat me to it."

Mom's hair cascaded down at her shoulders. Pink lipstick blushed her lips and smelled like flowers.

"I hope Jake was no trouble," Mr. Stanton's eyes glued to her.

"Jake's a fine boy. My stars, he resembles you," Mom replied.

"We hear that a lot, don't we Squirt?"

Tommy couldn't help but giggle at the baby name worse than his own.

Jake lost his cool demeanor. "*Dad,* you promised not to use my baby name in public."

"We're all friends here," Mr. Stanton said.

"I'm sorry I laughed at your name," Tommy said.

"Mary, I hope I'm not intruding on your plans. Truth is —I'm famished after work and didn't have much time to catch a bite." He grinned his full set of choppers and a glint sat in his eyes.

"You had time to shower and use aftershave," Tommy muttered. *Such big teeth you have, Mr. Stanton.*

Mr. Stanton turned his angular jaw line toward Mom and stroked a big hand against his hair. "It was kind of you to give him the guitar, but I insist you let me pay for it."

"Jake certainly earned it. No payment necessary, really. Except for this pizza, which smells ahhmazing." She smiled.

Tommy watched Mom's face blush pink. He folded his arms and studied her expression.

"Mom, the guitar belonged to Jake's *mother,*" Tommy said.

"Oh my." Her hand flew over her mouth. "That's

quite a coincidence. It's meant for Jake to have it." Mom's lips turned up at the edges.

Mr. Stanton nodded. "She's been gone for *years*... ghosted me. I'm surprised no one snapped this up before now."

"It's a funny thing. Tommy, Jake and I cleaned this place top to bottom. The first time I saw it in the shop was just the other day when Jake asked me about it."

Jake's eyes bounced to Tommy.

"It's like it traveled through time," Tommy said.

"Thank you for watching after Jake," he said. Then something awful happened. Mr. Stanton took Mom's hand in his, like he owned it.

Mom breathed heavily, even though she hadn't just run a mile. Tommy knew it. She was Googly eyed, mesmerized and cat nipped, just like Sadie. Tommy folded his arms over his chest. He watched Mom's face glow like Christmas tree lights. And worse of all, she didn't pull her hand back from Mr. Stanton as she should have.

Mr. Stanton held Mom's gaze.

Red-faced, Mom withdrew her hand. "We've

been knee deep in a mess. But we plan to open in early November."

Mr. Stanton's hand dropped to his side. He surveyed the newly organized spaces. "The place looks great."

"We're finally seeing the light of day," Mom said.

Then Mom toyed with her hair, just like Lana did at school when she was moony-eyed over Jeff. Tommy shook Mom's arm. "Your face is all woozy. Maybe you should go rest...upstairs...*alone* until you feel better." He knew it was rude, but he was desperate because he feared Mom *like-liked* Mr. Stanton and he wasn't ready for a new dad.

"Nonsense. I'm fine, Tommy." Mom shot him the stink eye. He was in big trouble for sticking a big toe over the line he wasn't supposed to cross, but always tried.

Tommy wracked his brains to think of something clever to say to remind her of Dad.

"Dad made perfect sized burgers for us." It wasn't clever, and didn't make sense, but it popped into his head. Suddenly, the air felt as thick as tomato paste.

Even Jake noticed as Tommy hurdled the line.

Jake shook his head and remarked, "Random comment, Dude. What's up with that?"

"I'm sure your dad made great burgers, Tommy." Mr. Stanton winked at him, not even upset with him. He didn't even notice he'd been rude, which infuriated Tommy even more than if he had.

"Tommy, why don't you and Jake set up the card table upstairs so we can enjoy this treat in a civilized manner," Mom said.

He and Jake pounded up the staircase and unfolded a table and chairs.

"Dude, what's the deal? You're acting super weird around my dad," Jake asked.

"I think my mom forgot all about my dad." Tommy eyed the floor and his eyes misted up.

"How could she? They loved each other. Right? I'll bet your mom is as lonely as my dad is. That's why he wastes his time with vapid women. None of them are special, like your mom."

"What's vapid?"

"Empty, tedious, uninteresting…boring. Your mom is smart and kind, not to mention, pretty."

"Oh." Tommy heard Mr. Stanton's boots thump up the stairs behind Mom's fast footfalls.

Mr. Stanton set the soda bottle on the table. "I'm famished."

Mom wiped her brow. "See, Jackson. I told you. More clutter up here too. We don't even own a proper table." Her voice dropped low. "We sold our furniture to pay medical bills."

They all sat around the small folding table in awkward moments of silence. Mom flipped open the pizza box and scouted around for paper plates and glasses.

Despite Tommy's discomfort, the cheesy oregano smells delighted his nostrils and made him forget he was so angry.

"Mrs. Delo, my dad renovated The Mill restaurant across from the school. Maybe we can all go for dinner there sometime. How about it, Dad?"

Tommy threw the stink eye at Jake. "Mom's too busy."

"Manners, Tommy. I can speak for myself. I've heard the renovation in the Old Mill is quite beautiful." She smiled as if she had a secret wish.

"Mary, once you're less busy, how 'bout it? Of course, we'd bring along the boys." Mr. Stanton gazed right into Mom's eyes.

Mom pulled her eyes away and dabbed the corners of her mouth. "I haven't been out in ages."

"It wouldn't be a date, just a nice dinner between friends," Mr. Stanton said.

Mom took a ravenous bite of pizza. "You know, I'd be delighted, Jackson… as friends. I'm not ready to date."

"Of course. We'd go just as friends." Mr. Stanton gulped the soda and burped.

Jake burped louder. "Bachelor food, right Dad?"

"You know it," Mr. Stanton said.

Tommy belched as loudly as could just to show Mom the bad habit he picked up from Mr. Stanton.

"Manners, Tommy," Mom whispered under her breath.

Tommy made his eyes widen, to pretend his rudeness was by mistake. "Oh, sorry, Mom. I was just being one of the guys." *Gotcha, Mr. Stanton.*

Mr. Stanton said, "I'm sorry too, Mary. Jake and I

are in need of etiquette training. We've been on our own too long and forgot our company manners."

"Mr. Stanton, can Jake stay over tonight? We have special research to work for school."

Mr. Stanton's voice was all rumbly and smooth when he said, "Sure, if it's ok with you, Mary."

"He's a pleasure. No problem," Mom said a bit too loud.

Jackson handed her a business card. "This is my cell number. Call me when you've had your fill of my kid and I'll pick him up. Or if you want to chat... anytime."

"Does Jake have any allergies, doctor numbers, food concerns?" Mom asked.

Mr. Stanton laughed as if she made a joke. "If he bleeds or gags, call me. Otherwise, we're all good." He took Mom's hand in his for just a moment. "See you soon, Mary."After the food was gone, the tall man strode out with the scent of his cologne and pizza lingering in the air.

CHAPTER 24

Ghost busting

The same night

"I'm full of pizza," Tommy said.

"Yeah, it's one of our favorite places. We go there a lot because Dad can't cook very well. He is great at pancakes, but that's about all," Jake said.

"Boys, I'll be organizing files on the second floor. Jake, make yourself at home. We have an extra sleeping bag rolled up in the Crow's Nest. There's a brand-new set of toothbrushes, paste, and soap in the cabinet by the sink. Clean towels in the wicker basket in the bathroom. Tommy can show you."

"Thanks, Mrs. Delo," Jake said.

They flew up to the third floor. "So, what's the plan, T?"

"I've got all the supplies we need to ghost bust. We'll head down to the shop and get rid of the ghost."

Jake unpacked his school bag. "I have a candle, mirror, salt, a cross, and Holy Water, just in case we need it. I think we should clear the shop level first. What do you think, T?"

"I agree. We'll do it once my mom is busy."

Mom was studying paperwork.

"Hey Mom, we're heading down to the shop to look at old stuff."

She mumbled a distracted, "Uh-huh."

"She wouldn't notice if a herd of elephants ran by," Tommy whispered.

They hammered down to the first floor.

"Did you find a good spell to get rid of the ghost?" Jake asked.

Tommy opened the book. "Right here on page ten. Hold the mirror up while we read the spell."

"I'll light the candle. We'll set the mirror on the

floor and recite the incantation together. Open the book so I can see it too." Tommy set the book down open to the right page.

Jake took a lighter and lit the candle. "Ok, ready."

"Me too. Together they recited, "*Ghost of old, hear our plea. Fly into this mirror and don't bother me. Cross to the light and leave this place, be gone your body and face.*"

"Nothing happened. Let's say it again like we mean it," Tommy said.

They recited, "*Ghost of old, hear our plea. Fly into this mirror and don't bother me. Cross to the light and leave this place, be gone your body and face.*"

A purple streak of light sparked across the room, the heater banged, hissed, and squealed. "I think that did it. Let's clear out and head to the Crow's Nest," Tommy said.

They dashed up to the third floor. Prayer Wheel was on his sleeping bag. "For once, it's right where I left it."

"I'd like to examine it." Jake gently rubbed the metal and it warmed in his hands. "Do you have a tissue?"

"You've seen the Aladdin movie, right?" Tommy handed him a tissue.

"Maybe a Genie will grant us three wishes." Jake buffed the barrel in small circles. "Ouch!" He dropped it from his hands, but there was no metal clang of metal on wood, only silence. "Where'd the heck did it go?" A vortex of light cracked open. A loop of light tied itself to Jake's wrist and pulled him inside.

"Tommy, help!" Jake muffled cry was almost lost.

Tommy watched helplessly as the bright spinning vortex burst open. "Jake!" He yelled, lunged forward, and yanked Jake's hand with all his might. Instead of pulling Jake out, the vortex sucked him in with Jake. It was useless to pull away. Both boys tumbled in the rainbow of swirling colors which made Tommy's stomach do gymnastics. Suddenly, they stood in a pitch-black silent void.

"Jake are you ok?" His voice echoed in the velvet black.

"I think so." Jake yelled.

A starburst of colors spewed them out. They somersaulted to a stop in a foreign land in front of a golden-domed temple with an intricate scarlet carved door.

Tommy rubbed his eyes, and held his gut, still queasy from the rainbow toilet twirl ride. He leaned over and vomited into a bush right in front of the temple.

"Gross, Dude." Jake rubbed his eyes to adjust to the bright light. "Where are we?"

Two children sat propped on a large boulder in front of the temple. Tommy guessed they were near his age. Their red silk tunics were tied with a golden rope, and moved in the breeze. Above them, colorful flags flapped and twirled on a long rope tied to poles, snapping their prayers in the bracing wind.

Tommy stared in awe at the sight of the golden-topped building. "Where the heck are we, Jake?"

"I can't believe it…I think we're in Tibet!"

They crept closer to eavesdrop on the conversation between a boy and girl who appeared to be Tommy's age.

The slight boy rotated a shiny object in his hands.

"Jake, that kid is holding our prayer wheel!"

Jake waved his hands in the air. "Hey! I'm Jake! Where are we? Just as I thought, they can't see us, T."

The girl said, *"Yeshe, I thought I heard someone whisper to me."*

"It's just the wind, Choden."

"Where did you get it from? A prayer wheel belongs in a temple."

"It dropped in my lap out of nowhere right before you joined me," Yeshe said.

"Are you telling me the truth? Did you monks give it to you as a birthday gift? If so, it's mine too, since we were born on the same day.

"No. I told you the truth," Yeshe insisted.

"Let me try. I think the girl heard you." Tommy moved closer and jumped up and down waving his arms front of them. "Kids on the rock, can you see me or hear me?"

The girl stopped and looked right through Tommy and smiled.

Tommy shook his head back and forth. "If she did hear me, she's not admitting to it."

"Can I see the prayer wheel, Brother?" Choden asked.

Yeshe held it tight pulling it to his body. "No. I want to examine it. There's writing on the barrel. You're just a girl and haven't learned translations."

"I can translate better than you can. And I can prove it." Choden folded her arms and set her jaw.

Tommy watched the curious boy examine the inscriptions on the barrel.

"First chance we get, we swipe it back and get out of here," Jake said.

"You have no idea what is says. Give it to me, Yeshe. I have a secret." Choden baited her brother with a sly brow raise.

"What secret?" Yeshe cocked his brow. "Tell me now. I demand it!"

Choden held her hand out. "You have no right to demand anything. I'll translate the words. The monks taught me how while you were playing tiddly-winks and wasting time watching flags blow in the wind."

He handed it to her. "Show me."

Choden gave her brother a satisfied grin, then wiggled the top of the barrel. "See?" She pulled a rolled paper from the barrel of the cylinder and unfurled it. *"The monks are training me for something special. I wasn't supposed to tell you.* **Past, present future all the same. Bring me to the karma of this life so I can go back and eliminate strife. Heal karma, and fix my life.***"* She re-rolled the paper and placed it back into the cylinder's center compartment.

"Let me have it!" Yeshe said.

"Here. Take it." She pushed the prayer wheel into her brother's hands.

All of a sudden, sparks flew from the artifact. Yeshe dropped it. "It's enchanted!" His eyes grew wide with fear.

The Time Wheel didn't hit the ground. It turned white hot and lifted in the air. With a thunderclap, a circle of light blasted open in front of Tommy and Jake.

"That's our ride home, Tommy!" Jake yanked Tommy's hand and they dove into the brilliant arc of light. With the force of a tornado, their bodies spun forward in time. The vortex coughed them out onto the wooden floor of the shop.

"Dude." Jake rubbed his head. "We just time traveled!"

"My head is spinning." Tommy turned and puked in a garbage can. "I should've popped a mint."

"Time travel overload." Jake rubbed his brow.

"Why did we go to Tibet instead of to a nice beach by the arcade?" Tommy grabbed his head in his hand.

"You tell me."

"I was thinking, I wanted to know where the time wheel came from."

Jake wiped beads of sweat from his brow." Don't you get it? The wheel gave you the answer. Did you hear the girl translate the words? Once she read them, the portal opened. We were in parallel time!"

"I wish I could remember the words she read."

"Something like past and present merging. Once we get the translation from Professor Banes, we'll try it out," Jake said.

The cylinder clanged and spun across the floor like a spinning top thrown from a tornado. It halted in front of Tommy's feet. "It's back!" He lifted it up. "It's icy cold!" He wiggled the top of the cylinder just like the girl did and clicked open to reveal a hollowed-out chamber. "It still has the paper in it. I was afraid it wouldn't be here."

"Be really careful with the scroll." Judging from what we just saw. It must be really old. Some writing holds up over time if the material it's written on lasts," Jake said.

"Parcheesi, again?" Tommy shrugged.

"Auspicious, Dude. Parcheesi is a board game." Jake slugged Tommy's arm. "The word parchment is used for an ancient scroll made of animal skin— kind of like a diploma with auspicious words written on it. You have to be extremely careful if it's linen or papyrus, since it will be more delicate."

"Suspicious?"

"Auspicious, you know… special," Jake said. "Remind me to buy you a dictionary for your birthday."

"Fun gift. Maybe you can buy me an ugly sweater, too."

Jake laughed. "Don't tempt me."

Tommy held the canister out toward Jake.

"No, T. You should take the scroll out. It's your

find. Just remove it slowly like the girl did."

Tommy squinted his eyes and flipped the artifact over. Tommy pointed to a small winged insignia on the top of the barrel. "Do you remember seeing this eagle stamped on the barrel? I don't."

"I don't either," Jake said.

"Alright, here goes nothing." The artifact warmed in his hands like melting butter on a biscuit. Tommy felt a surge of confidence coursing through his veins. With care, he pulled the rolled paper from the inside of the barrel and unfurled it. He scanned the unusual lines of symbols. "Squiggly writing with pictures on it." He handed it to Jake. "Take a look."

Jake felt the material between his fingers. "This feels like really old papyrus or linen cloth. I'm not sure which. These pictures appear to be Hieroglyphics, or maybe Sumerian cuneiform. Who am I kidding? I have no idea. The type of writing on the barrel is different than the writing on the scroll. Look."

Jake pulled his I Pad from his black backpack. "I'll look up cuneiforms on my I Pad to see if we can compare the writing," Jake said.

"How'd you know about auspicious stuff?"

"My other super power— antiquities research," Jake grinned.

"And vocabulary....and girls...and math....and school..." Tommy added.

"All true."

Tommy tapped on the computer and paused. "I'll check the word hieroglyphics, once I figure out how to spell it."

"Here, I'll jot it down for you." Jake wrote the word on a sticky note. "I know a professor from the Antiquities Department at Cathedral College. I completed an independent study with him last summer. Dad can drive us there tomorrow morning, if you want to go."

"Good idea. I'll put this prayer wheel here until the morning. Stay put." Tommy said to it.

"Do you think it understands us?" Jake asked.

"It must. We got to Tibet. I've decided from now on, this prayer wheel is a Time Wheel. The secret and magic part is just between us. Pinky swear to it." Tommy held out a pinky.

"Agreed." Jake linked his pinky with Tommy's.

"I think the *time wheel* might have a ghost in it," Tommy said. "But not a scary one, just a funny one who plays tricks on people."

"Interesting supposition. My guess is this time wheel is behind all the purple lights and weirdness you've been experiencing in the shop."

"I'm not sure if that makes me feel better or worse." Tommy's brain jumped like a monkey on a trampoline. He had time-traveled to Tibet and no one would believe him except for Jake.

"Let's decide on what we're going to tell the professor," Jake said.

"We'll keep all the weird stuff from everyone, *including* our parents, and *especially* the professor."

"I agree. Maybe the translation will be the key to how the time wheel works," Jake said.

"I hope so." Tommy pulled an extra sleeping bag from the closet for Jake.

"Time travel is exhausting."

"I agree."

Within a short time, both boys were snoring. Tommy dreamed of a spinning vortex of light. He saw himself walking through it, but this time he heard a girl's voice instructing him. "Time runs like a river. Parallel lines of past and present are two rivers. You can cross from one to the other. Then he heard the name *Professor Walter Banes*. My name is *Choden*. The names rung in his head. Right before he woke, he saw a quick vision of an old man, and a bell. He had no idea what the visions were trying to tell him.

CHAPTER 25

Visit with Professor Banes

Saturday Morning 9:00 am

The next morning, Mr. Stanton pulled his big blue flatbed truck up to the shop. He sauntered in as if he owned the place. Jake and Tommy were in the shop. Mom came down in her colorful top and jeans.

Mr. Stanton grinned and greeted Mom like she was a nice steak dinner he couldn't wait to have. "I hope Jake wasn't any trouble."

"None at all."

"Mary, Jake and Tommy asked me to take them to Cathedral College to meet with the antiquity's professor, Walter Banes, a good friend of mine. He offered to help the boys with their research project. Would you like to join us?"

"How nice!" Mom said.

Tommy caught a whiff of the tall man's cologne. It was obvious...Mr. Stanton was trying to swagger Mom. This college trip was a handy excuse for Mom to sit really close to Mr. Stanton jammed up in the crowded bench seat. Before Mom could answer, Tommy blurted out, "Mom's busy with the shop. She can't come with us." He shot Mom a disapproving glare, daring to leap over the lines of respect again.

"Mind your manners, Tommy," she scolded. "I can answer for myself."

He had to think of a logical reason she'd buy. He softened his voice. "It's just us guys today, Mom. Besides, there's no room in the truck for all of us."

Mom pushed a lock of hair from her pensive face. "Tommy could use a day to bond with the men."

Whew. She forgave his outburst. Tommy knew his clever deception worked, but an annoying mosquito of guilt buzzed around his conscience.

"Maybe next time. Let's get to it boys," Mr. Stanton said.

They left the shop and hopped in Mr. Stanton's ratty blue work truck. Mr. Stanton turned the key and the engine roared and rattled.

"Yeah, maybe next time." Tommy muttered.

Mr. Stanton looked right at him. "*Mano y mano,* man to man.... I get it. Your mom is very special to you. You don't want some guy giving her the look down. Am I right?"

Tommy was caught like a worm on a hook. Mr. Stanton saw right through his ploy and there was no denying it. So, he folded his arms and owned it. "Exactly."

Mr. Stanton pulled away to ride the fifteen miles to the college campus. His big blue flatbed truck rattled and bumpety bumped over the cobblestone driveway. Tommy admired the huge lion topped stone pillars and black iron gate they crossed. Green grass, tall trees, and winding pathways graced the sides of the private road snaking its way through the collection of campus buildings.

Jake whispered, "My dad has mad woman-powers. No wonder you're worried about him around your Mom."

"You know I can hear you, Squirt, even over this rattletrap."

"Jake, you have catnip genes too, and not the kind you wear," Tommy said. "The buildings look like old castles, just like you told me."

"Nice, right? And the girls...." Jake swooned and made an hourglass motion with his hands.

A perky blonde college girl walking past on the sidewalk turned and smiled at Jake seeing him through the truck's side window.

"Sweet!" Jake said. "Did you see her?"

"How does that even happen?" Tommy said.

Jake just smiled. "Lucky I guess."

"We're getting close to Bane's office, Tommy." Mr. Stanton turned the wheel and slowed the truck's approach. He swung into the parking area, turned off the truck, and pocketed the key fob. "Let's go."

Tommy leaped down off the running board and patted his backpack lightly to make sure he still had the artifact inside of it. He flung his backpack over his shoulder and repositioned it on his back.

"Prof's office, two doors down —dungeon level in the stone building dead ahead. He's expecting us by 9:30. He's very punctual." Mr. Stanton checked his watch. "Right on time."

"It's safe and sound right here in my backpack."

Despite himself, Tommy couldn't help but like Mr. Stanton. His emotions were battling each other, north and south, hot and cold, good and bad…Dad and Mr. Stanton. Two opposing forces and each one very different from the other.

They walked through the majestic archways into the stone building, a reproduction of a 1300 castle fortress.

"All I need is a sword!" Tommy mimicked swishing an imaginary sword in the air. He leaped left and right, dodging and play poking Jake with it.

Jake joined in the play fight. "Or a horse and chain mail! Touché!"

"We're about to visit the chambers of the educated, guys," Mr. Stanton said, *"Chill out."*

Tommy's dad never said clever things like chill out. He'd say, "Settle down, Sport," or "Calm down."

"K, Dad. I'm chill."

"I'm chill too," Tommy added.

Jake knocked on the door with fancy gold lettering, stamped *Humanities Department, Professor Banes Antiquities Specialist.*

Jake told Tommy that the professor acted 'socially awkward.'

Tommy didn't understand what Jake meant, until he met the professor.

The tall, lanky professor's skin was as white as a Vampire's. He opened the door, bowed. Then he pushed his wire-framed glasses against his nose with his two fingers, and announced, "Welcome, weary travelers."

It was an unusual greeting. Tommy checked with Jake to see if he'd bow, but since Jake didn't, Tommy didn't either.

Jake presented Tommy with a flourish gesture of his hand. "This is my buddy and research partner, Tommy, Prof."

"Pleased to meet you, Tommy," Professor Banes extended a smooth soft hand for him to shake.

Tommy took his hand and gave it a firm squeeze. The professor's hand was a cold dead fish, so different than Mr. Stanton's rough and ready shake. Dad was right. You could tell a lot about a man from his handshake. He could tell Professor Banes never used a hammer or screwdriver in his life. His baby soft hands were meant for research, paperwork, and books. He was as different from Jake's dad as he could be. But Mr. Stanton and Mr. Banes were friends.

"Pleased." Professor Banes pushed wire framed glasses back on his nose, an action he'd performed three times since Tommy entered the room. He realized the professor had a nervous habit, like biting nails, or squinting.

"Nice bowtie," Tommy complimented, remembering how much Mr. Taylor liked Jeff's comment about his tie.

"I do enjoy a fine bowtie or silk ascot. Let's see what your enquiring minds have brought to me. I'm intrigued to investigate your find."

Tommy noticed the fancy way he spoke using big vocabulary words, like *ascot and intrigued and investigate*. He slid the artifact out of his backpack, relieved it hadn't decided to spin away. "There's a Parcheesi inside of it—I mean parchment, or linen scroll. But I have to warn you, the artifact bites."

Jake exchanged swift glances with Tommy to warn him not to say too much.

"I see, like static electricity?" The professor clicked his tongue, shifted his glasses back with his forefinger and made a weird grimace.

"Something like that," Tommy said.

The professor lifted a curious brow and donned a magnifying headset over his forehead so he looked like a cave miner. He murmured, "Interesting. Fascinating."

"I'll just sit back and brew myself a cup of java while you three brainiacs do your thing." Mr. Stanton popped a coffee pod into the machine and pressed start. The hot water sizzled and steamed. The heady smell of coffee wafted into the air.

"Dad, make me a cup too, K?" Jake requested.

"Sure thing." The coffee maker beeped. Mr. Stanton popped in a second pod in to brew a cup for Jake.

Tommy gave a side eye to Jake. "You drink coffee?"

"Sure do." Jake seemed surprised. "Don't you?"

"Never. Mom says it will stunt my growth."

Jake laughed. "That's ironic."

"Tommy? You want a cuppa?" Mr. Stanton asked.

Tommy made his voice sound deep. "No thanks."

Mr. Stanton handed a steamy brew to Jake and said, "Banes, you want one?"

"Not while I have this precious article in my hands." Professor Banes held it in his palms as if it was a baby chick.

Mr. Stanton slid a book from the shelf, sat down, leaned back, and opened the book.

The professor said, "While I attempt to translate these inscriptions, use the archeological resource network, Jake. I've already logged you on as my guest."

"Right-o. Thanks Prof," Jake said.

Tommy dragged an extra chair next to Jake who was already tapping keys.

Professor Walter Banes continued to mumble with his head tilted forward. He slowly turned the artifact on the wooden stick base.

Tommy crossed his fingers that it wouldn't wake up and zap the Professor away.

"I see. Hmmm..." He gazed up at Jake and Tommy. "On first look, this appears to be a Tibetan Dharma wheel. I'll need more time to examine the inscriptions in greater detail."

"Don't rub the canister. Sometimes it lights up," Tommy warned.

"Did you say it lights up? In that case, I won't need my headset now, will I." Professor Banes cocked his head and laughed ever so lightly, as if Tommy told him an amusing joke.

Jake made a hand motion across his mouth to warn Tommy to zip his lips.

Tommy gave Jake a lopsided grin. "Oops."

Professor Walter Banes muttered a stream of "Hmmm, yes, I see, highly unusual..." While he wrote notes on a lined yellow pad. "I'm certain this is a Tibetan prayer wheel, but the inscriptions make it unique and puzzling. There's a mix of Sanskrit, Egyptian Hieroglyphics, and a most curious Roman insignia stamped on bottom of the metal canister. Perhaps it traveled many miles and somehow got inscribed. But how? Why? You say found this in the shop?"

"I did. It was on a tall shelf," Tommy said.

Jake wasted no time tapping words into the research address bar.

"Perhaps you can query the previous store owner?" The professor suggested.

"Mom said he's not well, but I can ask Miss Bell about him. She's his granddaughter and our history teacher," Tommy said.

The professor said, "I'm sure she might shed light on the subject."

Jake tugged on Tommy's arm. "Tommy, check this out, T. *A **prayer wheel** is a cylindrical object on a spindle made from metal, wood, stone, leather, or coarse cotton.* Ok, we knew that already."

"Check!" Tommy drew a check mark in the air.

"T, Listen to this part. *Traditionally, the mantra 'Om Mani Padme Hum' is often written in Sanskrit on the outside of the wheels. Dakinis, Protector Symbols are often used along with eight auspicious symbols.*"

"What's *suspicious* about the symbols?" Tommy

whispered to Jake.

"Not suspicious—*auspicious* which means *important, special, unique,*" Jake explained.

"I should've remembered the word from last time. Thanks for not rolling your eyes," Tommy said.

Jake continued. "*According to the Tibetan Buddhist tradition, the more the prayer wheel is spun, the more powerful it becomes over time.*"

"Karma? What's this part about?" Tommy pointed to the screen. He'd heard Jake's dad use the word when he talked about the old guitar. What did it mean?

Jake jotted notes and read, "*According to the lineage texts on prayer wheels, the canister can accumulate wisdom and merit... good karma to purify negativities... bad karma.* Listen to this T. *The most powerful canisters have a prayer or incantation inside,* just like ours!"

"Woah, *significant!*" Tommy rolled the latest new word off his tongue.

"Nice word choice, T." Jake hit Tommy's hand with a high five.

"I thought you'd like it. Karma sounds like an ice cream flavor. What the heck is it?"

"I see your confusion. *Caramel*, right?" Jake asked.

Tommy nodded his head. "The words sound so close."

"They do, but caramel makes no sense in this context, T," Jake said.

The professor turned and met Tommy's eyes. "Karma are the actions we take and what happens after we take action. For instance, if I am cruel in this lifetime, I will accumulate bad karma. If I am kind, I accumulate good karma, so good things will happen."

"Karma is a hot coffee, a great book, and a loving woman by your side. Two out of three ain't bad," Mr. Jackson remarked as he flipped pages of *A History of Architecture* book.

"I don't get it. Did I have bad karma when my Dad died?" Tommy shifted his gaze toward his sneakers and sniffed.

Mr. Stanton stopped reading and examined Tommy's expression. "No, Tommy. No you didn't. Let me take a stab at it, Banes. Do you know that game, Snakes and Ladder, Tommy?"

"Yes, I do," Tommy said.

"Bad karma is like the snake bite that gets you down off the ladder. Good karma is like the ladders which help you to rise up. A snake bite won't keep you down any longer once you realize you have free will to rise up from any situation." He grinned. "Got it? Your dad didn't die because he was bad, or you were bad, he died because he was ill and it was his time to go. His body was too weak to live. That's different. Sometimes bad things happen to good people, like your dad. Do you understand?"

Tommy nodded. "Mom told me the same thing."

Engrossed studying the artifact, Professor Banes didn't add to the conversation. He removed the magnifiers from his forehead. "Fine research, boys. I've translated the outer barrel. *Karma comes around and goes around. The wheel of time turns. Time is eternal, never ending. Past and present exist in the same plane of existence. Make peace with the past to live in the present.*" He smiled, satisfied and said, "Remarkable! Now to take a gander at the words."

Tommy's eyebrows knitted. The strange words sounded familiar to his ears. Did he hear them in a dream?

Time Wheel Book 1

"We learned a little bit about parallel universes at school," Jake winked at Tommy.

The professor paused to consider the term. "If parallel universes do exist, then past and present time overlap like so." He placed his right hand on top of his left hand to demonstrate. "Thusly."

Tommy added, "Can parallel universes explain moving back and forward in time?"

Professor Banes cracked a jack-o-lantern grin. "Fine assumption, young sir. Yes, it would. Einstein theorized that parallel universes and time travel are completely possible. The late Stephen Hawking, the great physicist, believed in the same time continuum theory."

"Just one more question. Is it possible for the wheel to spin off on its own?" Tommy forgot to zip his lips.

Jake elbowed Tommy in his ribs.

"What do you mean?" The professor raised his chin and looked right at him. "Like a top or a gyroscope?"

Tommy had to be sneaky. "Yes, but just for an example, not in real life."

"Highly unlikely." The professor dropped his question in a ditch.

Tommy figured Jake saw concern on the professor's face that Tommy didn't recognize because Jake asked the Professor, "Is everything ok, Prof?"

"I'm going to need a few days to work out these translations properly." He took a camera and photographed the object from all angles, and then photographed the scroll. "Put this artifact in a *very secure place and don't play with it*. It's quite unique."

"I'll say." Tommy winked at Jake.

"Tommy, I'll need your parent's email." He rerolled the linen paper and put it back inside of the metal barrel. He licked the copper lid to close it. He handed Tommy the artifact. "Remember, don't play with this."

"Oh sure." Tommy jotted it on paper and handed it to him.

"Thank you, sir. I'll keep this safe. And thanks for helping us for free." Tommy grinned. He stuffed the artifact in his backpack, and zipped it shut.

The pale man grimaced. "I wasn't going to charge you, Tommy."

"Oh yeah. I mean thanks for helping us because you wanted to," Tommy said.

"Thanks, Prof, for help, and the steaming java." Jake shook the professor's hand.

"Thanks for helping the boys, Walter," Mr. Stanton shook hands and said, "See you when I see you."

Professor Banes said, "I'm always fond of helping out good friends."

Tommy mulled over the stab of guilt that dodge-balled him in the gut. Maybe a bad choice made his stomach ache. He left Mom out. Did he make bad karma? Tommy's brain did mental gymnastics to understand the concept. "So, karma is like throwing a ball hard against the wall; sometimes it whacks you in the head and sometimes you catch it. Right, Mr. Stanton?"

"Yes, that's exactly right!" Mr. Stanton said. "What did you think of my friend?"

They all trudged back to Mr. Stanton's blue Ford truck. "He's nice and smart, but he talks weird."

"He does and always did. He was the top score on the SAT's in high school, but manage to fail the personality test to get a job at Tech Buy," Mr. Stanton said.

"Really?" Tommy dropped a jaw.

"No lie. He's book smart, but is clueless with social situations."

"I get it now," Tommy said.

CHAPTER 26

Buzzy bee sounds in the shop

At bedtime, Tommy trudged up to the Crow's Nest to finish homework without Mom prompting him. Mom needed to believe he didn't need a pretend dad to watch over him. At 10:00 pm, he dropped off to sleep. Around midnight, Tommy awoke when he heard an intense hum making the walls of his room vibrate. He shot up, grabbed his flashlight and metal bat. He cupped a hand to his ear and listened. Bat in hand, he tiptoed by Mom's room. She was still sleeping. He edged to the door which led to the shop and turned the dead bolt. He knew every rule in a horror movie... *never go down the cellar*. But, he gritted his teeth to investigate anyway. He crept down the short flight of stairs and listened, following the humming sound.

The whirring-humming noise increased in velocity, sounding like winds of a tornado spin. He unlocked the latch and turned the door handle, tip-toeing down the flight of stairs, bat in one hand, flashlight in the other. He continued to creep down the steps to the shop level in the dim light.

As he descended the final steps, he shined his flashlight down into the shop. Tommy felt a strong magnetic force pulling him toward the eerie purple light. The vibration blasted a shiver up his spine. Second rule of every horror story—*Don't forget the first rule*. But it was too late.

His feet froze to the ground.

Shards of light peppered the air, swirling upward creating a mini dust devil.

Tommy's hand squeezed the bat handle ready handle to strike any assailant. Before him, the bright arc of light swirled and leaped in a giant rainbow of colors. Stunned, he dropped the bat and it clanged on the hard floor. Goosebump-prickles chased up and down his body. His eyes glazed over and his head was dizzy and bubbly, like the time he drank champagne by mistake. His awareness drifted into a hypnotic, dazed half-sleep trance. Compelled, he moved toward the light.

Suddenly, the artifact appeared and spun wildly in front of him.

"It's you." Tommy murmured from the floor he sat on. Then his knees buckled under him.

A bolt of electricity coursed through him. Words spewed from his mouth that he couldn't have known or memorized. ***"Past, present, future; all the same. Bring me to the karma of this life, so I can go back and eliminate strife. No longer will I keep pain that lodged so deep. Bring me to the time of past, so I can free my soul at last. Reveal to me the truth I need to bring me peace I will succeed. The Guardian of the wheel is present."***

A wide arc of light cracked open and sucked Tommy right through it. He tumbled wildly, end over end, then landed in a room which appeared to be in his old house, yet it wasn't quite the same. The room had no ceiling, but glimmered with a starry evening sky twinkling above.

Tommy ran through the familiar dream room shouting, "Dad! Where are you?"

Dad emerged from his study holding a copy of Tommy's school book, *The Time Wheel* under his arm. "Son, you'll wake the dead with the racquet you're making." His father burst out into a hardy laugh. "I've been waiting for ages to use that joke on you. Come here and give your dad a hug, Sport."

Tommy couldn't believe his eyes. "Are you a ghost, Dad?"

"Do I look like a ghost?" He showed his arms, as solid as when he was alive. He set the book down on the end table, the one Mom had sold months ago.

Tommy ran to Dad. "Who cares if you're a ghost? I miss you a ton."

"The same moon shines on all of us." He pointed up to the moon above. "I love you to the moon and back, as always."

"Why are you reading my homework?" Tommy lifted a brow.

"Fascinating story line."

"Dad, weird things are happening all the time… like this. Are you the one doing them?" Tommy asked.

"I've not been party to those shenanigans. This visit is courtesy of your Prayer Wheel, or should I say, the Time Wheel and the sweet girl, Choden who brought you here."

"You *know* about her?"

"Sure do."

Tommy craned his neck around. "Where are we?"

"You're in a parallel dimension… a place between life and death," Dad answered.

Tommy scratched the top of his head. "I don't understand."

"*Parallel* means side by side. You heard clues and synchronicities everywhere at school. I exist in spirit form now, just like Choden."

"How did I get here?"

"Choden knew you needed a visit with me to set you straight."

"Is this the Better Place?"

"Not exactly. We're having an interdimensional visit."

"We create *a better place* with our love and memories. I wanted to you feel at home so I recreated our happy home. The actual *Better Place* is far better than this one, but since you're very much alive, this will have to do. The stars are a nice touch, don't you think?" He pointed up to the open ceiling where stars and full moon shone above.

"We had to sell our real house." Tommy hung his head low. "All the stuff in this room, like the real furniture is gone."

"But not gone from your memory or from mine. It's real here and still exists. Love makes a home, not the walls…or the ceiling for that matter. The shop is a fine place to make a new start. You and Mom did an impressive job with it."

"Mom and I have been so sad since you…left us." Tommy wiped tears from his cheeks.

"My body was as beat up as the old baseball mitt you found. But here I am as fit as a fiddle and singing a tune."

"You look good for a dead guy." Tommy gave Dad a hopeful smile.

He winked. "My spirit-self is vibrant and healthy. I'm proud of how hard you've been working at school."

Tommy bit his lower lip. "I'm keeping my promise to look after Mom, just like you'd asked me to.."

"About that... Jackson Stanton is a nice fellow, Sport. Give him a chance."

"You *know* about Mr. Stanton?" Tommy's face torqued. "Mom is married to you."

"Till death do us part. I want her to be happy. When you're older, you'll understand."

"Mr. Stanton's got too much swagger, Dad. I've been trying to stop Mom from liking him, but I can't. He has too many edges and is like catnip."

"I'm not angry with her—not one bit. You shouldn't be either. Life is for the living and *she's lonely,* Sport."

"She has *me.* She *said* so." Tommy knew she told him a lie. He saw it in her eyes.

"It's a different kind of lonely," Dad said gently. "Love multiplies, not divides."

"Are you lonely here, Dad?"

"I've been too busy to be lonely. I've taken up writing and painting. Just the other day, I had the most interesting conversation with Michelangelo. Einstein and I chewed the fat discussing time travel. And, I even tossed a ball around with Babe Ruth... but I had more fun tossing it to you. And sometimes,

I peek in on you at school to see if you're paying attention."

Dad's image started to shimmer and fade. "Don't go!"

Dad said, "Time's up. Walter Banes has interesting information for you. Hug Mom for me and be nice to Mr. Stanton, will you, Sport?"

The vortex of colored lights snapped open and sucked Tommy back in. It spit him out into the shop. Tommy rolled forward and slammed into the sales counter with a bang. He sat up dazed, as if he'd been on a wild teacup ride at the state fair. He had a million questions he wanted to ask, but time was up. Wisps of dream images floated away and vaporized.

Mom sprinted from her second-floor room, running down in her bare feet.

"You scared the devil out of me. You could've tumbled down these steps! Are you ok?" She gently touched his head with her palm to feel for a fever.

He rubbed his brow. "Where am I?" Confused and fuzzy he couldn't remember how he got down the stairs into the shop in the first place. He must have sleepwalked. But no…the details were coming back. It all started with the buzzing noise...and the bat...and walking down the stairs.

"I thought I'd locked this door. Let's get you back up to bed." She gently helped him up from the floor. "You gave me an awful scare, Punkin'."

The misty cobwebs cleared. "You don't understand. I was talking to Dad and he wanted me to hug you."

Mom kissed him and gave him a hug. "Back to bed."

Tommy knew she didn't believe him—not one bit.

He fell back into a deep sleep, dreaming of the spinning artifact turning through time. His clock alarm rang signaling 6:30 am. "Friday. TGIF." He sighed. His week was almost done. He glanced on the nightstand next to his bed where he set the Time Wheel before bed. It was gone.

CHAPTER 27

Ms. Moonshine English teacher

Monday 8:25 am

Miss Bell's Homeroom

Miss Bell was a slice of sunshine starting his day. Mr. Taylor was a humorous slice that sealed his day. In between was stuffed with subjects Tommy called stinky bologna and old cheese. Reading class was the biggest chunk of bologna and the toughest one to swallow. He couldn't digest all the details. He choked on every vocabulary test and he couldn't stomach comprehension questions. Nerves gave him gas. He hadn't met the new reading teacher and distress churned his gut. Surprises were never good. Surprise… Pop quiz. Surprise… Test today. All these worries rotated in his gut the minute his foot reached the pavement in front of Hope School.

Tommy scurried to his locker, then on to Miss Bell's homeroom.

Miss Bell greeted the students as they arrived. "Good morning! If you are in my history class, this is a reminder to complete your reports. To the rest of you, as you know, our dear Mrs. Otter has retired to sunny Florida. Ms. Moonshine is a rare treat, as you'll soon discover when you meet her today. Remember to give her a cheery Hope welcome." She waved her fluffy pen back and forth.

Tommy's stomach rumbled with a nervous bubble the size of a soccer ball. He leaned in toward Jake. "Surprises are never good."

Jake leaned in to whisper back, "Glad the Otter left."

"Mr. Delo, you appear to be green in the gills. Are you feeling unwell?" Miss Bell asked.

"I just don't like bologna."

"Well then, I hope you don't have any for lunch today," she remarked.

Tommy zoned out and imagined he spun far away from reading class. After homeroom, he motioned for Jake to join him at the teacher's desk. "Miss Bell, can you tell us about the prayer wheel in your grandpa's shop?"

"Hmmm, I recall Grandpapa locked it a glass cabinet in his home whenever I visited. He told me never to touch it without his permission—ever. I respected his wishes. He was careful with all of his artifacts. I'll admit, my feelings were hurt." Her eyes were misty. "Why do you ask?"

"We'd love a chance to talk with him about it. It'll help us finalize our research and I'm sure he's lonely. Do you think he'd like a visit from us this Monday after school?" Tommy asked.

"How kind of you! I'm sure he'd *love* the company. He's been asking about the new owner of his shop for months. He lives at the Cedar Rest Home." She cupped her hand near her mouth and lowered her voice, "Fair warning— he lives in a fantasy world. We play along with him and you should too. It makes him happy to tell his tall tales of travel."

"Thanks, Miss Bell," Tommy tugged on Jake's arm.

Tommy and Jake left for the Language Arts class.

Jake pulled Tommy aside. "T, you're a genius. I'll bet Mr. Bell could tell us fantasy stories we'd believe. I'll let my dad know it's on after school today."

Jake called his dad. "Would you be able to drop us off at Cedar Rest home after school today? Ok. Thanks. We have a ride."

Ms. Moonshine's Reading and Language Arts Class

Tommy and Jake headed to meet the new reading teacher. As Tommy approached, a squealing guitar riff drifted from the reading classroom. "What the heck?" He peeked in and caught sight of an older woman with a mop of gray curls propped and pinned in a wild disarray resembling a bird's nest atop her head. Tommy and Jake entered and took their seats. Ms. Moonshine's neck sported an electric blue feathered boa flung without apology. Tommy studied her. "She's nothing like Mrs. Otter!"

"Dude, check out her feet." Jake pointed down.

Tommy stole glance to the bottom of Ms. Moonshine's long flowery skirt. Unlike Mrs. Otter, there were no sensible black heeled shoes. She wore open-toed leather sandals revealing bright yellow toenails, each be-decked with a fluorescent orange smiley-face. A tattoo of a peace sign decorated her left ankle. Tommy never saw a teacher's toes before, much less brightly painted ones smiling at him.

She waved a greeting with gem ringed fingers. Her bangled bracelets clanged together with a soft metal clink.

As the group of students entered, the woman waved her hands around like she was shooing mosquitoes away. "Sit, stay, chill! As you have heard, our dear Mrs. Otter retired to Florida. My name is Ms. Moonshine, and I will be replacing her. I only hope I can fill her sturdy, sensible shoes."

Jenny stifled a full out laugh. "Are you a hippy, Mrs. Moonshine?"

"It's *Ms.* Moonshine dear. Define hippy."

"Someone who doesn't wear deodorant or shave their arm pits," Jenny snickered.

Joe burst out in a mocking roar and slammed his fist to his desk. "Good one, Jenny."

Ms. Moonshine didn't appear offended, just taken aback at the outburst. "Why you poor uninformed girl! You have such *limited and backward* view of a woman's role in history. Let me set you straight. The 1960's were a glorious, tumultuous era bearing witness to the strength and *value* of women. Gloria Steinman was our hero. We weren't fodder for lip-gloss and miniskirts. We had flower power... demanded equal rights...and lived fearlessly. *We changed history.*" Her eyes shifted down to Jenny's too-short skirt. "We were Goddesses, not eye candy for witless boys to ogle and leer. No offense to the fine gents in *this* room."

Jenny turned her gaze toward Sarah and tugged at the bottom of her skirt.

After that, Tommy decided he loved Ms. Moonshine.

"We have eons of time to explore many luscious books." Ms. Moonshine pointed to a stack of novels on her desktop.

Tommy grabbed his head in his hands dreading the big pile he probably wouldn't understand. Ice cream was a luscious treat. Books were stale bread.

"Our first in class reading book is *A Wrinkle in Time*."

Mom said synchronicities are coincidences that are supposed to happen, like road signs you can't ignore, Jake's guitar, and this time-bending book. It was another coincidence to add to the pile of I-don't-believe-this-is-happening events.

Jake jotted a note on his pad and showed Tommy. It read, "Did you hear from the Prof yet?"

Tommy wrote back and held up his notebook. "Not yet."

Math Class 2:40 Mr. Taylor

Tommy breathed a sigh of relief when 2:40 struck on the clock. Right after math, the last session of the day, he and Jake would be on their way to visit Mr. Bell and find out some secrets.

Mr. Taylor blew a bicycle horn twice to signal an important announcement. Tommy guessed Reese, Jeff, or Jake would earn the high score since they were the smartest kids.

"Our high score paper from yesterday's math session is... drumroll please..."

He and his classmates drum rolled fingers on their desk tops.

Mr. Taylor pointed to him. "Tommy Delo, my vertically challenged dynamo!"

Tommy's jaw dropped open. "Me? Are you sure?"

He tooted a party horn twice. "Sure tootin!"

"Nice goin' T!" Jake fist bumped him.

"Congratulations," Reese said.

"Nice!" Jeff commented.

Mr. Taylor donned a white chef's hat and mimicked an Italian accent. "Your name will appear on the 100% pizza chart. Thatza-so-nice, Tommy Delo! If it's not too cheesy to say, the pizza of success will carry your name until month's end." Mr. Taylor pinned up the chart. Tommy's classmates clapped for him.

Mr. Taylor said, "At month's end, all students whose name made the chart will enjoy a real pizza lunch with me in this very room!"

All the kids clapped.

"A real pizza?" Reese asked.

"Cheese and all," Mr. Taylor said.

Tommy burst with pride. He squeezed back an air biscuit ready to ruin his special moment. The word, *Archimedes*, flew into Tommy's head. What did this strange word mean? And why did it pop into his head.

"Great job, Tommy!" Reese said, "I hope mine will be on the chart soon."

The Time Wheel had a busy day. She visited Einstein, the famous physicist and the famous Greek mathematician, Archimedes. Tommy would be twelve in a matter of weeks. She couldn't wait until their connection was even stronger.

Cedar Rest Home Town of Hope

After school on Monday, Tommy and Jake hopped up on the running board on Mr. Stanton's truck and piled into the box seat.

"Hey, Mr. Stanton," Tommy said.

"Hey, Kiddo. I'm thinking I need to give you a nick name." Mr. Stanton said.

"Not Squirt or some other baby name, Ok? Jake calls me T. My dad called me Sport, even though I'm lousy at all of them," Tommy said.

"You're a good sport all the time," Jake quipped.

Mr. Stanton said, "Jake told me you like time travel books. How about TT for short."

Jake poked Tommy in the ribs. "Time Traveler Tommy has a nice ring to it. Don't you think?"

"TT it is!" Tommy agreed.

"I dub you TT," Mr. Stanton said.

After the brief drive, the boys headed out. Mr. Stanton called after Jake. "Jake, text me when you're done. I'll pick you up out front."

"K, dad." Jake waved his father on.

Mr. Stanton pulled away with the truck engine roaring and rattling.

Tommy and Jake left the parking area and followed the cement path leading to double wide glass doors.

"Let's do this. Follow my lead," Jake said.

The thin receptionist peeked over the red framed glasses propped on her nose. "Are you gentlemen lost or are you visiting a relative?"

Jake stepped forward, "Hello 'Mam. I'm Jake Stanton and this is my buddy, Tommy Delo." He shoved a hand toward hers giving Miss Gray the full-on-Jake catnip grin.

She blushed and giggled. "Oh my, such lovely manners from such a young man. "I'm Miss Gray, but you can call me Cindy."

Jake's magic charm did it again. Tommy stepped forward. "We're students of Miss Bell and she asked us to visit with her grandfather, Mr. Bell."

Miss Gray lifted the phone with a floaty hand gesture. "Sign in first, and sign out on this visitor log before you leave. I'll ring Mr. Bell's room to see if he's accepting visitors today." She pressed a button with her long pink fingernail and raised her voice to speak into the phone. "Mr. Bell, this is Cindy Gray at the front desk. Two young gents are here to visit with you. They say they're in your granddaughter's history class." She paused. "Oh, you were expecting them? Your granddaughter didn't mention it to me when she was here.   Alright. I'll send them down." She nodded and cradled the receiver. "He said he's been expecting you." She put her hand to her mouth and whispered, "Fair warning, he believes his fantasy stories are true. We play along when he prattles on about them."

Tommy shot Jake the *look*. "Sure thing."

"Mr. Bell is residing in Room 15 first hallway to your right. You have one hour to visit before his dinner service. Then you need to go."

Miss Gray tapped her watch and gave Tommy the hurry-up look he knew so well. He glanced at her name tag. Dad always said using people's names make them feel special.

"Thanks, *Miss Gray*." His cheek dimpled in a mile-wide smile which she returned to him.

Jake and Tommy followed the deep red carpet and turned right to room 15. Wheel chairs lined the walls. Rubbing alcohol, Lysol, lavender, and loneliness permeated the air and made Tommy pinch his nose. "This place smells worse than science class." He peered into the open doors and felt sad to see so many people alone.

"Yet, no frog guts anywhere in sight," Jake said.

"Just because you can't see them, doesn't mean they're not here." Tommy laughed.

As they approached room 15, Tommy peered in and saw an old man in a decorated veteran's cap sporting various military metals of honor.

Even though the door was open, Jake knocked on the door frame and asked, "Can we enter, Mr. Bell?"

"Sure. Don't just stand there and gawk at me. I've been waiting for you." Mr. Bell waved his arms excitedly. He pointed a bent finger to the folding chairs on the wall.

"Pull 'em over boys and close the door behind you." He watched Mr. Bell's age spotted hands move around with a life of their own.

Tommy closed the door and Jake unfolded the chairs.

Mr. Bell leaned forward on the overstuffed brown chair. In his lap, he held a leather-bound journal which looked familiar to Tommy.

The man laughed. "I see you got my message loud and clear, Tommy." His blue eyes twinkled with a cheery sparkle.

"Me?" Tommy pointed to his chest. "What do you mean?"

"Yes, you." Mr. Bell said.

"Hey, your journal looks like the one I found in my locker."

The old man burst out laughing. "Because it's the very same one, young man."

Jake shot Tommy a side eye. "*His* journal showed up in your locker?"

The man winked. "She dropped it off for me."

"Miss Bell?"

"Heavens no. You did read the journal entry, didn't you?" He held a page open to show Tommy the fancy black writing which said, "*Visit Mr. Bell at Cedar Rest Home.*"

"I did."

"Then you know I'm talking about the she in the prayer wheel."

"Ooooooh" Tommy said.

"I'm not following." Jake squinted his eyes.

"You'll catch up soon," Mr. Bell said. "Let's shake and get formalities over with."

"Tommy Delo, Sir." Tommy shook the man's large wrinkled hand.

"Your father taught you right. That's a good strong grip you got there, Son." Mr. Bell grinned in amusement.

Tommy filled with pride. "Dad said you can tell a

lot about a man by his handshake."

"And he was right," Mr. Bell said.

Jake shook Mr. Bell's hand. "Jake Stanton, Sir,"

"Another firm grip. Good for you, Son." Mr. Bell smiled and rubbed his palms together. "Now then, you've come to ask me about her."

Tommy shook his head. "*Her* who?"

Mr. Bell slapped his knee. "Choden."

"Just to clarify, who are you speaking about when you say, *she and her*?" Jake asked.

"The life force of a brilliant Tibetan girl who inhabits the prayer wheel. She is a kidder being your age and all, boys."

A chill ran up Tommy's spine. Somehow, he knew it all along. She'd whispered her name to him many times. "So, the artifact is haunted?"

"Not haunted—*inhabited*. There's a big difference. Choden was just twelve when she was chosen by the monks to be the first female Dalai Lama after Yellow Hat died in 1475."

"What happened to her?" Tommy asked.

"She died of a virus. She'll tell you more when she's ready. The important part is Choden pleaded with the monks to put her essence into the artifact so she could continue to help people. She was so insistent, the monks agreed. When Choden took her final breath, the monks released the former soul who inhabited the prayer wheel and she took his place. She's been in the prayer wheel since 1476. Her brother, Yeshe, took her place as the Dalai Lama."

"How did they do it? Put her in the prayer wheel, I mean." Jake asked.

"The monks performed a capturing ceremony. To this day, there's been no female Dalai Lama and the ceremony is kept highly secretive. Choden made it her mission to help twelve-year-old people to adjust their karma and to learn from past errors of judgement. Do you know what karma is, boys?"

"I do now." Tommy grinned.

"Tommy, Choden chose you to be her guardian. I knew it the moment you walked into my shop. I could feel it in my bones."

Tommy blinked and bit his lip. "Chose me, *how*?"

"Haven't you had strange dreams and visions ever since you moved into the shop?"

Tommy said, "I have. Mom said it was stress."

"Fiddle-faddle." Mr. Bell waved his hand as if he was swatting a fly away. "Don't you daydream about faraway place you've never been to?"

Tommy scratched the top of his head. "Yes, ever since I found the artifact." Tommy recalled the unexplained sunburn, the visions of Medieval England, and the weird daydreams. They all began in the summer when they moved into Bell's Treasure Trove.

"Tell him, T."

"Jake and I traveled to Tibet, and I got sunburn when I wasn't in the sun. In fact, I was in reading class."

"There you have it. She chose you like I said. And she's already decided you are both worthy of her time and travel efforts."

"But I'm not twelve yet," Tommy said. "Don't I need to be twelve?"

"Choden knows exactly why she chose you. Of course, she's had many guardians throughout the years, including me. She has others throughout time and space. I'd place the artifact on the second floor in a safe spot. But don't you know, Choden was so fond of people, she'd spin down to the the shop to sit on the high shelf just to watch customers arrive." He stopped to chuckle. His blue eyes glinted with merriment. "She's a curious soul and compassionate soul, just as you are, Tommy."

"Where does she go when she…disappears?" Jake asked.

The corners of Mr. Bell's eyes crinkled. He touched his chin and paused to think.

"Choden has a mind of her own. But sometimes, if you're lucky, she'll drop you off where you most desire to go. Like when you visited with your father, Tommy."

"You *knew* about the visit with my dad?" Tommy's eyes opened wide.

"Choden told me all about Thomas. He was a history buff and avid reader, just like Choden," Mr. Bell said.

"Does Miss Bell know about the prayer wheel?" Jake asked.

"When she was five, I took her on a trip to Egypt with me. She falsely recalls riding on an airplane to get there. I didn't dissuade her. It's where she developed her love of history. She is highly curious. I had to protect her from ever using the prayer wheel without me, so I hid it when she visited and never told her its secret or purpose."

"How did you get the prayer wheel?" Tommy asked.

"She came to me when I turned twelve. My father and I traveled to Tibet on a pilgrimage. One night, the prayer wheel spun into my room. I was so shocked when it first happened, I thought I'd dreamed her up. Choden and I have remained great friends throughout the years. She's allowed me an occasional trip with her, but I'm an old man."

Jake's face lit up. "T, the twins we saw…the girl's name was Choden!"

"Keep your voices low. The nurses here think I'm nuts in the noggin. No one believes a lick of what I say. I let them think I'm crazy, just so I can amuse myself. You both believe me. I can see it in your eyes."

"We do believe you for sure," Tommy said.

"Choden trusted you since she allowed to see her and her twin, Yeshe."

"Did Choden choose Miss Bell when she turned twelve?" Jake asked.

"No. Silva is a fact finder, a show-me-proof kind of gal. Choden chooses those with childlike wonder. Those who've seen rough times or experienced great loss, like you, Tommy. And she deems Jake worthy, too."

Jake held a hand up. "Wait...her name is Silva Bell?"

"My son loved Christmas, so yes. He named her Silva Bell."

"I get it. It sounds like Silver bells." Tommy laughed.

"Tommy, you and Jake are linked by friendship. A good friend is the key to a fulfilled life. What is a person without friends? Lonely." Mr. Bell held up the embossed leather journal. "This journal is yours now." He held it out to Tommy.

"Gee, thanks Mr. Bell. What should I do with it?"

"Keep it hidden. After a time trip, record what you learned and what your guests learned. There are many secrets hidden in this book. Each keeper of the prayer wheel must record their insights, proving to Choden they're worthy and have improved his or her life and the life of others. Don't open the journal until you are alone. Promise me you'll do all of it."

"I will!" Tommy exclaimed.

"Pinky swear." Mr. Bell held up a wrinkled pinky.

"Pinky swear," Tommy held up a pinky and linked it with Mr. Bell's.

"Then here you go." He handed it to Tommy. "I have a big request of you, Tommy. Before I kick the bucket, I'd love to take a final trip or two. I'd go myself, but now that Choden's chosen you, I'll need your energy boost to foist my wrinkled butt through the portal. I'm not as young as I used to be!" His eyes shined with merry laughter. "Will you boys go with me for my final ride?"

Tommy put a hand out. "I'll do it, Mr. Bell, as long as I'm home in time for dinner."

"We'll keep this quiet. No need for Silva to know about our travel plans." He smiled. "She worries about me."

"Anything else we need to know about the wheel?" Jake asked.

"The Keeper of the Wheel can directly communicate with her. You'll hear her hum when she spins and your dreams will link. When do you turn twelve?"

"November 4th. I've been hearing the humming sound ever since Mom bought the shop."

"She likes you, Tommy. Once you're twelve, return with her and I'll ride shotgun on the next trip. I'll show you a few tricks." Mr. Bell rubbed his hands together.

A buzzer sounded and a nurse wearing pink scrubs tapped on the door, then entered. "Mr. Bell, your dinner is ready. Boys, visiting hour is over."

"Yes, just entertaining the young folks with some stories." Mr. Bell said.

"I'm sure you are, Mr. Bell." The nurse in pink scrubs played along and winked at Tommy and Jake. She scurried from the room on quiet feet.

"She thinks I'm nuts in the noggin." He tapped his skull and laughed until his face turned red.

"Thank you, Sir," Tommy said. "We'll visit you again."

"My pleasure. I haven't laughed this hard in ages. Remember, karma is the cause and effect of actions, so choose your actions wisely."

"That would make a good fortune cookie saying," Jake said.

"It certainly would!" Mr. Bell said.

Tommy and Jake signed out at the desk and met Mr. Stanton outside the building.

"How'd your visit go?" Mr. Stanton asked.

Even though Tommy was bursting at the seams to talk about the visit, he held it in.

"Informative," Jake said.

"He expected us," Tommy said.

Mr. Stanton drove up Main Street. "Here we are."

"Thanks again, Mr. Stanton."

"No problem, TT."

That night, Tommy sat propped against bed pillows, anxious to read Mr. Bell's journal. He clicked the lamp by his bed, cracked open the leather cover. "What kind of joke is this?" All the cream-colored pages were blank. He flipped through the whole book. "No way!" Even the one Mr. Bell showed him was now blank. "It figures. Joke's on me." He was ready to fling the journal clear across the room when black ink letters rotated and revolved in front of his eyes. He stared mystified, as the inky squiggles dropped into a heap on the empty page. Fascinated, he poked the pile of letters with his index finger. They wiggled and settled into orderly lines of cursive right before his eyes. "What the..." Tommy squinted and soon he could decipher the words. His jaw gaped open. Not only did he witness magic, but he couldn't wait to tell Jake what he just read and how it happened.

Dear Tommy,

By now, you've figured out what I can do. Your free will is very important to me. Unless you agree to future time trips, I can't actually bring you along. Although you can invite a person who needs my special kind of help. I trust you'll use this new power wisely.

My name is Choden. You saw me with my twin brother when you time traveled with Jake to Tibet. I miss my brother. I suppose it's why I'm partial to twelve-year-old boys and why I showed you a part of my life. Soon, you'll be twelve and you'll hear my thoughts as if we were one mind. You are a kind and loyal boy. You can trust Jake. Tell Jeff about me. You can trust him, too.

Thank you for being my friend.

With fondness,

Choden

Tommy ran down the flight of stairs to the shop. He punched numbers on the shop phone.

"Jake, it's Tommy. You're never going to guess what I learned about the journal!"

CHAPTER 28

Researching the artifact

After School Tuesday

Jake slammed his locker shut. "Once the bells rings, we'll bolt to the shop. I'll show you a short cut to avoid crossing the bridge where the gorilla lurks. We'll take a right as soon as we pass the Old Mill restaurant. There's a hidden staircase behind Trout Alley which leads up to Main Street. Once we pass the stairs, we'll dash to the shop. Got it?"

"Got it!" Tommy memorized all of the directions Jake recited to him. At that moment, he realized his memory had improved. Now he'd score an A+ for outsmarting Joe.

The dismissal bell rang out the sweet sound of freedom. A flurry of activity began around him. He ordered his feet to walk, not run, to the nearest exit.

The crossing guard tooted a red whistle to halt him two seconds before he pounded the pavement with his usual after school sprint. Tommy careened to a stop. He and Jake eyed each other in a friendly challenge, then bolted. Tommy sprinted like a deer in hunting season, passing Trout Alley, taking the stone staircase two at a time, before heading up to Main Street.

Tommy arrived at the shop with heaving breaths seconds before Jake. "Beat you!"

Jake caught up to him panting like a dog. "Man, you're fast, T." Jake wiped his brow. "Have you thought about joining track in the spring?"

"Nah. I'm getting all the practice I need running from Joe and jumping to conclusions. I could even run faster if I had new sneakers. Mom can't afford the Air-Blast ones I wanted. Are you on the track team, Jake?"

"I ran track last year. No one could beat me at sprinting… until now." Jake said.

"Seriously?"

"Truth. There's spring tryouts every year."

Tommy felt a bubble of pride well up in his chest. He took the key from his backpack pocket and wiggled it in the lock. He pushed the sturdy glass entry door open, hearing the ting of the overhead bell. He ran to the steps leading to the second-floor apartment and tramped up the staircase to announce, "Mom, I'm here with Jake."

Mom opened the door and peeked out. She held a box of donations in her arms and set the box down. "Did you just run a mile?"

"Actually, yes," Tommy said. "Guess what? My name is on Mr. Taylor's pizza chart because I got 100% on my last homework."

Mom's face lit like sunshine. "Outstanding! Hi, Jake. Are you on it too?"

"Hey, Mrs. Delo. No, just Tommy."

"He is excellent at math," she said.

"Can we use the computer?"

"As long as you agree to stay on safe sites." She waggled her finger and gave Tommy a stern warning glance.

"Aww, Mom, not *that* again," Tommy groaned.

"Yes, that again. Here. Take a few snacks down with you." She walked back into the main room to sort and file papers.

Tommy grabbed two apples, juice, and two bags of veggie chips and handed one of each to Jake.

"I basically do what I want, with no mom to watch after me, T," Jake admitted. "Must be kinda' nice your mom cares so much."

Tommy laughed. "Seriously? Mom has rules for her rules. She repeats her cautions every stinkin' time. *enrichment.* and so on." He laughed. "Why'd you partner up with me instead of Jeff? He's super smart."

"Jeff spends tons of time with his brothers and likes to work solo. He's super intelligent, but doesn't know how to be chill about grades and can't joke around with me like you do."

They dug into the vocabulary words. "Recalcitrant? What kind of word is this?"

"Ah. It means stubborn natured," Jake said.

"Thanks!" Thirty minutes later, they were done.

Tommy checked the clock in disbelief. "World record finish." A wave of gratitude overtook him.

"Told you so." Jake brushed his palms together. "Now, let's research the artifact. I love history"

"Don't tell a living soul—I am thinking of going to college for archeological studies. Prof Banes really inspired me. I prefer to keep my smarts secret from the ignorant masses." He thumbed the loop in jeans pocket. "Occasionally I do something mad stupid on purpose."

"Why? If I was as smart as you, I'd want everyone to know."

"I don't want to ruin my laid back persona. Besides, once the teachers are on to me, they load me with busy work called *enrichment*. I don't want to get hassled, so I slow my roll."

"Geez, I could've gotten you a D with no trouble at all!" Tommy grinned.

"My dad insists women like a guy with an *edge*. Swagger gets a girl— not brains. I'm practicing my swagger potential."

"I think you have loads of it. My mom loved my dad. He was *really* smart. He was a history teacher and read a ton of books. You would've liked him," Tommy said.

"I'm sure, since I like you." He paused and lifted a brow. "I'll need to rethink my strategy about women if brains will earn me a woman like your mom— or the enticing Miss Bell. I'll let you in on a secret, my dad graduated college top of his class. He pretends he's all muscle and coolness, but he's very smart, too."

"Then you are both wrong to hide it." Worry creased Tommy's brow. "Your dad has too many edges and Professor Banes has none. They're so different from each other."

"Dad respects the Prof. They were in advanced classes together in middle school. They even crushed on the same girl —my mom, Lily. But as the story goes, Dad got her,and she left us…so it's not much of a win-win for Dad and I."

Tommy saw Jake's face drop, so he tried to lighten Jake's mood. "You and your dad have super powers."

"Not super enough. My mom ran off with a dude she met at a gig. I was a toddler and Dad was attending Grad school for his degree. At least, that's the way my dad tells it."

Tommy had to think of something to make Jake laugh. "Jenny stares at you like this." He batted his eyelashes, pursed his lips imitating Jenny's high timbered voice and said, "Oh Jakey, live on the edge with me." He pretended to apply gloss to his puckered lips and blew a kiss.

Jake burst out laughing. "You sounded *just* like the lipstick troll!"

"Really, Jake. All the girls gawk and giggle around you... or haven't you noticed?"

"Nah." Jake waved his hand to dismiss Tommy's suggestion. "Girls like to giggle."

"Haven't you noticed they giggle mostly around you? Even Miss Gray acted all goofy."

"She probably knows my dad. It happens a lot because I look like him."

"Seriously, what's so bad about being smart? I'd kill to have your brain in my head for even a second. I don't need to pretend to be dumb. I'm *authentic* at it."

"You're a smart kid...just vocabulary-challenged." He faked a punch on Tommy's shoulder.

"I like smart girls better than the giggle boxes."

Tommy grinned and thought, I like Beth.

"I prefer older women, like your mom."

"You're a perv. My mom is way too old for you," Tommy teased back.

"Like I said, all sixth-grade boys are pervs. You'll see. My hormones are raging. Dad says it's normal. All I can think about are boobs." Jake burst into laughter. "Besides, I'm just kidding about your mom. I *like Beth*. "

"Beth?" Tommy had no chance with Beth if Jake liked her. "I'd kill to know what it's like to be a girl magnet."

"Anyone you like, T?"

"Dina is pretty and nice," Tommy said.

Jake grinned. "I agree."

"Now back to our research." Jake clicked on his laptop. "Listen to this." Jake read, *"The Sumerians were one of the earliest urban societies to emerge in the world. They developed a writing system whose wedge-shaped strokes are known as cuniform used in years 3300 BCE to 100 CE.* My personal theory is the people who used it were super intelligent and...ok, this will sound weird... they may have had contact with aliens since many things can't be explained by old history."

"Aliens? No way."

"It's my theory. And no way will we share it...at school...ever," Jake said.

Tommy pulled up images. "See this picture? What do you think, Jake?" Tommy asked.

"Maybe there's a clue in Mr. Bell's journal."

That night, Tommy took a breath, made a wish and opened the journal.

Dear Tommy,

  I'm glad we're friends. The prayer wheel was created by monks, not aliens...Keep researching.

Your friend,
Choden

CHAPTER 29

Tommy learns a secret

Wednesday

Tommy wished for lazy fun filled days at the beach. Instead, he faced a tsunami of classes ahead of him. In his fantasy daydream, he imagined himself to be a fearless pirate using a sword to slay enemies. Then he imagined swabbing the decks of a creaky wooden ship. He could smell the salty air and feel the wind brace against his cheeks. Surely, a pirate's life would be easier than his own. Pirates had no homework. They could do anything they wanted to do. Life would be simple and trouble free.

Jake nudged Tommy to get his attention.

Tommy snapped to attention. "What?"

"I *said*, I have plans with Jeff after school today, so I can't come by the shop."

"Oh. Ok. But, remember our promise. You can't tell Jeff about the prayer wheel."

"I'll keep it on the down-low for now." Jake gave a Shazam finger wiggle and fist bump. "I wonder what Ms. Moonshine has up her bell-shaped sleeves today."

Tommy licked his lips. They tasted ocean salty. He touched his windburned cheeks. "Does my face look red to you?"

Jake examined him. "Actually, it does. Maybe you had an allergic reaction to something."

"Yeah, maybe." The bell rang for the next session. Tommy touched his scorched nose, wondering why it hurt so much.

They headed to Ms. Moonshine's reading class.

Ms. Moonshine's newest garish accessories included a chunky silver bracelet decorated with purple crystals, topped by a second wide, silver one. Each finger sported turquoise rings of various sizes and shapes. As she walked, her bracelets clanged together.

"Good day!" Ms. Moonshine raised her arms and drew her face upward, as if worshipping the ceiling tiles.

Tommy followed her glance and lifted his chin to see what Ms. Moonshine found so interesting up overhead. All he saw were white ceiling tiles. When she passed by him, an earthy scent of old socks, carnations, and stinky incense filled his nostrils. He recalled the funny names on an old perfume tin he found in the shop. The tin of Patchouli and Musk smelled so bad, he tossed in into the trash making a two-point score. Yet here it was again assaulting his nose.

While Jake seemed amused by her, Jeff cast a judgmental glance at Ms. Moonshine.

Tommy noticed a purple butterfly tattoo on the teacher's right ankle. It peeked out from the bottom of her long billowy skirt. He watched the array of layered necklaces dangle around her neck like a jumble of acrobatic snakes having a hug party.

"Boys and girls, I'd like to start our unit with an award-winning novella from the 1960's called *A Wrinkle In Time*, by Madeline L'Engle. She was not only an author, but a scientist." She bowed to an imaginary person and clapped at no one.

Tommy looked around at his peers. Was he supposed to clap at the imaginary person, too? No one clapped, so he didn't either.

She picked up a purple marker, walked to the whiteboard and scrolled A *Wrinkle in Time* in large flaring cursive script.

Tommy perked up to attention and waved his hand. "Ms. Moonshine, did you say the book is about *Time Travel*?"

"Yes, I did! Does this interest you, Dear?" She gave him a sly smile.

"It sure does!" After that, Tommy zoned in on her every word.

Ms. Moonshine danced around the room, instructing in her own unique style. "In her autobiography, A Circle of Quiet , L'Engle says that there are two types of time. Chronos and Kairos. Chronos is orderly and linear, or in a line. Think of our hours in day, or years that pass. Kairos is 'Universal time' and it's limitless. She says you can choose the correct time to remedy a situation."

Tommy propped forward on his elbows. He wondered, how could anyone can *choose* the right time? Time runs out, races, or crawls by —sand in an hour glass. It wasn't a choice. Time happens on its own.

"Past and present can exist side by side, two parallel moments in time. In her story, a tesseract helps the characters achieve time travel, jumping back and forth from Chronos to Kairos time."

Tommy waved his hand to ask, "What is Chronos time?"

"Chronos time is the one we use daily. Kairos is the time that exists in the past or the future."

Tommy, time watcher, only saw time tick away. "How can anyone jump back from Chronos to Kairos time? I don't understand."

"I suppose you'd need tesseract device to help you leap time. A tesseract is an object which allows a person to time jump. The theory states, when time stops, one can visit the past as if it just happened."

A lightbulb moment shined in Tommy's head.

Jake kicked Tommy under the desk and his face was just as excited as his own. Jake must have had the same switch turn on in his head.

Tommy sucked in a breath wishing to burst

from his seat and do a happy dance. He realized the artifact was a tesseract. The Kairos device allowed him to travel back in time.

Ms. Moonshine sashayed around the room to check student notebooks, "I see you are writing diligently. And your name is…"

Jeff sat up like a soldier when she neared him. "Jeff Milner."

"You and Jenny have the same last name. Is Jenny your sister?"

"Not even." Jenny snorted before Jeff could respond.

Jeff's voice got louder. "Jenny's my cousin. She's not my sister."

"I see." Ms. Moonshine lifted a brow and called out the attendance. She leaned in to view Jake's notes. "Interesting! And you are…"

"Jake Stanton." He gave her the full-on Stanton smile.

"Oh yes. *My, my,* you do resemble a young Jim Morrison…" she mumbled and held a hand to her heart. With a faraway look in her eyes she asked Jake, "Do you sing or play guitar, Dear?"

"Yes. How'd you know?"

"Just a hunch." Her face appeared misty. She floated over to Dina's desk and pointed to her notebook.

"Impressive, Dina. You have the makings of a true goddess."

"A true what?" Dina glanced up and wrinkled her nose.

"A true Goddess. It means you are a woman who *values* knowledge… a woman of the age of Aquarius." She held up her index and second finger forming a V. "This was a sign of the 60's and it meant peace for all humanity."

Dina grinned ear to ear. "I'm an Aquarius!"

"I knew you would be." Ms. Moonshine headed to Reese and patted her on the shoulder. She gave her a warm smile. "And you, my dear… such a fine effort." She leaned in to whisper words so softly only Reese could hear them.

Reese smiled and gestured Ms. Moonshine a peace sign.

Tommy watched the room transform from brick-heavy, to light and airy. Tommy tried to guess Ms.

Moonshine's age. Was she 60, 70, or older? She had a timeless quality and energy about her that defied time or age.

She eyed Beth's notebook and said, "My dear, you are very insightful."

Tommy saw Beth's face bubble happiness like soda fizz after you shake the can.

She glanced at Jenny's notebook. "Doodling won't help you in my class. But you are quite a talented artist, nonetheless."

A slight smile crossed Jenny's face despite her attempt to appear disinterested.

Tommy waved his hand like a flag snapping in the wind. "How did the author know how to time travel, Ms. Moonshine?"

Jenny snorted a mocking laugh. Joe burst into raucous laughter with her.

"Sir, you show your lack of gallantry when you mock another. You are too fine a gentleman to partake in such horseplay."

Joe went silent.

Ms. Moonshine glided across the floor and stood

near Tommy. "The author didn't travel in the way you'd expect. She *mind-traveled,* but we'll save our discussion of *astral* traveling for another day." She lifted her hands up to the ceiling.

Jeff tapped his temple to show Jake he thought Ms. Moonshine was crazy. Jeff waved his hand. "Ms. Moonshine, how do I earn an A in your class?"

Tommy heard annoyance lace Jeff's voice.

"I expect your mind to soar and your creativity to burst out! I expect you to think *outside* the box, breathe in joy, and breathe out worry. Can you do that, Jeff?"

"I'm not sure I can, Ms. Moonshine." Jeff let out a breath of air. "All I want to know is how do I earn an A?"

"I just told you. Follow my suggestions *precisely.*" She smiled. "Learning is not reciting facts; it's questioning, thinking, and evolving in your perspectives. The best thinking happens *outside the box*, not in it. When I lived in Greenwich Village in New York in the 60's, it was a tumultuous era of war. We experienced life, flew by the seat of our pants, and lived by experience."

Tommy wanted to shout, "I get it!" But instead, he

watched Ms. Moonshine work her brown-sandaled silver-beaded magic on everyone, except for Jeff, who appeared to be completely confused by her.

Jake leaned toward Jeff wearing a good-natured smile. "I like her."

Jeff frowned with displeasure.

Tommy waved his hand. "I meant to say how did she get the idea to write about time travel?"

"That's a wise question." She paused to check the name roster, "Tommy Delo. Ancient people have been traveling out of body since the beginning of time. This year, we'll read about the Aboriginal natives of Australia and their mind trips... but I digress..." Her expression was faraway lost in a misty memory casting her glance up to the ceiling.

Tommy looked up again to see what she was staring at, but nothing was there.

"Your face is turning red, Torch," Jake said.

Jake had told Tommy how Jeff wasn't satisfied with anything less than an A. It was Jeff's compulsion. Jeff understood school, but couldn't for the life of him understand Ms. Moonshine and it made him angry and off balance.

"Sally, please hand out these papers." She gave Sally a stack of purple copy masters.

"They're *purple*."

"Yes, they are," Ms. Moonshine said.

After Sally passed the papers out, she sat next to Jenny. "She's weird and smells funny. I don't like her," Sally said to Jenny.

Beth overheard them. "I like Ms. Moonshine and her fancy style."

"You would." Sally said.

Ms. Moonshine held the violet sheet out in front of her and propped purple reader glasses on her nose. "Who can sum up this passage for me?"

Jeff shot up his hand. "The author spoke of eleven dimensions. She mentioned parallel universes. We learned about those theories in our science class."

"Good observation, Jeff. But can you tell me more about how you *feel* about this revelation?"

Jeff shifted in his seat. "Feel? I don't understand what you mean."

"Tommy, can you help Jeff out? Use your heart chakra." She placed a hand to her heart.

Jeff folded his arms over his chest and tightened his jaw.

"My what?" Tommy asked.

"Your emotions, Tommy," she said.

Ms. Moonshine thought he could help Jeff understand. "I think time travel is possible. In fact, I'm sure of it." Tommy grinned.

"Really? Why are you so sure?" She asked.

Tommy couldn't tell her about the prayer wheel, so he came up with a good reason.   "At night I fall asleep and I can fly, invent stuff, and do all kinds of things I can't do when I'm awake. Even though it seems like I'm asleep for days, I wake up and it's been a few hours. We time travel in our minds every night when we dream!"

She clapped. "Excellent interpretation, Sir! Miss Bell can tell you more about the Mayan people, who believed time travel was possible."

"Reese, how do you feel about this passage?"

"The author references the concept of moving through time and space into parallel dimensions. She mentions the works of a math professor at Brown University, Mr. Tom Banchoff, and his theory of tesseracts. I think it's true. Maybe in another Universe, I'm different type of person."

"Are you still a gorilla girl in the other Universe?" Jenny mocked.

Sally burst out in a mocking laugh. "Good one, Jenny!"

Ms. Moonshine gave Jenny a stink-eye. "Reese, you are a fine and beautiful young woman. Ignore naysayers. Trust me. You will have the last laugh."

Jeff challenged Ms. Moonshine. "What does feeling have to do with science? This is ridiculous."

"I assure you I'm well-schooled, Jeff. I'd much rather know your opinion and emotions than facts you've gathered to test my expertise. I am a worthy opponent. True wisdom is admitting you don't have all the answers. So, what do you think, Jeff?"

Jeff said, "I believe time travel is conjecture. Even Einstein called it a theory. I don't think time travel is possible...ever."

Jake tossed Tommy a sideways glance.

"Don't be too sure of what you *think* you know. Not all truths reside in books. Much truth lies in personal experience," Ms. Moonshine said.

Tommy whispered to Jake. "I'll say." He wrote *"Parallel universe"* in his notebook. Strange coincidences were piling up. Mr. Bell talked about parallel dimensions, too.

"And now, a blast from my past. This song was popular in the 60's called The Age of Aquarius, by a group called The Fifth Dimension." Ms. Moonshine hit a button on her computer. She swung in an arc, holding her arms out as if she was hugging the room. She swayed with the music, her flowery skirt drifting around her legs. "Feel free to get up and move your body to the beat, boys and girls."

No one dared get up to dance, but the pupils watched her every move as if she were and exotic creature on display at the zoo.

Ms. Moonshine halted and glanced around at the seated students. "No takers? Pity. Please open to page 100." She stopped dancing and wrote the word 'Tesseracts' with a bold purple marker.

Jeff wrote tesseracts in his notepad and grinned. He was good at books.

Tommy wiggled a finger in his buzzing ears. The annoying hum continued until he dropped into a daydream. For a moment, he stood in front of a tall stone castle with a smelly moat. Knights on horseback rode past him on swift steeds.

"T, snap out of it," Jake poked him with the end of a pen.

He jogged out of his mindscape. "Just thinking," Tommy said.

Jake used his cell phone to define astral travel. "Hey T, listen to this. Astral travel is a term used for an out of body experience where the consciousness can travel throughout the universe by itself."

"Huh." Tommy said.

CHAPTER 30

Mr. Stanton likes Mom

Tommy was in a good mood when he entered the shop.

"Good news! No more drafts upstairs. Mr. Stanton fixed them for us pro bono, no charge!"

"You mean you were *alone* with Mr. Stanton and he fixed the window *pro boner*?" His emotions raged sky high. He shouted and wiped tears from his eyes. "Did he kiss you?" Her cheery announcement made Tommy's stomach dropped ten-elevator floors.

"The correct word is *pro bono*, not pro boner. Please calm down. No, he didn't kiss me. Mr. Stanton was a perfect gentleman. Why are you acting so disagreeable when he's been so kind to you?"

"He's got too many edges, Mom. He'll *swagger* you. Jake told me his dad says you're a *Peach*, Mom. A Peach — a sweet fruit and he wants to squeeze." Jake's big white teeth loomed in his head. *Wolf.* The thought of Mom with Mr. Stanton clawed at his stomach. "How could you do this to *Dad*?" He didn't mean to yell at her, but he did. Tommy threw down his book bag with a thud. His face flamed red. "Did you forget Dad *already*? You said Dad *sees everything* from the better place!"

"He's... gone..." Then Mom's eyes got watery.

Tommy didn't want to see her cry. He stomped his feet when he headed up the stairwell to the Crow's Nest. He flipped through the old photo album and wished with all his heart that he could see Dad again. Knots filled his gut and a watery flood wet his cheeks. He was too upset to apologize. So, he pouted, covered with a dark cloud of misery and his starry blanket.

Tommy heard Mom walk up to the second floor. He heard her head up the narrow stairs. He tossed the blanket over his head to hide from her.

"Punkin, are you okay?" She tugged at the blanket edges but Tommy held it tightly.

"What do you care!" Even though he yelled, his voice was muffled from beneath the cover.

"I miss him dearly, Tommy. I've cried my share of tears, and I have no more left to cry."

"I have *buckets* of them." Tommy dove his head deep into his pillow and cried. He felt her stroking his back saying, 'I love you, Punkin." He didn't answer because the flaming monster of anger was writhing in his gut.

"Go away! I want to be alone!" Nothing could ease the tidal wave of sadness pulling him down in the undertow. *Ker-plop.* Tommy was lost in Davy Jones Locker drowning in despair. Soon his eyelids were heavy anchors. He gasped a breath and dropped into an exhausted sleep, waking three hours later. His stomach was furious with him for missing an after school snack. It rumbled in protest. He trailed down the small flight of stairs, head down, toting his teddy bear like a kindergarten baby. "I'm sorry, Mom. I love you." He encircled her with his arms and sobbed bitter tears.

She wrapped her arms around him in a tight hug and kissed the top of his head. "No worries. Let's have dinner, Punkin. You must be starving."

Mom ladled chicken soup into his bowl. "Chicken soup cures everything."

Tommy dropped his head low. "Not everything, but almost. I'm sorry I yelled at you." He gave her a weary smile and wiped wet tears from his eyes. "Jake said maybe you're lonely like his dad. Are you lonely?"

"Sometimes, but you're good company."

"That's just what I told Jake." Tommy couldn't bear to see her pretty face crumble. She tried to hide her sadness with a smile. He saw the lie in her eyes. Mom was lonely. Dad wanted him to forgive Mom. His heart ached for what could have been…if only Dad didn't have to die. Then everything would go back the way it used to be.

CHAPTER 31

The translation

A few days later, Professor Walter Banes finished the prayer wheel translation. He checked his watch—1:00. He cleared his throat. "Mrs. Delo? This is Professor Walter Banes from Cathedral College. Jackson Stanton gave me your number."

"Oh, hello, Professor Banes. I want to thank you for helping Tommy out with his research. I haven't seen Tommy this excited about learning—ever." Her voice lilted like music. "Tommy told me to expect an email from you with the translation. I 'm surprised by your call."

He cleared his throat. "I thought it best to meet with you and hand deliver it instead."

Dead air filled the pocket. "Oh, is something wrong?"

"The translation is —highly unusual. Would it be alright if I dropped it off at the shop —1:30 today perhaps?"

"Sure. Come to the front entrance of the shop on Main. It used to be Bell's Treasure Trove, but we're the new owners We're not officially opened for business until next week, so knock and I'll open the door for you."

"Yes. Jackson mentioned it to me. Will do. Fare thee well until 1:30."

Tommy glanced at the digital clock on the wall. 1:08 during science class. Did Professor Banes translate the scroll? Without warning, he drifted into another realistic daydream. He imagined Einstein and Dad examining the artifact. Albert Einstein rotated the metal barrel and said to Dad, "This is a fine specimen, Thomas. I always knew Time Travel was possible and this tesseract proves it." Dad and Einstein shared a hearty laugh over it.

Tommy smiled as his consciousness drifted away. He snapped back to attention when Mr. Edwards called out his name.

"Do you think Einstein's theory of *twavel* was possible? I see you were in your own time zone."

"Could you repeat the question?" Tommy gave him a nervous grin.

"*Time twavel.* Do you think it's possible?"

Joe bellowed "Good one, Delo," from the back of the room.

"I think he was *100 percent* correct." He was sure of it. He just heard Einstein agree.

Mr. Edward said, "*Timewoop th-wee* shows Einstein believed time is not linear but behaves in a *woop*."

Tommy heard Sally and Jenny giggling at Mr. Edwards pronunciation of loop.

"Girls, what's so *vewy amusing*?" Mr. Edwards asked.

"Nothing at all, Mr. Edwards," Jenny said with a giggle in her voice.

The teacher wrote Einstein and Time Loop Theory on the whiteboard and Tommy copied the words.

Mr. Edwards drew a straight line and wrote the words Linear Time under it. The top of his bald head gleamed when the overhead light hit it. He jotted years in sequence under the straight line. "This is *linear time*." Next, he circled the first and the last date, drawing an arrow from the first date to the last one.

Sally raised her hand. "I don't get it."

"I'll show you with these two dots representing two different linear times, 1920 and 2020, a century apart. But when I bend the paper, past and present touch. 1920 and 2020 meet and time bends. This is Einstein's *time woop* theory, also called parallel time." Mr. Edwards smiled with uncharacteristic glee. This is a time *woop*. The first and the last date touch, just *wike* past and *pwesent* can touch."

Tommy's mouth dropped open. He swung his head toward Jake already writing a fury of notes into his spiral pad. Tommy's head swiveled back to Mr. Edwards, who had drawn two dots on opposite ends of a rectangular sheet of paper. Mr. Edward bent the paper so that both dots touched from the opposite sides of the sheet.

Jake whispered to him. "T, this explains *everything*."

Tommy couldn't dash down the words fast enough. *Time loop, Einstein, time travel, bending time. Does our wheel bend time?* He pondered the idea. *I saw Tibet, a time in the past, and how I visited Dad. It all makes sense!* After Mr. Edward's class, Tommy's mind was buzzing with scientific theory.

Jeff said, "I'd do anything to see my parents again...I sure wish I could travel back in time."

Jake eyed Tommy. "What do you think, T?"

Tommy shook his head, no, even though he felt guilty about turning Jeff down.

"What's going on?" Jeff asked. "Are you up to something? What gives?"

"Just a private joke," Jake fibbed. "Maybe we'll let you in on it later." He faked a punch to Tommy's arm. "Right, T?"

"Yeah. Maybe." He wiggled his pinky to remind Jake of their solemn secret swear not to tell anyone about the magical time wheel.

4:00 Thursday After school the same day

At 3:30, Choden spun back to Tommy's Timeless Treasures, formerly called Bell's Treasure Trove. She nestled behind the globe on highest shelf. *The globe reminded Choden of all the places she'd been and the people she'd helped. Her choice to inhabit the prayer wheel made a difference throughout time. Eager twelve-year-olds needed her help. She needed to rest because being an immortal was tiring. Tommy had all the clues he needed to know to become her best guardian yet. Soon, Tommy he'd be twelve and their connection would grow even stronger. She formulated a plan to help Tommy with his Joe problem. Medieval England might be just the place to bring a bully. It was just a matter of days until Tommy's birthday. She'd convince Jake of her plan, and then Tommy would go along with the idea.*

That night, the artifact sat on the nightstand near Tommy's sleeping bag. He drifted into a deep sleep. From the landmarks in the dream, Tommy realized he must be in ancient Rome.

He saw the artifact whirl through time and tumble into a large marble building with a golden eagle over the doorway. Stone Lion sentinels on pillars of marble guarded the entrance gate to the portico where a twelve-year old boy, Gabriel sat.

Gabriel turned the shiny copper object in his tanned studying it with curious eyes. "*What is this?*"

Olivia gazed at the object her brother held. "*I'm not sure what it is, but it's beautiful! Where did you get it?* Her almond eyes searched his for the answer.

"*I was sitting here and it dropped in my lap. It must be a gift from mighty Jupiter for my twelfth year!*"

"*You're teasing me.*" Olivia said. "*It had to come from somewhere. I don't think the mighty Jupiter even knows you.*"

The boy twirled the barrel around on its wooden stick. "*Ouch!*"

"*What's wrong?*"

"*It bites me.*"

Olivia laughed. "*It's not a dog, silly. Let me see it.*" She held her delicate hand open.

He slowed the metal canister with his palm and stared at the strange inscriptions on the barrel.

"Alright. Here." Reluctantly, he handed the artifact to her.

Olivia lifted the top of the barrel. *"Look! The top opens. There's a paper scroll rolled up inside."* She handed the emptied artifact back to him. "Hold this." She unfurled the paper with care. *"It has writing on it! I think I can translate the words."*

"How do you know how to read them?" Absentmind-edly, Gabriel turned the barrel with his fingertip while she deciphered the translation.

"I've been studying languages at school, unlike you, who wastes time playing Knucklebones. Oh, I did it!" Olivia recited the inscription **"*Past, present future all the same. Bring me to the karma of this life, so I can go back and eliminate strife. No longer will I keep pain that lodged so deep. Bring me to the time of past, so I can free my soul at last. Reveal to me the truth I need to bring me peace I will succeed. The Guardian of the wheel is present."**

Suddenly a flash of light blasted wide open. The Roman children were pulled inside the circle of light landing somewhere in time.

In the flash of light streamed into Tommy's eyes awakening him from the dream. He'd just seen firsthand, where the eagle inscription might have come from. His heart pounded in his chest. His mind just *astral* traveled with Choden. Now it made sense why his nose was sunburned and his cheeks were windburned after his daydream in class. It explained the many strange dreams, the song he heard in his head, and the buzzing whizzy bang noises in the shop. He was connected with Choden. He'd have to tell Jake all he'd learned. Tommy hoped, with practice, he and Jake could travel whenever *they* wanted to go. But he promised Jake he'd tell Jeff about the magical artifact too. Even though Choden asked him to tell Jeff, he wanted to keep his secret until the very last minute. His twelfth birthday was coming right around the bend after Halloween.

Tommy Delo, 11 ¾, a vertically challenged fatherless boy was in for more adventures. In just three short months, Tommy had managed to make two new friends (three if you counted Mr. Bell, and four if you counted Choden). His adventures were beginning and he wasn't even a full-fledged twelve-year-old guardian of the prayer wheel yet.

End of Book 1
Book 2 Wheel Guardian
Tommy discovers his unique connection to the artifact and travels through time with his best friend Jake.

REFERENCES AND DEFINITIONS

A Wrinkle in Time https://en.wikipedia.org/wiki/A_Wrinkle_in_Time

Stomp out Bullies- Hot line numbers https://www.stompoutbullying.org/get-help/helpchat-line

The Dharma Wheel, Dharmachakra, or Wheel of Dharma, is one of the many sacred teachings of Buddhism and other Indian religions, such as Hinduism and Jainism. It is one of the most important and sacred symbols in the Buddhist faith as it represents Buddha's teachings. Karma Wheel of cause and effect.

Dharma *Indian religion-* the eternal and inherent nature of reality, regarded in Hinduism as a cosmic law underlying right behavior and social order.

In Buddhism- the nature of reality regarded as a universal truth taught by the Buddha; the teaching of Buddhism.
an aspect of truth or reality

Einstein research https://study.com/academy/lesson/the-theory-of-relativity-lesson-for-kids.html

Time and space for kids. Albert Einstein, 1879-1955, was a German Theoretical Physicist.

England in the Middle Ages concerns the history of England during the medieval period, from the end of the 5th century through to the start of the Early Modern period in 1485. When England emerged from the collapse of the Roman Empire, the economy was in tatters and many of the towns abandoned.

Golden Eagle An aquila, latin for Eagle, was a prominent symbol used in ancient Rome, especially as the standard of a Roman legion. A legionary known as an aquilifer, or eagle-bearer, carried a golden eagle.

Kairos time The right time, the best time, for example, "harvest time, wintertime." The best time to sled is Wintertime

Karma (in Hinduism and Buddhism) the sum of a person's actions in this and previous states of existence, viewed as deciding their fate in future existences.

Khafra was an ancient Egyptian king of the 4th dynasty during the Old Kingdom. He was the son of Khafra and the throne successor of Djedefre.

According to the ancient historian Manetho, Khafra was followed by king Bikheris, but according to archaeological evidences he was rather followed by king Menkaure.

Khafra full name Khnum Khafra known to the Greeks as Cheops, was an ancient Egyptian monarch who was the second pharaoh of the Fourth Dynasty, in the first half of the Old Kingdom period (26th century BC). Khafra succeeded his father Sneferu as king.

www.https://brewminate.com/the-pyramids-of-Khafra -khafre-menkaure-and-the-great-sphinx-at-giza/

Knucklebones game

This is an ancient Roman and Greek game similar to Jacks.

The **player** throws the five **knucklebones** straight up with one hand, catching them all on the back of his hand (if he can). Then, he tosses them again from the back of his hand so he can catch them in his palm. You can use this figure to determine the order of **play**.

Kronos Time Exact measurements of time, for example, 7:05PM. (also spelled, **Chronos** is the time we use on a clock.)

Parallel Universe A parallel universe, also known as an alternate universe or alternate reality, is a hypothetical self-contained reality, also called a multiverse. It's a theory similar to Einstein's time loop theory.

Prayer wheel - a cylindrical wheel on a spindle made from metal, wood, stone, leather or coarse cotton. Traditionally, the mantra Om Mani Padme Hum is written in Newari language of Nepal, on the outside of the wheel. www.https://en.wikipedia.org/wiki/Prayer_wheel

Rome www.https://rome.mrdonn.org/ Ancient Rome for kids

Author's note: In my first draft, Choden was named Tenzin. Then I rewrote and thought it would be an interesting story plot to have the twin girl from Tibet be the same spirit in the prayer wheel. I changed her name to Choden because it's easier to remember and to read. It's a Tibetan Name which means devout one.

Tenzin is a Tibetan given name, meaning «the holder of Buddha Dharma». Tenzin can alternatively be spelled as Tenzin or Stanzin. The name can be used for a boy or a girl.

Tesseracts In geometry, the tesseract is the four-dimensional analogue of the cube; the tesseract is to the cube as the cube is to the square. Just as the surface of the cube consists of six square faces, the hypersurface of the tesseract consists of eight cubical cells. The tesseract is one of the six convex regular 4-polytopes.

Time Loop Theory-Two Point of times (past and present) meet at the same juncture.

Yeshe is a Tibetan term meaning wisdom and is similar to jnana in Sanskrit.

ABOUT THE AUTHOR

Rosemary DeTrolio loves to write for children. Teaching children and engaging students is her passion. She is a retired full-time educator of 32 years, member of the NJEA and NEA, mentoring many new teachers.

Rosemary holds an MED in Education with a reading specialization from East Stroudsburg University and is a NJ past recipient of teacher of the year.

She's also a Reiki Master Teacher, member of the International Association of Reiki Professionals, and Who's who for professional business owners and educators. Find her primary books and adult spiritual book, Divine Messengers on Amazon. Grow your spirit with her delightful books to enrich your mind and entertain you.

Interested in contacting her? info@rosemaryd.com She loves to hear from readers.

Grow Your Spirit

Made in USA - North Chelmsford, MA
1179519_9781733986953
10.13.2020 0829